The
Secret of
Splint Hall

The
Secret of
Splint Hall

Katie Cotton

ANDERSEN PRESS

First published in Great Britain in 2022 by
Andersen Press Limited
20 Vauxhall Bridge Road, London SW1V 2SA, UK
Vijverlaan 48, 3062 HL Rotterdam, Nederland
www.andersenpress.co.uk

2 4 6 8 10 9 7 5 3 1

British Library Cataloguing in Publication Data available.

ISBN 978 1 83913 196 7

Printed and bound in Great Britain by Clays Ltd, Elcograf S.p.A.

For two beautiful sisters:
Chloe and Aubrey

Part One: A New Start
September 1945

CHAPTER ONE

Mum said the War was over, but Isobel thought that it was not. She could see it in the tight lips of the women as they queued to buy sugar, butter and bacon. She could feel it in the dust from the rubble that used to be kitchens and bedrooms, but now were nothing at all. That was what had happened to their house. One evening it was there, the next morning it wasn't. It had become a pile of rocks, like something you walked over to get home in a storybook. But they didn't have a home to get to any more.

They were the lucky ones, Mum had said, holding Isobel's hand too tight. They'd been in the shelter when it happened. Not like Mrs Potts and her children, Sammy and Kit, from number forty-eight. Isobel knew that they were the lucky ones, but she hadn't felt very lucky, at the time.

Most of all, the War was in the eyes of the men that had come back. Or it was in what *wasn't* in them. Like a light had gone out. How they looked without seeing, like they were miles away. She'd said that to Flora but Flora said she didn't know what she was talking about, and she should be quiet and stop looking at people anyway. Nosy parker.

Isobel thought that maybe Daddy would have looked like

that if he'd come back from the War. She wanted to ask Flora about it, but she'd only get cross and tell her to stop talking about him. They'd known he wasn't going to come back ever since the boy came with the telegram that had made Mum bend right over like she was going to be sick. The boy, who hadn't looked much older than Flora, had patted Mum awkwardly on the back, then turned red, like he wasn't sure he should have done that. Then he'd left. And Flora had taken Isobel's hand and they'd gone upstairs and huddled under the covers and read *The Little Prince* until Mum knocked on the door.

Isobel thought that Daddy not coming back was the reason they were going to Aunty Bea's. It was either that or because their house wasn't there any more, and they were living with their neighbour Mrs Dooley, who sniffed loudly if you banged a door by mistake. Or maybe it was both. Mum called it a New Start. In the country. Isobel knew that some children had been sent to the country during the War. It was children in the city that were sent there, and Mum had said they didn't live in the city or the country, they lived in a town, so they could stay where they were all together and be safe. Which they were, Isobel supposed, until their house had got bombed.

Isobel pressed her face to the cold glass of the car window and looked out.

'Don't do that,' Flora said. 'You'll leave a mark.'

Isobel ignored her. It was only September but the day had been damp and dark, and now it was getting darker. They were travelling along a road with stone walls on either side that was winding up and down and sometimes around huge hills. Beyond the road, apart from the hills, all Isobel could see were fields with

4

white blobs of sheep on them. If this was the country, Isobel thought, then really the country was nowhere at all.

She settled back against the soft leather of the car. Aunty Bea's husband, Mr Godfrey, had sent it to pick them up from the station. It was bottle green with pale cream leather and a loud, honking horn, which the driver had already used twice – once when a cow stumbled on to the road, and the second time shortly afterwards, when the farmer had taken too long to get it off. Isobel had never been in a car before. There were lots of nevers that were becoming nows. Maybe that was what growing up was.

'Are we nearly there yet, Mum?' Flora said, her voice loud and plaintive.

Mum turned round. Her eyes were big and dark underneath her hat. She didn't normally wear hats – during the War she'd had her hair tied up under a grey scarf because she worked in the factory, sewing fabric on to the wings of planes. Everyone knew you had to keep your hair away from the machines, otherwise you'd come to a Bad End.

Today Mum's hair was hovering on her shoulders in soft, bouncy rolls, her small black hat balancing on top like a bird settled on its nest. She reached back and squeezed Flora's arm, then Isobel's leg.

'Not long now, girls,' she said, turning back to the front. She peered forwards through the windscreen. 'Look, we're just coming through the village.'

Isobel looked. It didn't look like much though. Not like home, where there were roads full of houses all pressed up together like best friends out for a walk. Here, there were only a few houses scattered about. They were all white or yellow, wearing thatched roofs like low-brimmed hats. The bottle-green car drove past these houses and then they passed a larger, darker building, streaming yellow light from the windows, with a sign with a picture of a bird on it. As they drove by the door swung open, revealing a man in a tweed cap and overalls. He went to light his cigarette but saw the car and watched it go past instead.

'That's the public house,' the driver said. 'Though I don't expect you'll be frequenting that sort of establishment.' He gave a little chuckle, as if the thought were preposterous.

'Actually I'm quite fond of a gin and lemon,' Mum remarked cheerfully. 'It's what got me through the War.'

The driver looked at her in surprise, then gave a small shake of his head. Mum didn't seem to notice. She was peering through the windscreen again.

'Oh, my goodness, look at the cottages,' she said, her hand flying to her mouth.

Isobel and Flora turned their heads to look as they drove past. They had seen similar things at home: the fronts of houses blown clean off, so you could see inside them like dolls' houses. Often there was still furniture left inside. These, though, were empty. All you could see were spaces where rooms used to be.

'Bea said they had been bombed,' Mum said. 'I couldn't believe it when she put it in her letter. It's such a small village. What bad luck.'

'Not if someone forgot to black one of their windows,' the driver said, his tone surly.

'Is that what happened?'

The driver sniffed. 'Don't see why else it would have. As you said, we're only a small village. And the family who lived there, they'd be the sort.'

Mum didn't say anything, but Isobel saw her press her black gloved hands together tightly. 'Were there any casualties?'

'Everyone got to their air-raid shelter in time,' the driver replied, his tone making it sound like it was a pity.

Mum turned to look out of the window again. 'Look, Isobel, look, Flora,' she said, her voice brightening. 'There's the house!'

This time, the driver made a small, irritated *tsk*ing sound, then immediately tried to cover it up with a cough.

'What?' Mum said, sounding on the edge of cross.

He cleared his throat uncomfortably. 'It's just that round here, we now call it the Hall. Splint Hall.' He flicked a look at her from underneath his smart black hat, whose brim sat rather low on his forehead. 'That's how the Master likes it.'

Mum stared at him for a few seconds before peering out into the dark again. 'Well, when I grew up in it, we called it the house,' she said. 'Can you see it, girls? It's only a mile or so from the village.'

Isobel pressed her face to the window again. This time she was joined by Flora, who seemed to have forgotten that she had told Isobel off for doing the same thing only five minutes before. Flora *always* did that. They couldn't see much anyway, the trees were in the way.

'Why's it called Splint Hall?' Flora said, her forehead furrowing like it did when she didn't understand something. 'What's Splint?'

'No one knows,' Mum said, turning to look at the girls, her eyes sparkling with mischief. 'It's quite the mystery, actually. It should really be called Burlington Hall, after Lord Burlington.'

'You mean Grandpa?' Isobel said. She'd never met Mum's father – he died before she was born – but Mum had told them about him.

'No. Well, yes, Grandpa was Lord Burlington, but his father was Lord Burlington before him, and his father's father was one before that. There's been one for hundreds of years, as far as anyone can remember.'

'There isn't one now, though, is there?' the driver said. Then he looked at Mum, like he thought he'd been rude.

'No, there isn't,' she said. 'My father never had a son. Girls, look, this is the best view you'll get.'

The trees parted to show Splint Hall, which loomed over the fields like a general over his army. It was the biggest house Isobel had ever seen, built out of dark red brick with a huge chimney at the back. Three pointy roofs stuck up like witches' hats, a flat stretch of roof in between them. At the front, a massive flight of steps reached up to a huge wooden door. At home, houses were tall and thin – there were only two rooms on each floor. But this house was different. In Isobel's house there was a window in each room, so she thought that if she counted the number of windows at Splint Hall she'd know how many rooms there were. She started to count and had got to ten when her mother said, 'Is Mr Godfrey home?'

She hadn't looked at the driver when she'd said it; she'd been busy smoothing her skirt.

'Yes, Ma'am,' the driver replied. 'The Master's home most of the time, these days. Since the War ended.'

Isobel knew that Mr Godfrey was Aunty Bea's husband. She didn't know what a Master was though. She opened her mouth to ask, but before she could, Flora said, 'Have you met him, Mum? Mr Godfrey, I mean?'

'Once,' her mother said, a little stiffly. 'You have too, actually. Both of you. But you were too young to remember. We visited once when Isobel was only a few months old, but—' Mum broke off. It looked to Isobel like she wasn't sure what to say. Isobel was going to say, 'But what?', but then Flora gasped suddenly.

'What's that?'

Isobel looked at where Flora was pointing. All she could see were the flat blue-green fields, with darker lines of hedges criss-crossing them into patchwork. The sky was darker now, giving everything that dark blue tinge that says night is coming, and quickly.

'What's what?' she said.

Suddenly, about 200 feet away, sparks shot up from the ground. It was like the top of a bonfire, but Isobel couldn't see the fire underneath. Also, these sparks were blue, not red, bright against the dark sky. As soon as she saw them, they'd disappeared.

'How odd,' Mum said.

The driver made the strange *tsk*ing sound again, but this time it was louder. He shook his head slowly from side to side. 'It'll be those wastrels again,' he said. 'Master won't like that.'

Mum's shoulders stiffened. 'Wastrels?'

'Thieves,' the driver said, as if to explain. 'We've had all sorts of trouble with them, and not just recently neither. All through the War too. People coming into the garden, thieving vegetables from their beds, even meat from the kitchen, can you believe?' He shook his head. 'Worst thing is, some of them used to work here.'

'What do you mean?' Mum said.

'What I said, Ma'am. Some people have got nothing better to do than roam around the countryside, taking what's not theirs. Even if they used to work at the house they're stealing from.'

'But who is it?' Mum said, perplexed. 'I know everyone who used to work here, they were all local. None of them were thieves. Perhaps they're simply hungry. Rationing has been difficult. Do you know their names?'

The driver looked at her shiftily. 'Not my place to say, Ma'am. Anyway, you can't go taking what's not yours, even if you are hungry. It's not right.'

From her position in the back seat, Isobel could just see the top of her mother's face. Her eyes looked dark and worried, the skin between them crinkled.

'You don't have to worry, Ma'am,' the driver said, misunderstanding her distress. 'About the kiddies, I mean. If the wastrels come knocking, we know how to deal with them.'

Mum was quiet for a few seconds. 'I rather thought,' she said eventually, her voice low, and as clipped as horses' hooves, 'that if this dreadful War had taught us anything, it was how to look after our fellow countrymen.'

The driver looked at her in surprise. Then something cold and hard crept over his face, and he shrugged.

As the driver swung the car onto the narrow, tree-lined road that led up to Splint Hall, Isobel kept her face pressed against the glass, until it turned warm under her breath. But she didn't see the sparks again.

CHAPTER TWO

At breakfast the next morning, Isobel met Mr Godfrey again. Afterwards, she was relieved she hadn't remembered him the first time, when she had been a baby. The housekeeper had set his toast down next to his plate smartly and said, 'Your breakfast, Master.' He hadn't said anything at all, hadn't even looked up from his newspaper, but she'd nodded once, curtly – maybe because someone had to nod, if he wasn't going to – and then left the room.

Not that Isobel felt that sorry for her. The housekeeper was called Miss Stewart. She had a face like a fishwife's and a temper to match. When they had finally arrived the night before, they had knocked on the huge, heavy wooden door and she had answered, saying with pursed lips that they were later than expected and everyone was already in bed. Mum had pointed out she had written to Aunty Bea to let her know the time of their train, so she wasn't sure why they had been expected earlier. The housekeeper hadn't said anything but pressed her lips together even tighter and led the girls to a small room outside the kitchen, where they had a glass of milk and a small (too small) slice of bread with marge. Then, after saying goodnight to Mum, they were bundled up two

11

flights of stairs to a small, cold white room with two beds and handed a plate with a stub of candle on it. 'There's still candle rationing you know,' the housekeeper said defensively, though they hadn't said anything. Then she had left.

As the girls got into their flannels Isobel had asked Flora what 'Master' meant. She had said it was someone who was in charge and told everyone else what to do. Isobel had asked her how she knew this and she said that at school there was a Headmaster and he was who you got sent to if you were naughty, to decide what to do with you. Isobel had never been to school. She'd only been four when the War had broken out and the school in their town had closed, so she'd had no idea if Flora was telling the truth. And anyway, after Flora had said that she had got into bed, pinched the candle out and turned over and gone to sleep, so Isobel couldn't ask her any more questions. But, looking at Mr Godfrey, sitting at the breakfast table, she thought it made sense.

He was thin, with watery blue eyes and a ginger moustache. His long neck stuck out from his stiff white collar, in which a paisley tie was nestling. Isobel supposed his hair was ginger like his moustache, but she couldn't tell. It was dark with oil and combed neatly to the side, showing pink stripes of scalp underneath. She watched as Mr Godfrey spread a piece of toast thickly with butter and jam. His movements were very slow and deliberate, like he had all the time in the world. When he was finished, he carefully brought the toast to his lips and bit into it. Little ginger moustache hairs drowned in the red jam as he chewed silently.

Isobel only realised she was staring when Mr Godfrey looked up and caught her eye. She looked quickly down at her plate and her own piece of toast. Like Flora's and Mum's, this had only a tiny scraping of butter, and no jam at all. Even though the War had ended months ago, there still wasn't enough food to go round, so you had to be careful. Unless you were Mr Godfrey, apparently.

He finished swallowing and wiped his moustache with a napkin, leaving a red smear on it. Then he looked at a place on the wall just over Mum's head. 'I trust your room is comfortable?' he said. His voice was soft but cold, like a cloth Mum might put on Isobel's forehead if she were ill.

Mum smiled. 'Perfectly pleasant, thank you.'

Isobel wouldn't have described their small, cold room as pleasant, particularly. It was too plain for that. There were no books or toys at all, just a dark chest of drawers in one corner and a little table in between the beds. There wasn't even a rug on the floor, just cold floorboards. And there was only one window, high up on the wall the beds were pushed against, and strangely it was small and round, like the porthole of a ship. When Isobel was lying down she could just see the moon out of it. She had gazed at it for ages, trying to ignore the scratchiness of the blankets and the growling of her tummy.

'It's so wonderful to be home,' Mum said. 'I hadn't realised how much I'd missed the old place! But where's my sister? I thought I would see her last night. I was surprised that she had already gone up—'

'I'm sure she will appear when she has a mind to,' Mr Godfrey said curtly. 'My wife spends a great many hours in bed.'

'Oh,' Mum said. She looked like she was going to say something else but thought better of it.

Mr Godfrey took another piece of toast. 'What are your names?'

Isobel looked up. She thought he was asking her and Flora, but she couldn't be sure because he wasn't looking at them. He was buttering his toast and looking at his newspaper, like he'd never even asked the question. Flora was staring at her plate, like she didn't know who he was talking to either.

'Um . . .' Isobel began.

Mr Godfrey's pale blue eyes flicked to hers instantly. 'Don't say "um",' he said. 'It shows dithering, which shows a lack of intelligence. One must always say what one means and mean what one says.'

He looked back down at his newspaper as Isobel's cheeks flared hot like a match. Mum squeezed her hand comfortingly. 'This is Isobel,' she said. 'And my eldest is Flora.'

Flora, perhaps unsettled by what had just happened, went to put her teacup back on its saucer but her hand trembled, and the cup slipped. It didn't break but landed with a clatter. Mr Godfrey's watery eyes flew up again and this time they stayed fixed on Flora's for a few, horrible seconds. 'Do be careful with the china,' he said, his voice even colder than normal. 'It's extremely valuable and I won't have it broken by foolish little girls.'

Isobel heard Mum breathe in sharply next to her. Flora sat on her hands and looked down at the table miserably. 'Sorry,' she whispered.

Mr Godfrey put his paper down. He clasped his hands gently in front of him, and looked from Flora to Isobel, then back to Flora. 'As you are Beatrice's family, I have no choice but to welcome you to this house. But you *will* obey some rules. You will not touch any of the ornaments, paintings or furniture without permission. You will not shriek or run along the corridors. You

14

will not speak until you are spoken to. You will play quietly and nicely in your room, which has been placed high in the attic so that I cannot hear you. In the garden, you will keep to the paths. You will not go into the summerhouse or the air-raid shelter.' He looked slowly from Flora to Isobel, and then finally to Mum. 'Do I make myself clear?'

'Yes,' Flora and Isobel mumbled. Mum's cheeks had gone the colour of beetroot.

Mr Godfrey grunted, then went back to his paper. For a time, the only sounds were the rustling sort, of him turning the pages. Isobel wanted to finish her toast – her tummy was clenching with hunger – but she was too terrified of doing something wrong.

After a few minutes, Mr Godfrey folded his newspaper neatly, then got up out of his chair. That was when Isobel noticed that his right leg gave him trouble. He swung it out to the side, then used the edge of the table and the top of his chair to pull himself upwards. Collecting his walking stick from where it was resting against the table, he stiffly moved towards the door, careful not to put too much weight on his bad leg.

'I'll be in my study,' he said.

As soon as he had closed the door softly behind him, the room seemed to breathe out a sigh of relief. The light from the tall windows seemed brighter. Isobel, whose attention had been gripped by Mr Godfrey since entering the room, looked around. They were sitting at a long, thin wooden table in a room that was also long and thin. It had windows on two sides, out of which Isobel could see a garden and what looked like an apple tree. Dark oak panelling rose up nearly to Isobel's height and above that the walls were wallpapered in a sky-blue colour with twisting plants and pale red berries. Isobel followed the vines up to the ceiling, which was so high above her she had to tilt her head to look at it.

Mum pushed Isobel's plate towards her.

'Come on,' she said. 'Stop staring and eat up.'

Isobel took a bite of her toast and chewed.

Next to her, Flora was still staring at the crumbs on her plate.

'I didn't mean to,' she whispered, looking at Mum with wide eyes. 'My hand just slipped . . .'

'I know, darling,' Mum said. 'You mustn't worry.'

There was a timid knock on the door and then it opened, slowly. A woman with the same colour hair as Mum was standing shyly in the doorway. Isobel knew immediately that it was Aunty Bea. She was a little smaller than Mum, not just in height but all over, and her eyes had dark circles underneath. But she had Mum's mouth, a mouth that widened into a smile when she saw them. 'I'm sorry I didn't come before,' she said, her eyes flicking to Mr Godfrey's empty chair. 'I was . . . I had some letters to write—'

'Bea!' Mum said. Actually, it was more like a sob. Her hand flew to her mouth as if she wanted to stuff the word back in, then she pushed her chair back clumsily and stood up. 'Why on earth did you knock, you silly goose? It's your house!'

Aunty Bea's face coloured. 'I . . .'

For a couple of seconds, the two sisters just stayed looking at each other. Then in the next moment, Mum had flown round the table, leaving her chair rocking in her wake, and they were hugging. Mum pushed Aunty Bea away again so she could look at her properly.

'Julia,' Aunty Bea said simply. Her hands were clinging to the tops of Mum's arms a little too tightly and her eyes were searching, looking deeply into her sister's. Suddenly, she flung her arms around Mum again. 'Poor Peter,' she whispered fiercely into Mum's ear. 'Poor, poor Peter.'

Peter was their father's name, though Isobel wouldn't have called him that, of course. She would have called him Daddy. *Did* call him Daddy, though she hardly remembered him. She had been only four when he left. Sometimes, she thought she could remember a feeling, of his beard scratching her face as he tickled her, but she was never sure. When she tried to picture it more closely the feeling dissolved, like sugar in tea. But even though she didn't remember him she knew he had been nice. Everyone said so. And even if they didn't, she would still have known that he had been nice. It was just something that *was*, like how summer was hot and winter was cold and the War was bad.

From where Isobel was sitting, she couldn't see Mum's face after Aunty Bea spoke. But she saw how Mum's back tensed as she squeezed Aunty Bea even tighter than she had before. And she saw a single tear inch out of Aunty Bea's eye and roll down her cheek. She thought she would wipe it off but she didn't. She just stayed hugging Mum for ages, so hard it was like there was no one else in the room or even the world. Isobel looked away, feeling a little left out.

Eventually, Aunty Bea and Mum pulled apart. 'You're really here,' Aunty Bea said with a little laugh. She wiped her eyes. 'I can't believe it.'

'Of course I'm here,' Mum said. 'I said we were coming, didn't I? You look exhausted. Sit down and have something to eat.'

'I will,' Aunty Bea said. 'But first I want to say hello to my

17

beautiful nieces.' She turned to them, her arms outstretched. 'Who's got a kiss for Aunty Bea, then?'

Flora was nearer so she was first. Then it was Isobel's turn. She stood up awkwardly, wincing at the scrape of the chair against the wooden floor, but Aunty Bea didn't seem to mind. 'The last time I saw you, you were still sucking your thumb!' she said after she'd let her go, smoothing Isobel's hair where it had come loose from her plaits. 'Now look at you, all grown-up. How old are you now?'

'Ten,' Isobel replied.

'And Flora's nearly thirteen,' Mum said.

Aunty Bea smiled, but her eyes filled with tears again. 'They've grown up so fast,' she said. 'This War went on too long. I should have come to see you—'

'Don't be silly,' Mum said, ushering her sister into a seat. 'I'm sure you had your hands full here. You didn't mention it in your letters, but the house must have been requisitioned?'

Aunty Bea's smile wobbled, then vanished completely. 'Well—' she began.

'What's requisitioned?' Isobel asked, struggling over the funny word.

'Don't interrupt, darling,' Mum said as she sat back down. 'Requisitioned means when a house was needed by the government in the War. There are lots of big houses all over the country, just like this one, and they became training camps for the army, or hospitals, sometimes even schools.' She turned to her sister. 'What was the house used for, then? I've been trying to work it out but I can't. We've been lucky, anyway. I've heard dreadful things . . . I read in the paper that in Cottlemore Manor they took all the

18

wooden fretwork and chopped it up for firewood, and in Waterford Abbey all the statues were blown to bits during training exercises. But there's no sign of what happened here at all, not even any marks on the walls or dirty footprints. Was it a hospital? That's my guess, given all the bedrooms we've got . . .' She trailed off as Aunty Bea stayed silent. She was sitting in the chair looking at her hands. 'What on earth's the matter, Bea?'

'It wasn't requisitioned,' Aunty Bea said quietly.

Mum's eyebrows shot up in surprise. 'It wasn't? But I'm sure the government could have used a house like this.'

'Charles didn't want it to be,' Aunty Bea continued, her voice so hushed that Isobel had to lean forward to hear her. 'They asked, but he was working for the Ministry of Defence during the War. Quite high up, I think, but he didn't tell me about it. He wasn't allowed, I suppose. Anyway, after we got the letter from the government, he spoke to someone, and then they left us alone. He said he needed peace and quiet at home to do his job.'

'Oh,' Mum said, like she wasn't sure what else to say.

'I know you must think that's selfish,' Aunty Bea said in a rush, her words tumbling over each other in her haste to get them out.

'I didn't say that,' Mum said. She went to hold her sister's hand, but Aunty Bea picked up her teacup instead, even though it didn't have any tea in it. She had two high spots of colour in her cheeks.

'Everyone thinks it's selfish,' she said. 'I know what people think. But they don't understand. Charles has suffered enough. More than enough.'

In the silence that followed, an image of Mr Godfrey pulling his bad leg behind him flashed through Isobel's mind. She supposed that was what Aunty Bea meant, about him suffering.

19

'Well, it's probably for the best, anyway,' Mum said, folding her napkin and putting it on the table. 'I would have been dreadfully upset if anything had happened to Splint Hall. I'm so looking forward to showing it to the girls. And I expect you're excited to see it, aren't you?' She looked expectantly at her daughters.

'Did Mr Godfrey hurt his leg in the War?' Isobel asked.

Flora dug her elbow into Isobel's side.

'Ow!' Isobel said.

'Flora,' Mum warned.

'But she's not meant to ask things like that,' Flora hissed out of the corner of her mouth. 'It's rude.'

'It's all right,' Aunty Bea said. 'Charles's injury happened in the war, but not this one. The First World War. He was only seventeen when he went to France and he took a bit of shrapnel in his thigh, only three months in. He says it's never been the same since.'

'Does it hurt him?' Flora asked curiously.

'Oh yes,' Aunty Bea said. 'Every day. The doctors say that the muscles grew back all twisted and that's why it aches so much.'

Mum put her teacup down with a clatter nearly as big as Flora's earlier. 'Still,' she said, 'it could have been worse. He was lucky to come home alive. There's many who didn't.'

'He knows that.'

Isobel supposed that she should feel sorry for Mr Godfrey. It must be awful to be in pain all the time, like when you had a headache, but forever. She tried, but the picture of him biting into the jam-covered toast filled her mind.

'Was the other war like this one?' she asked.

Aunty Bea and Mum shared the Look. Isobel had seen this

look before, many times. It was the sort of look that said she was asking too many questions, and the questions she was asking were about things adults didn't want to talk about or didn't think she should know about yet.

The seconds ticked by, slowly.

'Enough of this gloominess,' Mum said, clapping her hands the way she always did when a meal was finished. 'Let's talk about what we're going to do today, shall we? Girls, I'm sure you'd love to explore the house while Aunty Bea and I have a walk round the gardens.' She turned to Aunty Bea and smiled. 'I'm dying to see the lily pads again.'

Aunty Bea smiled too. 'They're even more glorious than when we were little.' She stood up, her green striped dress rustling against the smooth oak of the table. 'Come on, then.' Her voice deepened as she said the next bit. 'Time waits for no man . . .'

'Though it often waits for nosy children,' Mum joined in, and they both collapsed into giggles.

'What does that mean?' Flora asked.

'Nothing,' Mum said, when she'd stopped laughing. 'It's just something your grandpa used to say. Now come on, you two.'

'But Aunty Bea hasn't had any breakfast,' Isobel protested.

The atmosphere in the room darkened, ever so slightly. Flora shot Isobel the Look. Isobel quickly glanced at her mother to see if she was in trouble, but she wasn't. Mum was frowning but it wasn't at her. It was at Aunty Bea.

'She's right,' she said. 'You must eat something, Bea. Look, there's still some toast left, and a bit of butter.'

Aunty Bea hesitated, her fingers clutching the table, as Mum pushed the butter towards her. Quickly, she sat down again, then

21

took a piece of dry toast and bit into it. 'I prefer it this way,' she said quickly, looking at them all. 'I like saving the butter for . . . for special occasions.'

As Mum's face tightened, Isobel thought of Mr Godfrey and how much butter he'd spread on his toast. Perhaps breakfast in Splint Hall was a special occasion, for him at least. But it hadn't felt much like one.

CHAPTER THREE

Whaile Mum and Aunty Bea went for their walk, Flora and Isobel had been told to explore the house, with very strict instructions to be quiet and not to venture down the long corridor that snaked behind the staircase. At the end of that corridor was Mr Godfrey's study, and it was very important, Aunty Bea had said – looking intently at both of them – that he wasn't disturbed. Did they understand?

Isobel had nodded but she didn't, not really. At home there weren't any rooms that she couldn't go in. She had to knock first, of course, if it was Mum's room or the outside toilet they shared with next door, but there was no one that she shouldn't disturb.

'It's because he's working,' Flora announced, following Isobel as she skipped down the large hallway. 'Aunty Bea said he was high up at the ministry, didn't she?' Flora stopped. 'Which way shall we go?'

They were standing with their backs to the great wooden door through which they'd come in yesterday. Before them was a grand hallway, painted the colour of custard, from which a dark staircase ascended upwards and then turned to the right. There was wooden panelling all over the hallway – as Isobel was to discover, it was everywhere in Splint Hall – which could have made it look sombre, but someone had clearly realised this, and done their best to avoid it. Next to the door there was a big armchair with a pink cushion and on the walls there were a variety of colourful pictures. They were mostly of flowers and fruit but one of them, beaming out from the top of the first bit of the staircase, was of a man. He was about fifty years old and wearing a soldier's uniform, with his hand resting on a sheepdog. He wasn't smiling, but there was a glint in his blue eyes and a twitch in his mouth that suggested a smile wasn't far off.

'Who's that?' Isobel said, pointing at the picture.

'How should I know?' Flora said. 'Shall we go through this door?'

She pointed to a set of double doors on their left. They'd come through the doors directly opposite, which led onto a corridor, off which was the Breakfast Room, which opened out into the Morning Room (which was where Aunty Bea said she liked to sit and write letters). Then you had to go further down to find the small room that Flora and Isobel had been served milk and bread in the previous evening. Behind this room was the kitchen, which Flora and Isobel had been told not to go into by Mrs Fishwife (Miss Stewart), who said she didn't like to be disturbed while she was cooking.

It seemed that a lot of people in Splint Hall didn't like to be disturbed.

Isobel nodded and Flora pushed open the doors. They swung open gently, without even the faintest murmur of a creak. Isobel was expecting to see another corridor but instead they found a huge dining hall, dominated by an enormous table – Isobel thought forty people would be able to sit down easily – which jutted forwards as proudly as a ship.

'Maybe this is the Dining Room?' Flora said doubtfully, tiptoeing inside.

Isobel was looking at the walls, which were hung with tapestries showing all sorts of things: men hunting with dogs, women dressed in long silvery robes lying by rivers, people at parties.

'Do you think Aunty Bea is rich?' Isobel said, craning her neck to look up at the ceiling.

'Mum said so, didn't she,' Flora said, a touch impatiently. 'Before we came here. Remember? Mum used to be rich too. This was her house, when she grew up. But then she left when she married Daddy and now the house is Aunty Bea's. It was left to her when Grandpa died because she's the eldest.'

Isobel could have stayed and looked for hours but Flora was already at the door on the right.

'Come on!'

Isobel followed her through. This time, they did find another corridor. Off it were even *more* rooms: a sage-green library with books stretching up to the ceiling; a musty, dusty brown room that was filled with glass cabinets full of butterflies and stuffed birds; even a room that had nothing but a piano and chairs in it, like a miniature concert hall. And there were countless rooms that were hard to understand what they were for, because they had white sheets over everything.

'Do you think we're allowed to look?' Isobel said, in a smallish room which had a large bay window, looking out onto a pond.

Flora said nothing, but cautiously picked up an edge of sheet and looked underneath.

'It's just a chair,' she said.

After that, they peeked under all of the sheets. It seemed that most of the rooms weren't used for anything except sitting, as all they had in them were paintings and chairs. They were filled with chaises longues, Chesterton armchairs squatting by empty fireplaces, chairs with straight backs, chairs with curved backs, wooden chairs, tweed chairs, plaid chairs in every size, shape and colour.

'What's the point of having all these chairs? They're all covered in sheets so no one sits in them anyway,' Isobel said.

'*I'll* sit in them,' Flora sighed, sinking into a blue velvet armchair with curved arms. 'This is heaven.'

'Can we look at the butterflies again?' Isobel asked, a little bored.

'Let's go upstairs first,' Flora said, leaping up and pulling the sheet back over the armchair. 'When we've explored the whole house, then we can go back.'

Back in the hallway, they nearly collided with the driver, who was carrying a large brown paper bag down towards Mr Godfrey's study. He shifted it in his arms and something inside clinked.

'What's that?' Flora asked.

'It's none of your business, is what it is,' he replied, scowling.

'I was only asking,' Flora said, under her breath.

The staircase was old, with the soft, slightly polished sheen of wood that has been smoothed by thousands of hands and feet. After the excitement of downstairs, upstairs proved a bit disappointing. It was just bedroom after bedroom after bedroom, and most of the furniture was covered in sheets too. There were so many rooms that the two girls couldn't help wondering why the one they'd been given was so small.

'Why can't we have this one?' Flora grumbled as they entered a rose-pink room with two single beds in it. 'I know Mr Godfrey said he didn't want to hear us, but we're not that noisy. Look, it's got electric.' She snapped the light on and off. 'Like home. And this is so soft!' she marvelled, touching one of the pretty, flower-sprigged eiderdowns. 'Feel it, Isobel.'

But Isobel had uncovered a brown chest in the corner and was busy with her own discovery. 'Look!' she cried, holding up a doll. 'Toys!'

Flora rushed over, nearly forgetting that she was – at nearly thirteen years old – getting to be a little too old for dolls. 'Look at this one!' she said, holding up a wooden clown. It had red rosy cheeks and a bright white smile, with a tangle of orange wool for hair. Flora turned it over and found a silver knob at the back, poking out of its yellow shirt. She twisted it and put the clown on the ground, where it started to walk with sudden, jerky movements.

'I've never seen that before!' Isobel said, open-mouthed.

'It's a wind-up toy,' Flora said knowledgeably. 'I used to have one when you were really little. It was a dog that barked and everything, but you broke it.'

Isobel frowned. She wasn't sure if you were supposed to say sorry for something that you didn't remember doing, but she decided to anyway. 'Sorry,' she said.

'That's all right,' Flora replied, rummaging in the chest. Isobel nudged next to her and they spent the next fifteen minutes thoroughly exploring the contents. There was a wooden train which you pulled on a string, complete with little wooden people sitting in the carriages, which they got bored of very quickly. There were also wooden blocks with letters painted on them which, as Flora pointed out, were for babies; four porcelain dolls and a velvet bag that clinked promisingly and turned out to have marbles in it – beautiful, glorious marbles.

Flora said. 'Is that everything?'

Isobel peered into the chest once more. 'I think so . . . wait.'

At the bottom, hidden in the gloom, something gleamed. Isobel reached in, then drew her hand out quickly. 'Ouch!' she said. 'There's something sharp.'

Flora looked at her witheringly. 'I'm sure there's not. Don't be such a baby.' She reached into the chest too and brought out something small, crouching in her palm. It had spikes running down its back – this is what had pricked her, Isobel thought – and a long neck and even longer tail with another spike on the end. Wings stuck out from its scaled body and its mouth was slightly open, showing sharp teeth.

'It's a dragon,' Isobel said.

'I think it's made of metal,' Flora said, fingering the scales. 'Like a tin soldier, but different.'

'Can I hold it?' Isobel asked.

'In a minute,' Flora said. 'Do you think they meant to paint it, but forgot?'

The dragon was dull silver. 'I don't know,' Isobel said, looking in the chest again. 'Wait! There's another one!'

This dragon was even smaller than the other and was browney-black, like the colour of the night sky in cities. It had horns on its head as well as spikes on its back. Isobel held it up to the light, looking at the tiny splayed claws on its feet.

'Do you think they were Mum's and Aunty Bea's?'

Isobel looked at Flora in surprise. She hadn't thought of that. She looked around the room, seeing the rose-pink walls and two little beds as if for the first time. 'Maybe this was their bedroom,' she said.

Flora nodded. She seemed about to say something else, but before she could, the two girls heard a single dry cough from the corridor outside.

They froze.

The next sound they heard was the clunk of a walking stick hitting the wooden floor, then the *swish* of a leg being pulled forwards. Clunk, *swish*. Clunk, *swish*. Clunk, *swish*.

'It's him,' Flora mouthed. 'Mr Godfrey!'

Isobel nodded, wide-eyed with fear. The two girls sat, motionless, as the clunk, *swish* got louder and louder and louder, until Isobel thought Mr Godfrey was right outside. They were sitting in the corner behind the door, so he shouldn't be able to see them, unless he decided to look inside. For one horrible moment the clunk, *swish* faltered, but then it started up again, and got quieter and quieter as Mr Godfrey got further away. Eventually, they heard the quiet click of a door shutting.

The girls put all the toys back in the chest as silently as they could. The doll, the marbles and the two dragons they – without speaking – decided to keep. Noiselessly, they slipped out of the room and up the stairs. Isobel's heart was pounding so loudly she was sure Mr Godfrey would be able to hear it, but there was no sign of him. When they got to their bedroom, Flora shut the door behind them. Isobel let out a long, nervous breath.

'It wouldn't have mattered, if he found us. He didn't tell us we couldn't go in there,' Flora said, but she didn't sound like she believed herself.

Isobel said nothing. She was nervously fiddling with the bag of marbles, turning it over and over in her hand. Somehow the string came loose and the marbles tumbled out, dropping loudly on the floor and scattering in all directions.

'Iso*bel*,' Flora cried, saying the last syllable much louder than the first two. She always did that when she was cross. 'You're so clumsy!' she said, getting down on her hands and knees.

'I didn't mean to,' Isobel began.

'Never mind, just help me!'

The marbles were mostly found under the two beds, but one had managed to roll all the way underneath the small chest of drawers in the far corner. Isobel stuck her hand underneath but she couldn't reach.

'We'll have to move it,' Flora said.

Gritting their teeth, they managed to shuffle the chest of drawers back as far as it could go, against the bed. Satisfied, they turned to look for the marble.

'Oh,' Isobel said.

The marble (black, fire-flecked) lay against the skirting board, forgotten. Because the chest of drawers had been covering a door. It was as wide as a normal door but only about half as tall, with a heavy black lock about halfway up. Flora pushed it, hesitantly at first, then harder.

'It won't budge,' she said.

'What's in there?' Isobel said.

'I don't know, silly,' Flora said, trying the door again. She looked at Isobel, and Isobel thought she'd never seen Flora quite look like that before. Her cheeks were red and her eyes were shining. 'We need to find the key,' she said.

CHAPTER FOUR

Isobel and Flora knew exactly where the keys to the house were kept. The problem was that they were kept on a huge metal ring tied to the strings of Mrs Fishwife's apron. Over the next couple of days, Isobel and Flora watched her closely and never once saw her take her apron – which was as white and as smooth as a sheet – off. The good thing about it, Isobel thought, was that you always knew when Mrs Fishwife was coming, because you could hear the clinking. The bad thing about it was that it would be very, very difficult to take the keys without Mrs Fishwife noticing.

'We'll have to wait for the right moment,' Flora said, eyeing Mrs Fishwife one day as she disappeared into the coal cellar.

While they waited, life in Splint Hall settled into a routine. Every morning, Flora and Isobel washed their faces using a tin bowl and jug of water, combed their hair and got dressed in one of their dark blue or grey knitted dresses and woollen socks. Then they went downstairs for breakfast. Isobel had dreaded this on their second morning but to her surprise she had found that Mr Godfrey wasn't there. Mrs Fishwife, her lips pressed into a ruler-straight line, told them that he would be taking breakfast in his study from now on. From the way Mum hummed a tune as she poured the tea, and Flora confidently picked up her teacup, Isobel didn't think anyone minded. She was also quite sure that it was the reason Aunty Bea now appeared every morning, smiling as she slipped into her seat next to Mum.

After breakfast, it was time to study. The same thing had happened to Burlington Village School as had happened to the school in their old town. When war had broken out, it had shut down, and it hadn't yet reopened. So every morning, and some afternoons, Mum had made them practise sums and spellings and dates, and it was the same in Splint Hall. They used the green library, which had had its sheets taken off but Mum said they weren't allowed to touch any of the books. Isobel thought this was silly. What was the point of having all of those books if no one was allowed to read them? She thought it must have something to do with Mr Godfrey, and her heart set against him even more.

Isobel didn't normally like studying. Sums were all right but spelling was impossible – she knew which letters words began with, and usually what they ended with, but in between was a complete jumble. Her 'a's and 'e's always got mixed up and she didn't know how to make them behave. It made her eyes itch and her head hurt. But Mum never shouted. She just patiently put the letters in the right order, her head close to Isobel's so that Isobel could smell her smell (soap and lilies), her face lighting up when Isobel finally got it right.

When studying was done, it was usually time for lunch, which was Isobel's least favourite time of the day. Mr Godfrey was always there, which meant she was conscious of every knife squeak or every pea falling off her fork. Plus, Mrs Fishwife's food was horrible. Isobel knew that there was still rationing, but there had been rationing at home too and Mum had made much nicer things. Vegetable pies and pasties, cheese on toast, even mashed potato and sausages once a week. All Mrs Fishwife seemed to make was watery soup, or even more watery vegetables and potatoes.

Flora had hoped they could get the key when Mrs Fishwife was cooking, as she had a different apron for that. They had seen it once when they had been playing with their marbles in the main hallway. Mrs Fishwife had come upstairs, holding a wooden spoon quite threateningly, and told them they were being too loud. She was wearing a wider, sturdier apron made of brown hessian, and the keys *weren't there*.

In another house, they might have been able to help with the baking (as children are asked to sometimes) and then they could have slipped off with the keys that way. However, in Splint Hall it was clear that Mrs Fishwife did not want help. One morning at breakfast, drinking over-stewed tea and eating burned toast, Mum had asked Aunty Bea if she could do some of the cooking. It would help Miss Stewart out, she said, seeing as she had such a big house to look after. Aunty Bea had smiled and said it was a good idea. She would ask Mr Godfrey.

That day at lunch, Aunty Bea's voice wavered like a wireless when you are turning the dial as she put Mum's suggestion to her husband. She was passing the salt at the time and Isobel saw her hand shaking, very slightly. Isobel nearly asked her why her hand was shaking but then wondered if it was a question that would get the Look, and she thought it might be, so she stayed quiet. Mr Godfrey looked at Mum in that funny way he had, like you'd done something wrong but you didn't know what. Then he said, 'I'm sorry that you're not enjoying the food.'

Mrs Fishwife had just come in to serve the main course – boiled fish and potatoes – and she glanced at Mum angrily, then set the dish down on the table with a bang. Mum blushed as red as a radish and said that wasn't what she'd meant at all, she'd just enjoyed cooking during the War.

'Thankfully the War is over,' Mr Godfrey said, leaning back in his chair and patting his moustache with his napkin. When he brought it away, Isobel saw a green slimy soup smear on it. 'Many things happened in the War that should not have,' he continued. 'Including women of our class doing messy, sometimes dangerous work. Now that the country is no longer in need, I'm sure they will be grateful to return to more appropriate ways of spending their time.'

'I hardly think that working in a Spitfire factory was inappropriate,' Mum said. 'The country needed the planes.'

Mr Godfrey looked at Mum with something like a sneer. 'I'm not surprised you think so. I understand from my wife that *your* desire to do things that are beneath you started before the War.'

'Charles!' Aunty Bea protested.

'Leaving Splint Hall to live in a three-bedroom semi in Romney,' Mr Godfrey continued, practically spitting out the last word. 'A middling town in middle England.'

'We moved after we got married, as Peter's practice was based there,' Mum replied, her lips pressed into a thin line.

'Ah, yes, the solicitor,' Mr Godfrey said, definitely sneering now. 'I expect Lord and Lady Burlington were very proud.'

'Charles, stop it,' Aunty Bea pleaded, but Mum had already stood up to leave the room. Isobel had wanted to follow her but had been too nervous of Mr Godfrey to ask to be excused.

After the dreadful lunch was over, Isobel and Flora were free to roam the house and the grounds.

'She must leave the house sometimes,' Flora moaned as they walked in the rose gardens, still thinking about Mrs Fishwife and the keys.

'What would she leave the house for?' Isobel said, looking up at a blood-red rose with petals that furled into points.

'To go to the baker's or the butcher's,' Flora pointed out. 'To go to the post office. Or to see a friend. I don't know.'

'I don't think Mrs Fishwife has any friends,' Isobel said, carefully picking up a ladybird from a dog rose.

'You're probably right,' Flora sighed. 'She is awful. It's so maddening.'

Isobel said nothing. Part of her wanted to see inside the door, same as Flora. But part of her wasn't sure what all the fuss was about. It would probably just be a cupboard full of old clothes or boxes of boring grown-up things. Even if it were an attic, which Flora thought it was, it would probably be the same story. That was what their attic had been full of, at home.

'Let's go back to the house,' Flora said. 'I want to look at my dragon again.'

Isobel watched as the ladybird crawled across her hand. She wanted to look at her dragon too. She *always* wanted to look at it. Not to play with it. Isobel had experienced that strange feeling you get when a toy is somehow too real for make-believe. She had tried imagining that the dragon had to protect the locked door from an evil witch (who looked suspiciously like Mrs Fishwife), but as she flew the dragon up and down, she'd caught sight of its eyes. It seemed to be looking at her, not angrily or unpleasantly but with gentle laughter, like she was being a bit silly but it didn't mind. She had let her hand fall and since then had contented herself with tracing the patterns of its scales on its back.

'Why do you think Mr Godfrey said that, about Daddy being a solicitor?' she asked. 'Is it a bad job?'

'Of course not,' Flora said. 'He just said it because he's horrible. And because he doesn't know anything. Daddy wasn't just a solicitor. He was a pilot, during the War.'

'I know that. But what's a solicitor, anyway?'

'Mum said it's someone who helps you when you need to get something important done, like buying a house.'

It didn't seem like a bad job, but Isobel supposed Mr Godfrey had his own ideas about it. He had ideas about everything. Like how you mustn't run in the corridors, or play hide-and-seek outside (too noisy) or touch the bannisters (it would leave sticky fingerprints). And how if you were a child you shouldn't speak unless you were spoken to, which didn't seem at all fair. Especially as Mr Godfrey never spoke to them. It was like he didn't want them to speak at all.

The ladybird, which had been crawling up Isobel's thumb, suddenly got bored and flew off. She followed the speck of it in the air as it zigzagged past the brightly coloured roses, past the elegant white curve of the summerhouse, then away into the world. She frowned, sheltering her eyes against the sun.

'Flora, what's that?'

A stone's throw from the summerhouse, partially hidden by a clump of fluffy white cabbage roses, was a squat, square roof. It looked like it was made out of corrugated tin, with grooves running down its length like stripes.

'It must be the air-raid shelter,' Flora said. 'Let's go and see.'

Their air-raid shelter at home had been the one most people had – an Anderson. It had a curved roof stuck out of the ground and you had to go down steps to get into it. But this air-raid shelter was different. As Flora and Isobel approached, they could see it was much bigger – maybe twice the size. The roof was flat rather than curved, and though there was the same square opening, there weren't any steps.

'How are you meant to get down?' Flora said, peering into the murk.

'Jump?' Isobel suggested.

Flora bit her lip, like she wasn't sure that was a good idea. 'We don't know how far down it goes . . . Wait a minute. What's that?'

She grabbed at something in the dark, making Isobel think she'd gone mad for a second. But then Isobel saw what she had reached out for. It was a rope – pale yellow and dusty looking. Attached to the end of it was a round piece of wood, perfect for a child to sit on.

'It's a swing!' Flora said, surprised. She tested it in her hands, looking up at the roof. 'It's tied to that beam there, look. I think that's how you're meant to get down.'

Isobel looked, but her eyes hadn't yet adjusted to the gloom and all she saw were strange, swirling blots.

'I'm going to try it,' Flora said.

'But what if it breaks?' Isobel said, then remembered something. 'Anyway, Mr Godfrey said we weren't supposed to go down here.'

Flora pulled a face. 'Hang Mr Godfrey,' she said. Putting the rope between her legs and sitting on the wooden seat, she pushed off, and disappeared into the dark.

'Flora?' Isobel called, her voice trembling a little.

'It's all right,' she called back, after a few horrible seconds of waiting. 'It didn't break. Here, I'll pass it back to you and you can come down too. Don't worry, I'll catch you.'

Isobel felt a little scared, but she grabbed hold of the rope – which felt prickly in her hands – and sat on the wooden seat. As soon as she'd done that, it felt like any other swing she'd been on, and she was no longer afraid. Letting go with her feet, she swung forwards. In less than a second, Flora grabbed the rope, and Isobel was at the bottom.

She shuffled off the swing and looked around. As her eyes gradually got used to the dark, she realised that the air-raid shelter wasn't empty. There were shadowy lumps everywhere she looked which – when she ran her hands over them – turned out to be chests and crates. There were so many that you had to be careful where you walked, as Isobel found out after banging her shin painfully.

'What's in all of these?' she wondered out loud.

As if to answer, Flora snapped one of the crates open. She brought something out, something long and floaty and rustling, and peered at it in the half-light.

'What is it?' said Isobel.

Flora didn't answer but took what she had found closer to the rectangle of light that was the entrance. 'It's . . . it's a dress,' she said, a note of disbelief in her voice.

Isobel didn't believe her at first. She was used to seeing the dresses that women wore during the War. Those were simple and plain, made out of faded cotton, linen or wool. The prettier ones had flowers on, like the yellow and pink one Mum liked to wear in the spring. But none of them were anything like this. This had beads and sequins that shone like tiny pieces of mirror as they caught the light and it was long – longer than any dress Isobel had ever seen. But Flora was right – it had two holes for arms and a low neckline that made Isobel think of a bird swooping. Flora moved and the dress moved too, glistening silver like a mermaid's tail.

'It's so beautiful,' Isobel breathed, reaching out.

'Don't touch it!' Flora scolded. 'Your hands are dirty. Look, you've made a mark.'

It was true; there was now a grey smudge on the arm. But Isobel hadn't meant to, and she couldn't have stopped herself touching it, even if she'd wanted to. She stuck her tongue out at her sister, even though – perhaps because – she knew Flora wouldn't see it in the dark. 'Your hands are dirty too,' she said.

Flora wasn't listening. She was reaching past the dress to pull out another. This one was sunshine yellow, soft and slippery. 'Why are these all down here?' she said. 'It doesn't make any sense to hide them away. They're so lovely. Look at this green one! It's got feathers on it.'

Isobel looked, but as she did so, the air-raid shelter suddenly darkened. A figure had appeared in the doorway.

Flora's gasp echoed the panic Isobel was feeling. Her mouth went dry, but when she looked more closely, the silhouette was too small to be Mr Godfrey. And whoever it was didn't seem to have noticed them. They grabbed the rope, like they'd done it before, and made to sit on the seat.

'Who are you?' Isobel blurted out.

The figure said nothing. It stayed completely still for a second, then dropped the rope like it was red-hot, and vanished.

'Iso*bel*,' Flora complained. Rushing to the entrance, she put her hands on the ledge and hoisted herself up. She stood and Isobel saw her black plimsolls turn one way, then the other. Then, 'Wait!' she called, running off.

Not wanting to be left out, Isobel rushed to the entrance too, but it was a little too high. She could just reach the ledge but only with her fingertips, and she couldn't pull herself up with those. She tried bravely until Flora returned, breathing hard like she'd been running.

'It was a boy,' she said, reaching down to pull her sister up. 'About your age, I think. I tried to follow him, but he was too quick.'

Outside the shelter the day was too bright. Isobel closed her eyes for a second then, as the colours slowly returned to normal, looked around the gardens. The roses, the summerhouse and the grass were all just the same as before.

'He's not there,' Flora said, sighing. She turned and started trudging back to the house, muttering under her breath. 'He's the first person who's not a grown-up we've seen since coming here. We could have made friends, maybe. Why did you say something? Why do you *always* have to say something?'

CHAPTER FIVE

Flora sulked for the rest of the day and the following morning. Even though Isobel said sorry, she wouldn't play hide-and-seek or hopscotch out in the driveway. She wouldn't search for the boy in the gardens, even though she clearly wanted to find him. She wouldn't even *speak* to Isobel. And when the bell rang for the dreaded lunchtime, she didn't wait but ran as fast as she could down to the Dining Room, even though she knew Isobel couldn't run as fast as her.

Isobel arrived, out of breath, to see her sister sitting at one of the best seats – the one nearest the door, with an empty seat between her and Mr Godfrey, who always sat at the head of the table in a red velvet chair. Mum was sitting opposite her, in the other best seat. Swallowing hard, Isobel sat in the seat next to Mum. This meant that she would be next (though at a right-angle) to Mr Godfrey. Her tummy did a little jump as he entered the room, not greeting anyone as he walked over to his seat. Aunty Bea followed, also not saying anything. She sat in the seat opposite Isobel.

Mr Godfrey sniffed, hard, and rested his white-shirted arms on the table. They were so close that Isobel could see the hairs poking out from his cuffs. She hoped that he would move them when the food came, or she might spill something – like a fleck of soup or crumb of bread – on them, a prospect which put chilly fear into her heart. Keeping her hands tightly folded in her lap, she sneaked a glance at her sister. Flora was looking down at her lap too, but, sensing Isobel's eyes on her, she looked up. She didn't say anything, or even smile, and after a second or two she looked away. But then her lips curled upwards into an expression of complete smugness.

A hot wave of anger flashed through Isobel as the door opened again. Mrs Fishwife placed a huge pot on the table and stood back, a grin hovering on her lips. 'It's bacon and vegetable stew, Master,' she said, pulling the lid of the pot back with a flourish. 'The butcher had bacon in for the first time in weeks.'

Even if Mrs Fishwife hadn't said what was in the pot, Isobel would have guessed from the smell, which hit her as soon as the lid was taken off. It was salty and smoky and it made her mouth water instantly. At home they had had bacon only very occasionally. Mum would save it for Sunday morning, which was the only morning she didn't go to the factory, and they had it with eggs. Mum always used to complain about the eggs, which were made by mixing water with a powder, but Isobel couldn't remember any other kind and they tasted fine to her.

Isobel dragged her gaze away from the round black pot and looked at Mrs Fishwife, who was still standing by the door, the keys on her belt glinting invitingly in the midday sun. Then she looked at Mr Godfrey, who had turned to Mrs Fishwife. Isobel thought he was going to say thank you, but he didn't. 'Will that be all?' he said instead, his voice mild.

42

Mrs Fishwife's smile drooped, then vanished. A little pink, she did a strange bouncing thing with her knees, then turned for the door.

'Miss Stewart, kindly ask Rigby to come into the Dining Room,' Mr Godfrey called after her.

With a tight nod, Mrs Fishwife left.

After a few seconds of silence, Aunty Bea cleared her throat nervously. 'Bacon!' she said. 'What a treat. Shall I be mother?' She got up, smoothing her skirts, and reached for the ladle.

'Leave it,' Mr Godfrey said.

Aunty Bea's hand froze in mid-air. Mr Godfrey's voice was cold, like the voice he used with everyone else, but deeper and angry too – like the jagged pieces of brick you got after a raid. He looked at Aunty Bea, who was still hovering, unsure what to do next. 'Sit down,' he spat.

'I have something important to say,' Mr Godfrey continued as Aunty Bea returned to her seat and folded her hands in her lap. He clasped his hands together in front of him and stared at Flora and Isobel. 'It is better to tell you before we eat because I know what children are like with their food. I want everyone's full attention and I don't want to hear disgusting chewing noises while I'm talking.'

Isobel squirmed in her seat, just a little.

'Sit still,' Mr Godfrey barked.

Mum's hands clenched into fists. 'Charles,' Aunty Bea said, looking from her husband to her sister, then back again.

Mr Godfrey looked at his wife angrily, but at that moment the door opened and Rigby came into the room.

Rigby was the driver who had picked them up from the

43

station and taken them to the house. But today he wasn't dressed in his driver's hat. Instead, he was wearing grey overalls and a flat cap because he was working outside in the garden. It had become apparent during Isobel and Flora's stay at Splint Hall that as well as being the driver, he was also the gardener, gamekeeper and even butler, though there had been no call for his services in that area yet. In the week that Isobel and Flora had been there, no one had come to visit.

At Rigby's feet, there was a little Jack Russell called Jake. This dog went everywhere with him. Isobel normally loved animals, but not Jake. The first time she'd met him she'd tried to stroke him and he'd shrunk down to the floor and gone extremely still – the sort of stillness that a wolf has before it pounces. Suddenly, he'd bared his yellow teeth in a growl, making Isobel snatch her hand away, then trotted off to find his master.

'You asked to see me, Master?' Rigby said.

'Yes, Rigby,' Mr Godfrey said. 'It is about what you said yesterday.' He turned his icy blue gaze to Flora, Isobel and Mum. 'Something has come to my attention. It concerns people going where they shouldn't.'

Isobel felt, rather than saw, Flora stiffen across the table. She looked down guiltily, staring so hard at the white china bowl that the roses on its rim dissolved into pink blurs. Had Mr Godfrey seen them going into the air-raid shelter?

'A boy has been spotted in the gardens,' Mr Godfrey continued.

Isobel looked up with relief. Then she immediately thought of the boy Flora had seen.

'I don't need to remind you that this house is full of many valuable and beautiful things,' Mr Godfrey said. He gestured to the oak dresser which ran along one of the walls, silver candlesticks and other ornaments on top. 'Things that are the envy of people who live in the village, and beyond. This boy is no doubt a thief, after whatever he can get his hands on.'

'Comes from a thieving family too,' Rigby muttered under his breath. Jake yapped, as if to say he agreed.

'You mean you know who he is?' Mum said, looking at Rigby with barely concealed dislike.

'That's correct,' Mr Godfrey said. 'This boy and his family are known to us. Before the War they were work-shy scoundrels and I'm sorry to say that the War has effected no change in their character.'

Mum said nothing.

'We used to see him in the vegetable patch and the chicken coop,' Rigby explained. 'During the War, I mean. It weren't just once, either. He always got away though. He's quick, that's for sure.'

The mention of the vegetable patch made Isobel eye the black pot longingly. The stew, and the bacon inside it, would be getting cold. Her stomach felt hollow. Perhaps this was how the boy had felt, she wondered, and that was why he had tried to steal.

Mum was clearly thinking the same thing. She looked at Aunty Bea, as if trying to decide whether she should say something. Then her expression became determined. 'If a child is hungry, then I would be inclined to give him some food, rather than have him before a policeman for theft.' As she took in a deep breath, Isobel noticed angry red patches on her throat. 'If a child is suffering—'

'We have all suffered, Mrs Johnson,' Mr Godfrey snapped.

His bad leg clunked under the table as he shifted it. 'Rationing means that he is no hungrier than anyone else. If people desire extra food then they must earn it. That is the way the world works.'

The blotches on Mum's neck and throat got angrier. 'I was always taught to share what we had with people less fortunate,' she said. 'Our father—'

'Oh, your *father*—' Mr Godfrey scoffed.

'Please,' Aunty Bea said, standing up suddenly, her chair grinding loudly against the floor. 'Please don't. I can't bear it.'

In the silence that followed, Isobel kept her eyes firmly on the table. She heard the ticking of the grandfather clock in the hall and, from somewhere far away in the house, the echo of footsteps. It must be Mrs Fishwife, she thought, doing her afternoon polishing, and she felt a sudden, surprising rush of jealousy. She hated chores, but she would have given anything to have swapped places with her just so she didn't have to be in this room, with the air thicker than normal and no one speaking. Eventually, she heard a small creak as Aunty Bea sat down.

'Well, if any of you see the boy,' Mr Godfrey said, his voice quiet and cold, 'you will alert Rigby and me so that he can be dealt with. Is that understood?'

Isobel glanced quickly at Flora. They had already seen the boy yesterday, when they were in the air-raid shelter. Mr Godfrey hadn't asked him to tell them if they'd *already* seen him, only if they *did* see him, but she was old enough to know that it was the same thing. So was Flora. So it was a surprise when Flora looked up and said simply, 'Yes,' before looking down again.

Mr Godfrey's cold blue eyes met Isobel's.

'Yes,' she repeated.

Mr Godfrey let the silence stretch out for a few seconds. 'Good,' he said. There was a heavy gold bell on the table next to his plate which he rang, making a loud clanging noise. Then he waved his hand in the direction of the stew and Aunty Bea got up immediately. She reached for his plate first, but he snatched it back, setting it on the table with a clunk.

'Master?' Mrs Fishwife said, entering the room.

'I will be having lunch in my study,' Mr Godfrey said, standing up and taking hold of his stick.

'Of course, Master,' Mrs Fishwife said, her face blank as she moved aside to let him and Rigby pass through the door. When they had both left she went over to the table. Aunty Bea was still standing there, slightly helplessly, with the ladle.

'Let me, Ma'am,' Mrs Fishwife said, her tone almost gentle.

Mrs Fishwife took the ladle and served the stew. Isobel had thought that she would do Mr Godfrey's first, but she didn't. Instead she put bowls in front of Aunty Bea, then Mum, then Flora, then Isobel, who looked down at the curled bits of bacon floating on the top. Her mouth watered again. She had a low, pulsing headache, like someone knocking at a door quietly.

'Thank you,' she said, not knowing she was going to say it until she did.

Everyone looked at her. For a second Isobel thought she was going to get the Look, but she didn't. Instead, Mrs Fishwife's face was smoothed by surprise – the lines on her forehead disappeared, and her mouth opened.

'Yes, thank you,' Mum said, picking up her spoon. 'I'm sure you must have had a fight on your hands to get that bacon.'

Mrs Fishwife's face tightened again. 'It would have been nicer if it were hot,' she grumbled. She took Mr Godfrey's bowl out of the room, closing the door firmly behind her.

As soon as Flora had finished, she asked to be excused. She had clearly forgotten that she was meant to be cross, because she wiggled her eyebrows at Isobel to make her get down too and, when that didn't work, even kicked her under the table. Still smarting from having to sit next to Mr Godfrey, Isobel ignored her, making sure every last delicious drop of her stew was eaten before she got down.

Flora grabbed her hand and dragged her out the room, then out of the front door.

'What are you doing?' Isobel complained as Flora ran down the steps, still pulling Isobel after her.

'We've got to find him,' Flora said.

'Who, the boy?' Isobel said.

Flora stopped running and turned to glare at her sister. 'Sssshhhhhh!' she said, putting her finger to her lips. 'You don't want Mr Godfrey to hear. Or Rigby or Mrs Fishwife. They're on his side, you know.'

Isobel thought about it. She found she was perfectly convinced that Rigby was on Mr Godfrey's side, but she was less sure about Mrs Fishwife. There was something about the way she had taken the ladle from Aunty Bea, like she had felt sorry for her.

'Why do you want to find the boy?' Isobel whispered.

'Cos we've got to warn him that Mr Godfrey is on to him, of course,' Flora said. She hesitated. 'And . . .'

'And what?'

Flora pulled Isobel behind a neatly trimmed hedge. She looked around to check no one was in hearing range, then said, 'You know how Mr Godfrey said he was a thief?'

Isobel nodded.

'Well?' Flora waited, tapping her foot against the stone path and looking at Isobel intently. Isobel knew she was supposed to understand what her sister meant, but she didn't. There was an empty space in her brain where the answer should have been. Eventually, Flora rolled her eyes. 'If he's a thief, he'll be good at stealing things, silly,' she said. 'He can help us take the keys from Mrs Fishwife! He'll know all sorts of things that we don't. Then, if we've got the keys, we can open the door and find out what's behind it, at last.'

'Why do you want to know what's behind the door so much?' Isobel said, a little cross at being called silly. 'I bet it's just a cupboard, full of boring grown-up things. Like old clothes and books.'

Flora shook her head. 'You're wrong,' she said. 'If it was just that, why would it be locked?'

Isobel shrugged. 'The kitchen's locked and I bet there's nothing exciting in there,' she said.

Flora flapped her hand dismissively. 'That's just because Mrs Fishwife doesn't want us in there, getting under her feet,' she said. 'The door in our room's different.' She gazed at Isobel thoughtfully. 'There's something different about this house,' she said. 'Something's going on, I'm sure of it. It's like it's got a secret. Can't you feel it too?'

Isobel shrugged again. Her head was still hurting – it had turned into a dull, thumping ache – and she suddenly felt tired.

But her sister was looking at her expectantly, so she thought of Splint Hall. She thought of Mrs Fishwife and Rigby, and Mum and Aunty Bea walking round the gardens, and, most of all, Mr Godfrey, lurking like an icy stone at its heart. There was definitely something going on, something not very nice, but she couldn't have said exactly what it was. Anyway, she didn't think that was what Flora meant. She had the same expression she had when they'd decided to climb to the top of the bombsite in Morley Road, back home. She was talking about something exciting.

'Getting into that room's the first step to working it out,' Flora said, her eyes burning with determination. 'I'm sure of it.'

CHAPTER SIX

That afternoon, Isobel and Flora searched for the boy. They started with the gardens. As well as the rose garden, which was where they'd found the air-raid shelter the day before, there were two others. One was centred around a pond the size of a swimming pool, with steps leading down to it on all sides. The pond was dark green with pink and purple lilies floating on it – the lilies that Mum had been so excited about seeing again. Isobel could see why. There were so many that it looked like a flowerbed, with strange soil – so dark it was almost black, and shimmery. The other garden was even stranger because it had stone walls round it. Isobel had never seen that before. You had to get in through a wooden door, which wasn't locked. However, Rigby was in there, viciously attacking some ivy that was creeping up the grey stone in the left-hand corner, and he scowled at the girls, Jake snarling alongside him, before going back to his task. Isobel only got a glimpse of neat square flowerbeds before Flora hurried them out.

Another garden had an outhouse – a small wooden shed that smelled of mildew and wood smoke. The girls peered through the tiny window to see a huge number of brown heavy-looking sacks, stacked on top of each other.

'What do you think those are?' Isobel asked.

'It looks like flour,' Flora said, then was distracted by Mrs Fishwife, who was walking past with an armful of potato peelings.

'I'd stay out of there if I was you,' she said, glaring at the two girls. 'Those packages are to do with Mr Godfrey's work and Mr Rigby won't be best pleased if they're moved.'

She stalked off to the compost heap, her shoulders slightly hunched with the weight.

'All right, all right,' Flora muttered. 'Let's go, Izzy.'

They were searching behind the huge oak trees in the sweeping driveway when a car arrived. Instinctively, Flora pulled Isobel behind one of the trees so they wouldn't be seen. Some men wearing bowler hats got out. One of them opened the boot then took out some white sacks, so big that they had to bend their knees and wrap both their arms around to lift them. They staggered to the front door in stops and starts. One of them balanced his sack on his knee so he could knock, but Rigby suddenly came round the side of the house, wiping his hands on his overalls. They exchanged some words and then the men used wheelbarrows to take the sacks round the back of the house, working quickly. When they came back, one of the men handed Rigby a brown paper bag, smaller this time. Rigby reached into his jacket pocket and gave the man some money. He looked left to right before he shut the door.

'What was that all about?' Isobel said as the men were driving away.

'It must be something to do with Mr Godfrey's work, like Mrs Fishwife said,' Flora answered. 'Come on, let's look round the back of the house. The boy might be in the coal cellar.'

But you could only get to the coal cellar through a huge, heavy black trapdoor.

'If we can't lift it, he probably couldn't,' Flora reasoned, after they'd given up and were both rubbing the red grooves on their hands. 'There's only one of him, and he's small. I don't think he's in there.'

Isobel was shielding her eyes against the sun – she still had the headache from the day before, and sunlight always made it worse – as she looked at Splint Hall. She wondered if the boy was somehow hiding inside rather than out. There were so many rooms, after all, she thought, looking from window to window. As she was turning her head, she caught sight of something at the edge of her vision: something black, clinging to the side of the house like a spider.

'Flora, what's that?'

'What's what?'

'There, just below the roof.'

Flora followed her finger to where she was pointing. She squinted with concentration. 'It's a staircase,' she said.

They moved closer to the house to get a better view. The staircase was made of iron and looked a little spindly, like you wouldn't want to be walking on it in a storm. It went from a wooden door at the top of the house all the way to the ground, twisting and turning on its way.

'Where do you think it goes up to?' Isobel said.

'I bet it's Mr Godfrey's room,' Flora said. 'He probably did it so that he can get out if the house got bombed and there was a fire. Never mind anyone else. Come on, the boy's not going to be up there, is he?'

A few hours later, after Flora and Isobel had unsuccessfully searched the whole house and gardens, the late summer sun dipped below the grand roof of Splint Hall.

'He must not have come today,' Flora said, her voice heavy with disappointment. 'We've looked everywhere.'

'We didn't look in the air-raid shelter again,' Isobel pointed out. They hadn't been able to as Rigby had, after receiving the mysterious delivery, spent the rest of the afternoon pruning the roses. It was impossible to snoop around the air-raid shelter without him seeing.

'If he was in there, we'd know about it,' Flora said. 'Rigby would have seen him. We'll just have to look again tomorrow.'

So they did. In the afternoon they searched the gardens again, from top to bottom, left to right, looking behind bushes and inside the greenhouse and even glancing at the air-raid shelter (they were both too nervous to actually go inside, in case Mr Godfrey saw them). But there was still no sign of the boy.

They searched the next afternoon too. When they got to the main lawn, Rigby stopped pouring petrol into a lawnmower and put his hands on his hips, adding more oily streaks to his overalls. 'You girls are always in these gardens, snooping around,' he said, his eyes narrowing to slits. Jake lifted his head up and growled toothily. 'What are you up to?'

'Nothing,' Flora said innocently. 'We're just exploring. It's what children do.'

Rigby shook his head, muttered something inaudible under his breath, and went back to his task. He set the can down, pulled what looked like a string high above his head once, twice, and the engine coughed loudly. 'I'd explore somewhere else if I were you,' he said as he started mowing the grass, straight towards them. 'You don't want to be caught in front of these teeth.'

The metal glinted as grass flew up behind him, and the girls ran back to the house.

The next day there was no chance of exploring. It was raining. Hard, heavy rain that pooled on the roof of the air-raid shelter and on the steps leading up to the house.

'Where is he?' Flora said crossly.

She was standing on Isobel's bed (not that she had asked), looking out of the porthole window at the gardens below.

'He's not going to come in this weather,' Isobel said. She was sitting at the foot of the bed, out of the way of her sister's legs, reading. 'I wouldn't.'

'But he didn't come yesterday either, or the day before that.' Flora pressed her nose to the glass.

'Maybe he's given up,' Isobel said, turning the page. 'Anyway, what if he's not a thief? Mum didn't think he was.'

'What would he be doing in the air-raid shelter if he wasn't stealing those dresses?' Flora said.

Isobel hadn't thought of that. Her brain whirred. 'But why would he steal dresses?' she said. 'Boys don't wear dresses.' She thought of the mermaid dress, trailing on the floor, and the small outline of the boy in the entrance. 'Anyway, they'd be too big for him.'

Flora smothered a laugh with her hand. 'Not to wear them, silly. To sell them. That's what thieves do. Don't you know anything?'

Isobel bit her lip. '*You're* silly. No one would buy them. No one wears dresses like that.'

'They don't now, but they did before the War.'

'How do you know?'

'Cos I've seen pictures,' Flora said loftily. 'Mum used to wear stuff like that too, you know. Hasn't she shown you the pictures?' She looked down at Isobel. 'Maybe she will when you're older,' she said.

She didn't say it unkindly but in that moment, Isobel hated her. She stared at her book so hard that the letters swam into each other and – even though she was called a baby, pathetic and a nuisance – refused to speak to her sister again for the rest of the day.

The next morning, Isobel still wasn't speaking to Flora. When Flora said, 'Isobel, can you pass the sugar please?' very politely, Isobel gave the bowl to her, but didn't say anything. When Flora said, even more politely, 'Thank you,' Isobel just took another bite of her toast. Even when Flora said, 'I slept very well. Did you sleep well, Izzy?' Isobel ignored her.

Normally Mum would have told her off. But today she didn't even seem to notice. She was either staring into space or looking at her watch. The only thing that got her attention was Aunty Bea coming in, looking even more tired than normal. She glanced at Mum warily, said sorry for being late, then sat down. She proceeded to cut her toast into tiny squares, each the size of a stamp. She did this every morning and every morning Isobel wanted to ask why, but didn't. She knew it was the sort of question that would get the Look. If Isobel had done the same thing, Mum would have told her off for playing with her food. But Aunty Bea was a grown-up, which meant – as far as Isobel could see – that she could do whatever she wanted with her breakfast.

'I thought we might go for a day out today,' Mum said.

Aunty Bea looked confused for a moment. 'A day out?'

'Perhaps we could take the girls into the village.' Mum's face brightened at the thought. 'Or even to Burley Caves!' She turned to her daughters. 'Would you like that, girls?'

'What's Burley Caves?' Flora asked.

'The caves are what made Burlington famous, a long time ago,' Mum said. 'They're not real caves. Well, they are, but they're manmade. They used to be mines. Men dug up flint and limestone for centuries upon centuries, and now the caves and tunnels go on for miles and miles.'

Isobel swallowed, her bread sticking in her throat even more than usual. 'Miles and miles?' she said.

'Oh, so you do talk,' Flora said.

'Whatever do you mean, Flora?' Mum said. Her eyes narrowed as Isobel dipped her head back towards her toast. 'I hope you two haven't been quarrelling.'

'*I* haven't,' Flora replied.

Mum rubbed the skin on her temples, the way she sometimes did when she had a headache. 'Well, how about it, then?' she said finally, letting it pass. 'Do you want to visit the caves?'

Isobel thought about it. She imagined the caves and tunnels stretching on underground, all that earth on top of them. She supposed that rabbits and mice and moles didn't mind it. But there was something so horrible about the idea. How did you know the earth on top of the tunnels was going to stay where it was? What was to stop it from falling in? As a reflex, she reached into her pocket, where her dragon was waiting. She held it tightly, her palm curling around the long, ridged tail, and instantly felt better.

'I want to go,' Flora said. 'But Isobel won't. She doesn't like dark places. She gets scared.'

'No, I don't!' Isobel protested, even though it was true.

'What have you got in your pocket, Izzy?' Mum said, her eyes narrowing.

'Nothing,' Isobel immediately replied.

'Yes, you have, you're holding something. Show me.'

Reluctantly, Isobel took the dragon out and put it on the table. Then a strange thing happened. Aunty Bea and Mum both stopped eating and stared at the dragon. Aunty Bea let the square of toast she was holding drop back on to her plate.

'The dragons,' Mum said. 'I'd forgotten all about them.'

'Where did you find it?' Aunty Bea said.

'I . . . we . . .' Isobel glanced at her sister, but Flora just looked angrily back at her, cross that Isobel had got them discovered. 'I found it in a chest, in the pink room,' she admitted.

'The pink room?' Aunty Bea echoed, alarm ringing in her voice. 'But girls, you mustn't . . .'

'Should I not have taken it?' Isobel said. 'Will Mr Godfrey mind? I can put it back—'

'Don't be silly,' Mum said. 'They're our dragons anyway, and they're meant to be played with. Aren't they, Bea?'

'Yes, yes,' Aunty Bea said. 'Of course you can have it. It's just . . . you must tell me beforehand if you want to go into a room. Will you?' She looked beseechingly from Flora to Isobel, then back again. 'I mean, do you promise? It's just, Mr Godfrey doesn't like people snooping.'

'They were hardly snooping,' Mum protested. 'We told them to explore.'

'I know, but . . .' Aunty Bea trailed off. 'You know. I didn't mean . . .' She turned to the girls and gave them a trembling smile. 'Of course you can play with the dragons.'

'We weren't playing,' Flora said at once. 'We're too old to play. Well, I am, anyway,' she said, with a pointed look at Isobel.

Isobel stuck her tongue out at her.

'Don't do that, Izzy,' Mum said.

'There's nothing wrong with playing,' Aunty Bea said. 'No matter what age you are.'

'We used to take them around with us everywhere,' Mum marvelled, remembering. She picked up Isobel's dragon and turned it over and over in her hands, a strange expression on her face. As she touched it, perhaps because of the warmth of her fingers, the metal changed colour. Only very slightly, but Isobel could see it. It was a warm, coppery glow. 'Your grandfather gave them to us. He loved dragons,' Mum said. 'He used to do hundreds and hundreds of drawings of them. Your grandma used to get so cross because she'd bring him tea in his study and she couldn't get across the room, there were so many papers left lying about. She used to say that if he loved her half as much as he did dragons, she'd be the most beloved wife in England.'

Aunty Bea giggled but Isobel didn't understand. 'But dragons aren't real. Are they?' She stopped, uncertain.

'Of course not,' Mum said, stroking Isobel's cheek.

'That one was yours,' Aunty Bea said unexpectedly, looking at the copper dragon. 'Mine was silver. I don't suppose that was in the chest too, was it?' she said, a little wistfully.

After a moment, Flora took the silver dragon out of her pocket and gave it to Aunty Bea, who held it up, reverently, to the light.

'I always used to love the way it shone,' she said. 'Like moonlight in a pond. We were only girls when Daddy gave us them.' She looked up suddenly. 'Around the age you two are now, in fact! How funny.' She smiled as she looked back down at the dragon, stroking it softly. 'That would have made Daddy smile. He was the type of man who always had a smile in his eyes.'

'Like the man in the picture on the stairs,' Isobel said.

'Of course!' Mum said. 'I'm so used to his portrait by now that I don't even notice it. I should have shown you before.'

'You mean that's Grandpa?' Isobel said, surprised.

'I knew it was,' Flora said immediately, though Isobel didn't think she had, because she'd never said. 'I've met him, haven't I Mummy?'

'You have, but you were only a baby,' Mum replied. 'You can't have remembered it.'

Flora went a little red. 'I still knew it was him. I just *knew*.'

Aunty Bea's eyes were sad. 'He got that portrait done around the time you visited, just a few months before he died. And then Mummy died only a year after that. It was over ten years ago, now. Before the War had even started. And before I met Charles . . .' She sighed as she looked at the dragon, then gave it back to Flora.

Mum handed Isobel's dragon to her and she put it back in her pocket. For some reason, the air got thicker, like Mr Godfrey was there even though he wasn't. Flora put her dragon away too, then pulled the newspaper towards her.

'So, what about these caves?' Mum said, after a few moments. 'It would be nice to get out of the house for a bit, wouldn't it?'

Isobel looked out of the window. The only sign of the rain

from yesterday was the wet grass, which was glittering in the bright sunshine.

'I'd like to go,' she said, feeling a sudden longing to be outside.

'I don't know,' Aunty Bea began.

'Please?' Isobel said, suddenly desperate. 'Please can we?'

Aunty Bea looked at her for a few moments. She sucked in her bottom lip sharply, then smiled, but it didn't reach her eyes. 'Of course we can,' she said, giving Flora's arm a squeeze. 'I'll just need to let Charles know. I'm sure he'll be glad to have us out from under his feet for a bit,' she added, sounding like she was trying to convince herself.

Mum looked at Aunty Bea with an expression Isobel didn't understand. It was all knotted like when Mum was worried, but there was something else there too, something that made her grip her knife too tightly. She turned to Flora, doing her best to smile. 'Would you like to go, Flora?'

Flora looked up from the newspaper she was reading, her face as troubled as her mother's. 'There's been another one,' she whispered.

'Another what?' Mum said. She put the knife down and snatched the paper. 'Flora, I've told you not to read the news before I have.'

'Another what?' Isobel said, as her mother scanned the paper quickly.

Flora sat back in her seat, her face pale. 'An unexploded bomb,' she said.

A cold ripple shivered through Isobel and she huddled down in her seat. Now that the War was over, and the Nazis were no longer coming, unexploded bombs were everyone's greatest fear.

No one knew where they were or how many there were. They were hiding in the rubble or deep underground, and if you hit one with a car or a digger they could blow up. Isobel didn't think it was fair. There was all this mess from the bombs that *had* exploded. But when people tried to clear it up, they just found more bombs, which made even more bricks and dust and other mess. Maybe it would never end, not ever, it would just go round and round in circles, and eventually there'd be no houses left.

'That's a bad one,' Mum said, sucking in her bottom lip just like Aunty Bea did.

'How many?' Aunty Bea asked.

'Fifteen,' Mum said, flicking a glance in Isobel's direction.

Isobel didn't know why they didn't just come out and say it. They were talking about the number of people who had died. But she didn't say anything, she just picked at the lace doily underneath her plate.

'They were clearing a bombsite in East London,' Mum sighed. 'They got hit so bad that way.'

'Are there any unexploded bombs here?' Isobel asked. 'Maybe we shouldn't go into the village after all.'

'No, I don't think so,' Aunty Bea said, frowning at the thought of it. 'That would be very unlucky. We only got hit once during the whole War. And it was on George Street, nowhere near Burley Caves.'

'I'm sure there aren't any,' Mum said, putting her arm round Isobel. 'There are only nice things to see. Like shops and the church, and the caves, of course. That sounds fun, doesn't it?'

'Do we have to?' Flora said, leaning her head on her elbow.

Mum tutted. 'Flora, you said you wanted to earlier.'

Isobel nodded. The thought of a morning away from Splint

Hall, and therefore Mr Godfrey, was too good to miss, even if it did mean going underground. She imagined it, and something else popped into her mind, something so brilliant that she hardly dared say it, for fear it would dissolve into dust.

'Could we have lunch in the village?' Isobel asked.

'That's a good idea!' Mum said.

The door opened and Mrs Fishwife came in. She nodded at everyone, did the strange bouncing thing, then started to clear away the crumb-covered plates.

'I don't know if anything's open,' Aunty Bea said, sounding worried. 'There's only the public house these days. Is the Eagle still doing food, Miss Stewart?'

'Just on Saturdays, Ma'am,' she replied.

'It's Thursday today,' Flora pointed out.

Mrs Fishwife stood up, the plates expertly stacked in the crook of her arm, and looked at Mum thoughtfully. 'Are you wanting lunch out? Ma'am's right, there's not much about in Burlington. It all stopped during the War and it hasn't come back again.' She glanced out of the window. 'But I could put together some bits and pieces for a picnic. It's still nice outdoors, though it's not far off October.'

'That would be wonderful!' Mum said.

She sniffed. 'That's overdoing it a bit, Ma'am, if you don't mind me saying so. It'll only be bread and cheese and maybe a bit of corned beef.'

'It'll be perfect,' Mum said. 'What do you think, girls?'

Even Flora couldn't resist the thought of a day without lunch with Mr Godfrey. With any luck, Isobel thought, they wouldn't have to see him at *all*.

'Yes, please!' they chorused.

Mum laughed. 'Well go on then, go and get your coats and we'll be off.'

Aunty Bea stood up awkwardly, her hands gripping the table as she pushed her chair back. 'I'll just tell Charles,' she said, the words trembling a little as they came out. 'I won't be long.'

'Don't you worry about that, Ma'am,' Mrs Fishwife said, her voice firm. 'I've got to get his breakfast things and I'll let him know then.'

Aunty Bea hovered, unsure. 'But—'

'You just get yourself off and enjoy that sunshine,' Mrs Fishwife said, pressing down gently on Aunty Bea's shoulder so that she sat down again. 'There's no harm in spending some time with your sister and nieces, is there?' She stopped, the colour rising in her cheeks, as if she thought she'd said too much. 'I'll have the picnic basket ready in ten minutes,' she mumbled. The door clicked shut decisively as she went out.

'Well,' Mum said, looking after Mrs Fishwife. 'That's that, then!'

Aunty Bea looked at the shut door and smiled hesitantly. But her hands were still gripping the table, like she'd forgotten to stop.

CHAPTER SEVEN

Fifteen minutes later, Flora, Isobel, Mum and Aunty Bea shut the huge wooden door of Splint Hall behind them and set out for the village.

Aunty Bea had said they could take the road (because of petrol rationing there were hardly any cars on it these days anyway) but the path was nicer. So they took the path that wound through the trees at the bottom of the driveway and across the fields.

Isobel couldn't help agreeing that it was nice. Trees grew either side, bending their branches to meet each other overhead like they were lined up in two rows, ready to dance. The air smelled of old leaves, warming in the sunshine.

'It's not even cold in the shade,' Mum remarked. 'Mrs Fishwife's right. It is warm for this time of year.'

Since leaving Splint Hall, Aunty Bea was behaving differently. Instead of looking at the floor or her hands, she was stopping to peer at things in the trees or look up at the sky. Her footsteps seemed lighter, like she had shrugged off a particularly heavy coat.

'Look, the woods end just there,' she said, pointing ahead and then taking Flora's hand. 'Let's run in the sunshine!'

Aunty Bea and Flora ran off. Mum grabbed Isobel's hand and

they followed, their coats flapping and their feet kicking up leaves as they giggled. In no time at all, the path curved out from the trees and they were standing in a meadow full of warm sunshine and long green stripes of bushy plants.

'What's that?' Isobel asked. 'Are they cabbages?'

'Potatoes,' Mum explained, slightly out of breath. 'You can only see their tops. They grow in the soil underneath.'

'They'll be harvested next week,' Aunty Bea said, bending down to inspect the green leaves. She pulled one up and a potato emerged, soil still clinging to it. 'Miss Stewart will be pleased. She's been complaining that she's running out.'

'Do you think she might make us chips?' Flora asked hopefully.

'Ooh,' Mum said, nudging her in the ribs. 'Now there's a thought!'

'Chips with salt and vinegar . . .' Isobel said dreamily.

'Steaming in the paper . . .' Mum added.

'What are chips?' Aunty Bea said.

Flora stopped dead in her tracks. 'Aunty Bea, do you mean you've never had them?'

'I don't think going to the chippie would be the sort of thing Mr Godfrey would approve of,' Mum said under her breath. She'd meant it as a joke, but Aunty Bea stopped smiling.

'Come on,' Aunty Bea said, quickening her pace. 'We'll never make it to the village at this rate.'

They followed her down the edge of the field to the bottom, where they crossed over a stile and into another field, this one filled with yellow grasses that swayed in the wind. ('Mustard,' Mum explained.) The path cut a green trail diagonally across the crop, so narrow that Isobel could feel the grasses scratching gently on her legs. At the furthest edge of this field there was a dark green hedgerow, which they followed up to the road. They only had to walk along the road for a couple of minutes before it swerved to the left and headed sharply downhill, showing them the village nestling below.

Aunty Bea had started to look nervous again, Isobel thought. She was twirling a lock of hair between her fingers, faster and faster, and her quick, darting look had come back.

'Perhaps we shouldn't go after all,' she said.

'Why ever not?' Mum said, her eyebrows pulling together in a frown. 'Don't be silly, Bea. We've just walked all the way from the house. Why wouldn't we go?'

Aunty Bea stopped twirling her hair and put her arms straight by her sides. She breathed out a deep, quick breath. Then, without answering Mum, she continued walking down the road.

Isobel thought it was strange that Burlington was even called a village. It seemed to be just one road with a few buildings on it. The first had a red post box set into the brickwork, with *Burlington Post Office* written above the door.

As they walked past the post office and a shop with vegetables and powdered milk in the windows, Isobel began to understand why Aunty Bea thought they shouldn't have come. The shopkeepers were staring. Not the kind of curious staring that people do when strangers come. This was a different kind of staring, like they knew exactly who they were, and they didn't like them being there one bit. The woman in the grocery was wearing a headscarf and wiping the counter when she saw them. She put the cloth down and leaned against the counter, folding her arms as she watched them go by. It made Isobel's skin prickle.

Aunty Bea just looked at the floor and said nothing.

Mum tried to smile and say hello to people she recognised. She peered through the window into the butcher's, her face lighting up when she saw an old man leaning against the carving block. 'Tony!' she cried, rushing inside to take his hand. 'You made the best sausages in the whole of South England. That's what my father used to say, anyway. It's me, Julia,' she said, her smile faltering as he stepped back. 'Don't you recognise me?'

'Of course, Ma'am,' Tony said, not meeting her eye. He took his hand away and dropped it to his side, like he wasn't sure what to do with it.

'You don't have to call me "Ma'am",' Mum said. 'Don't be silly, Tony.'

Tony looked quickly at Aunty Bea, who had followed Isobel and Flora inside and was standing in the entrance, holding the door half open. She flushed red and looked away. Tony's face twisted in dislike as he returned his gaze to the floor. 'Things have changed round here a bit, since you left,' he muttered.

'What do you mean—' Mum started, then stopped as the old bell fixed to the top of the door clanged loudly. Aunty Bea had left.

'Bea!' Mum called, then rushed after her. The bell clanged for a second time.

Flora and Isobel were left in the shop, which was dark and gloomy. There was a marble counter behind a single pane of glass, which looked like the place you'd display all the meat. However, it was empty except for two parcels, each the size of a fist, wrapped in brown paper. Isobel's eyes travelled upwards to see a row of empty hooks above Tony's head. Then she looked at Tony. He was old, she could tell that from his grey hair, and the way he was standing awkwardly, like his hip gave him trouble. He sniffed once, loudly.

'I don't know what you're waiting in here for,' he said gruffly. 'You got your rations through Miss Stewart. You can't have any more. Even if you're the Burlingtons.' He said the last word in what Isobel knew was a 'hoity-toity' accent – the 't' sharp and the rest of it soft and musical. 'You'll have to make do with the same as the rest of us.'

'We know that,' Flora mumbled. She grabbed Isobel's hand and tried to pull her towards the door, but Isobel shrugged her off.

'We're not Burlingtons actually,' she said, her voice coming out loud and clear as she looked straight at Tony. 'We're Johnsons. Our daddy was called Peter Johnson.'

For the first time, Tony looked at her properly. From the way his eyebrows shot up, she thought he was surprised.

'Before he died,' Isobel added, to explain. 'He was a pilot.'

Tony's mouth dropped open.

'Iso*bel*,' Flora hissed. 'Come *on*.'

Isobel could feel Tony looking at them as they crossed the green-and-white tiled floor and left. Outside, Mum and Aunty Bea were nowhere to be seen. There were two ladies walking down the street towards them, one holding the hand of a toddler who was taking unsteady steps. The little boy saw Isobel and Flora and pointed. His mother smiled at the two girls, until her friend whispered something in her ear. She picked the boy up quickly and the two women quickened their pace, their shoes making a clopping sound as they went past.

'What's going on?' Isobel whispered to Flora.

Flora folded her arms. 'I don't know, but you're not going to make it any better by saying silly things.'

'What do you mean?'

'Like just saying our daddy's name was Johnson and he was a pilot and he died in the War to that man.' Flora brushed a piece of hair off her face angrily. 'That's private. We'll never make friends if you keep blurting out things like that.'

'Why not?' Isobel said.

'Because it's not how people do things.'

'But why?'

'Because it's *not.*'

Isobel looked at her shoes. 'Well, I didn't know you wanted to make friends with that old man, anyway,' she said.

'Of course I didn't!' Flora replied hotly. 'That's not the point!'

Isobel felt a small flash of satisfaction at rattling her. Then she noticed her mother and Aunty Bea walking towards them. Mum was smoothing her hair and Aunty Bea's face was pale.

'Come on, then, girls,' Mum said briskly. 'The caves are on the other side of the village.'

If they were at home, the other side of town would have taken two buses, perhaps even three. Here, it was just a five-minute walk. It felt quick even though no one was speaking. Isobel kept her eyes on Flora's white socks as they moved up and down in front of her. Mum said it was wrong to hate people. You should always try to see it from their side, and forgive them. But she had never said anything about hating socks. She had never said anything about hating the way they were so clean and perfect, or hating how their frills were so *frilly*.

'Here we are then,' Mum said.

Isobel looked up. She'd been so busy hating Flora's socks that the change in landscape came as a complete surprise. The houses had petered out and now there was a huge green hill looming above them. Directly in front, the black mouth of the cave yawned open. A small painted sign said in cracked black letters, *Burley Caves, entrance 1 penny, ha'penny for children*. Underneath there was a black box with a slit for you to put the coins in.

'There used to be someone here,' Mum said, 'taking the coins. What was his name? Albert, I think. He was ancient!'

Aunty Bea nodded. 'He died a few years ago. Now they just have the box. People are generally honest and, well . . . the caves don't get as many visitors as they used to, anyway.'

Mum nodded. She fumbled with the metal clasp of her handbag, then reached inside and found enough coins for everyone. They clanged as they hit the bottom of the box.

Mum, Aunty Bea and Flora stepped inside the entrance, but Isobel hung back. Suddenly, she was afraid. She gulped, then imagined what Flora would say if she was too scared to go inside. She dug her fist into her pocket and clenched the dragon, then followed.

Just inside the cave there was a box with fat, creamy candles, and matches.

'Girls, here, you have one each,' Mum said, lighting the wicks carefully and passing them on. 'Just in case. But I don't want you getting separated, do you understand? We've all got to stay together. It's easy to get lost down here.'

'How far are we going?' Isobel asked.

'Don't worry, we won't go too far,' Mum said. 'I know you don't like the dark, Izzy.'

'That's not true!' Isobel protested.

'No, course it's not,' Flora said under her breath.

The floor was covered in a mixture of stones, some small, some large, so you had to watch where you were going. Aunty Bea went first, then Mum, then Flora, then Isobel. The flickering light made shadows dance on the walls, which weren't grey but a brownish yellow colour, like dirty sand. Isobel stopped, reached out and touched a wall. It was soft and crumbly – a small piece of it broke away and fell on to the floor, where it scattered. Something caught in her throat. *It's not safe*, she thought.

'Hurry up, Izzy,' Flora said, her voice sharp. 'We're all waiting for you.'

As Isobel caught up, Mum started to explain the history of the caves. 'They date back to Roman times. They used lime to make mortar for their buildings.'

'What's mortar?' Flora asked.

'Sticky stuff that you use to hold bricks together. They used it for roads too.'

Isobel felt a little better when she heard that. Limestone was obviously sticky, so hopefully it would all stick together. Instead of coming crashing down on their heads.

'They used to have hundreds of people working down here,' Mum said. 'There were some dreadful accidents. One time, twenty men were trapped when a tunnel collapsed behind them. That's why most of it's closed off. They don't let people go down too far now. Only about a mile's open to the public, I think.'

As Mum walked on, Isobel felt panic bubble up again at the thought of the accidents. The candle felt slippery in her hand.

'Isobel, stop wobbling the candle like that,' Flora said,

sounding exasperated. She stopped so that Isobel could catch up with her. 'Give it to me.'

'No.'

'Come on, you'll drop it and it's dangerous,' Flora said, trying to grab the candle. Isobel stepped backwards, her foot twisting awkwardly in the stone.

'I won't drop it! Why do you always think I'm such a baby? I'm only two years younger than you.'

'Two and a half!' Flora said. 'And maybe I wouldn't treat you like a baby if you didn't act like one.' She looked down the corridor. 'Now Mum and Aunty Bea have gone.'

'That's not my fault.'

Flora let out a deep, long-suffering sigh. 'Look, it doesn't matter if you're scared. I know it's a bit dark and horrible down here. I know it reminds you of . . . of before. Of at home, during the raid. Just give me the candle, then we can go and find Mum and Aunty Bea and say you want to go. They won't mind.'

'I said, I'm not scared!' Isobel shouted.

Flora didn't say anything, but in the next moment, she lunged for the candle again. Isobel jumped backwards, then turned and ran, ignoring Flora's shout behind her.

She meant to run straight back outside, but they must have gone further than Isobel had realised. The corridor felt longer than before, with more twists and turns. There was a fork that Isobel didn't recognise and – without even really thinking about it – she took the left path. Her anger with her sister was making her legs go faster than normal.

'I'm *not* scared,' she whispered to herself. 'I'm not.'

After a few minutes, it slowly dawned on her that it seemed to be getting darker, not lighter. There was a strange thickness in the air. Eventually, Isobel shuddered to a stop, and realised she was lost.

The blackness closed in. It swooped from the walls and pressed on her cheeks, her shoulders, her eyes – which Isobel promptly shut. She swallowed, hard, then opened them again and took a deep breath, trying not to panic. *I'll just go back the way I came*, she thought. *Easy.*

She took one slow step backwards, then stopped. She had heard something from further down the tunnel. It was a long, slow hiss, the kind of noise a balloon makes if it has a tiny hole in its neck. Almost a whistle, but not quite.

Isobel gripped her candle tighter. 'Hello?' she said, trying to be brave.

Her hello bounced back to her – once, twice, three times.

There was silence. Then the hiss started again. It went on for a few seconds then stopped, then started again, but a little deeper. It sounded almost like someone – or something – was breathing in and out. Suddenly Isobel realised why the air felt thicker. She had expected it to be cold and damp this far underground but it wasn't – it was warm. So warm that tiny pinpricks of sweat were breaking out on her forehead and upper lip. There was also a strange, smoky smell, but it wasn't quite wood smoke, or even the smoke from the factories back at home. It had something oilier mixed in. It was almost like, Isobel thought, someone was cooking meat . . .

Isobel had just taken another nervous step backwards when she heard a new noise. It was a sharp clunk, like bone hitting rock. Then there was another one. The hissing got louder as whatever was making the noise got closer.

Run, Isobel told herself, but her body betrayed her and stayed right where it was. It felt like her muscles were frozen solid. She fumbled in her pocket, her palms slippery with sweat, for the comfort of her dragon, then jerked her hand back in surprise. The dragon was burning hot.

But there wasn't time to think about that now. The clunks stopped, leaving the hissing, which was now louder than ever. With a trembling hand, Isobel lifted the candle into the darkness of the tunnel.

At first, she couldn't quite understand what she was seeing. It looked like a branch, but it was gunmetal grey instead of brown, and strangely twisted. Then it moved, very slowly, like something waking up. A fist-sized knot on the end uncurled into what looked like a hand, except the fingers were too long, twice the size of normal fingers at least, and they weren't that odd square, roundish shape at the tips like normal fingers, these were points . . .

Slowly, Isobel realised she was looking at five long, razor-sharp claws.

Then, she ran. She ran as fast as she could, the candle jack-hammering up and down, throwing crazed shadows onto the walls. She heard the thing hiss behind her and the clunks start up again but faster this time. *It's following me,* she realised, and she closed her eyes against the terror of it. She willed her legs to go faster but the clunks and the hissing were getting louder. It was so close she could almost feel the claws on her back . . .

Without thinking, she turned blindly and flung her candle in the darkness. The thing howled, but Isobel didn't stop to listen. As she ran, she became aware of a faint, milky glow up ahead, and her heart soared. Ignoring the burning in her legs, she sprinted forwards, letting the glow guide her until she barrelled out of the caves into the blinding grey of the morning, and into her sister.

'Isobel!' Flora shouted, pulling her upright, then shaking her a little. 'Where have you been? Mum and Aunty Bea have been worried sick. They're still inside, looking for you!'

'Wha— what?' Isobel turned back in a panic, thinking Mum and Aunty Bea had to come out, they had to get out of the tunnels *right now*, but immediately felt relief when she saw the two of them at the black mouth of the cave. Mum saw Isobel and her face flashed from worried to cross, then to concerned. 'There you are!' she said. 'Thank goodness. I told you not to get separated! Izzy, whatever's the matter?'

Isobel had thrown herself into her mother's arms. 'There was a monster,' she choked. 'In the tunnel. It made this hissing sound and it chased me and it . . . it had *claws*.'

There was a moment's silence, in which Mum stroked Isobel's hair soothingly. Eventually Isobel looked up, wiping her eyes with the back of her hand, to see Mum and Aunty Bea looking at each other with an expression she couldn't read. Then she saw Flora looking at her, her arms folded with satisfaction and her cheeks round and smug.

'You see?' Flora said, in her most irritating I-told-you-so voice. 'Didn't I say she was too young to go into the caves?'

CHAPTER EIGHT

Ever since she could remember, Isobel had had headaches.

Mum said it was because of the War – not because the planes and the bombs were noisy (though that was a part of it) but because of the fear and worry. But if that were the case, Isobel reasoned, now that the War was over, the headaches should have gone away, and they hadn't. Sometimes it was a sharp, bright twang, like the stroke of a violin played diagonally across her temples. Sometimes it was a dull drumming, like the kind of rain that you think is never going to stop. Sometimes it was a rattling when she moved her head, and sometimes – like the night after Isobel went to Burley Caves – it was a whole orchestra, different parts of her head ringing to create the tune.

Mum used to try giving her aspirin. Isobel always liked to see the way it fizzed in a glass of water, but even though she swallowed every last drop, it never worked. Sometimes Mum put a cold cloth on her forehead and that didn't work either, though it felt nice. But Isobel hadn't told Mum about the headache she currently had anyway, because since they had returned from their day out she hadn't really spoken to anybody. No one had believed her about what she had seen in the tunnels. Flora said she was just imagining things, like in her dreams. Mum said that she believed Isobel had seen something, but it can't have been a monster. It must have been another person. Maybe they needed help. She had even telephoned the police station when she got home (they said they would take a look tomorrow). Aunty Bea hadn't said anything at all, but Isobel had caught her gazing pityingly at her when she thought Isobel was busy eating her sandwich.

The night that their house had got bombed, Isobel had had the worst kind of headache. It was like someone rolling their knuckles over the top of her head, hard, like they really wanted it to hurt.

She had sat there in the shelter on the cold bench, her eyes screwed up tight. Mum had her arm round her and she'd tried to pretend that they weren't in the shelter at all, that it was a night when the Germans hadn't come. That they were in Flora and Isobel's bedroom and Mum was reading them a story – one of the best kind of stories, with everything turning out all right in the end.

But she couldn't pretend very well because of the noise. The sirens wailed on and the planes sounded like thunder or they buzzed like huge bees, depending on how big they were. Isobel knew they weren't interested in them. They were flying over, heading for a city where there were lots of people all together in one place. They were too small, Mum always said so. She said so that night too, and Isobel snuggled closer to her.

Then it happened. They heard the whine of it before the explosion. Flora said, 'What's that?' and Mum looked up, her mouth half open, not believing it, and then the bomb hit. There was a huge crash and then a boom that seemed to go on forever, and the sound of tinkling glass. The whole ground juddered and Flora was screaming and Mum was holding them too tight and Mrs Dooley was praying and Mum was *really* holding too tight, Isobel was trying to get out, she was pushing against Mum's arms but Mum wouldn't let go. She couldn't breathe. And then Isobel turned her head away from Mum's jumper and she did breathe, and the air was full of something thick that made her cough and her eyes water. And what felt like hours later, when the juddering finally stopped and the All Clear sounded, Isobel thought she couldn't see, but it was because there was something blocking the air-raid shelter entrance. They had had to wait for some men to move the rubble before they got out.

Mum said they had never been in any danger, but Isobel had never forgotten the feeling of being shut up in the dark. It liked to sneak up on her. At breakfast, or when she was walking to the shops, or – like now – when she was trying to get to sleep. Though she would never admit it to Flora, Isobel *was* scared of the dark. At Mrs Dooley's she'd wanted to sleep with the lamp on but Mum said no because it was an old gas one and it was dangerous. Here, they only had a candle, so it was out of the question. But Isobel wanted light more than ever. Because now, as well as remembering the raid, she also couldn't stop remembering what she had seen in Burley Caves.

What was it? Isobel wondered as she turned over in her cold, hard bed. Her blankets were tucked in so she could hardly move her legs. Normally she pulled the sheets out but not tonight. It felt safer, somehow, this way.

Isobel knew the thing she had seen wasn't a bear or a wolf.

They were furry, and though they had sharp claws they weren't as big as the ones on the creature. Plus, those animals walked on all fours, and even though Isobel hadn't seen the whole of what was in the cave, she knew from the position of its hand that it had been standing upright. She also knew, despite what her mother said, that it wasn't a person. She shivered, remembering the thin, twisted thing that must have been its arm. No human's arm could look like that.

Mum had kept Isobel with her until it was time to go to bed. When she sent Isobel up to get ready, she had taken Isobel's face in her hands and looked at her, her hands gripping so tightly it almost hurt.

'What are you doing?' Isobel asked, her voice a bit squashed.

'I'm drawing the bad dreams out,' Mum said, kissing her forehead.

It probably wasn't possible to draw dreams out, though Isobel didn't say anything. Anyway, it didn't seem that she would get a chance to find out tonight. She'd just heard the clock strike two and she was still awake.

What if the thing left the cave?

The words had appeared, uninvited, in her head. Isobel swallowed, wishing she could unthink them, but she couldn't. There wasn't any reason for it to stay underground. Unless it liked the dark, but if that was the case, wouldn't it come out during night-time? It could be creeping across the lawn right now, coming up to the house, its claws scraping against the door as it pushed it open . . .

On legs that were slightly wobbly, Isobel stood up in her bed. The springs creaked gently as she turned around to face the window.

Flora murmured something in her sleep and Isobel paused, but her sister soon fell quiet and Isobel heard the slow, regular sound of her breathing resume. She leaned forwards and peered out of the small round window.

The grass was dark and as still as a lake. Isobel waited for a few minutes and nothing crossed it – not even a flicker of a fox or the rush of an owl. Isobel breathed out slowly, unaware that she'd been holding her breath. She looked up at the moon, or the thin, frosted sliver of it that was visible. She sighed and was just about to get back into bed when something caught her eye.

It was a car, moving softly and quietly up the driveway. It didn't have its lights on and if Isobel's eyes hadn't been so used to the dark, she might not have seen it at all. But she would have noticed the wobbling light of the lantern that made its way down the steps towards the car. And seen the car stop and a couple of men get out, light lanterns themselves and then get on with helping Rigby load white sacks into the boot. Isobel was quite sure that they were the same sacks that had been delivered a few days before. She wondered what was in them. Mrs Fishwife had said it was something to do with Mr Godfrey's work. But why would they need to be taken away in the dead of night? It was almost like they wanted to make sure that no one saw.

It was only a few minutes before the job was done and the car was driving away, as quietly as it had come. Isobel breathed out, misting the glass. As she wiped it away, she saw something else, something that made her heart jump in her chest.

It was a shower of blue sparks, like they had seen on the way to Splint Hall, over a week ago now. Isobel pressed her face against the window, and waited. After a few seconds it happened again.

The sparks almost looked like droplets from a fountain – they seemed to shoot high into the air from the ground, then cascade down again. Isobel knew they weren't the kind of sparks that came from a normal fire. She just didn't know what kind of sparks they were. Like the locked door, the men coming in the night and the secret staircase, it was a secret that Splint Hall was hugging close to its chest.

But strangely, Isobel didn't mind this one. For some reason, it made her feel safer. She realised, as she snuggled deep into the blankets, the dragon safely under her pillow, that her headache had finally started to lift.

Mr Godfrey didn't join them for lunch the next day. Once again, Isobel and Flora were relieved. When they found him absent for the second day, they were delighted. But then he didn't join them the day after that, and the day after that as well, and Aunty Bea started looking at his empty chair anxiously, and Mum started looking at Aunty Bea anxiously, too. After the lunches where Mr Godfrey wasn't there Aunty Bea would go to his study. There was no shouting, just cold, empty silence. While this was happening Isobel learned something: that anger wasn't always easy to see, and sometimes you couldn't hear it at all. When the door to the Drawing Room was open one morning Isobel saw Aunty Bea touch Mr Godfrey's arm as he was reading the paper. He brushed her off like she was nothing more than a fly, and Aunty Bea turned round and Isobel saw her face. That was when she realised that maybe the worst thing of all – even worse than being shouted at – was being ignored.

'He's cross because we went to the village and the caves and *he* can't go because he can't walk very well,' Flora said. 'So he doesn't want anyone else to go either. You see?'

'No,' Isobel said. 'I don't see. He could ask Rigby to drive him there in the car.'

Flora bent her head back over her sums, not saying anything. She never said anything when she thought Isobel was right, and this always gave Isobel a small flicker of satisfaction. She hadn't said anything when Isobel had told her about the men coming in the night either, only that they should mind their own business and not be nosy.

'Well, Mr Godfrey can't go inside the caves. Not far, anyway,' Flora said eventually.

Isobel put her pencil down on the table and leaned back on the hard wooden chair. They were in the library again. She looked down at her sheet of sums but she had that horrible feeling that she got after a long headache, like tiny ants were crawling on her forehead with spiked feet. Instead, she got her dragon out of her pocket and sat it on the table.

'Mum says we've got to finish this page,' Flora said, without looking up.

'I can't do it,' Isobel said.

'I'll help you.'

'I don't want you to help,' Isobel said, knowing she was being childish.

'Suit yourself,' Flora said. Soon, all Isobel could hear was the scratching of Flora's pencil as she worked. Still holding her dragon, she got up and went to look at the gleaming leather spines on the bookshelf opposite the table. There were all sorts of colours – red, blue, green. She peered closer to read the spidery

83

gold letters on one of them. It said, *A Child's Garden of Verse*. The gold ink was so thick Isobel was sure she would be able to feel its ridges if she touched it. She stretched out one finger, just to see.

'We're not supposed to touch,' Flora said.

Isobel let her hand fall to her side. Irritation – with her sister, with Mr Godfrey, with sums – crawled through her. She walked over to the window and looked out. It was another hot, cloudy day. Except for the odd day of rain, it had been hot ever since Flora and Isobel had arrived. No one could understand it. It put Rigby – who spent most of his time labouring in the gardens – in a foul mood. He swore under his breath as he mopped his sweaty forehead, his shirt ringed by sweat around his armpits. Mrs Fishwife said she'd never seen anything like it and complained of the milk turning bad before its time. Even though it was nearly October, it seemed to be getting hotter, not colder, like winter had simply decided not to come this year.

The leaves were still falling off the trees, Isobel thought, gazing at an old oak tree in front of the stone wall. That was what made it so strange. It looked like autumn, but it wasn't.

Isobel blinked. She was sure she had seen a bit of the trunk detach itself, then pop back into place.

She looked more closely. There it was again! But it wasn't a bit of the trunk at all. It was a figure. Someone wearing a dark shirt. Someone who looked about Isobel's height—

Suddenly, Isobel was running, round the table, swerving to avoid her chair, then out the room and into the corridor.

'Where are you going?' she heard Flora shout behind her, but she didn't stop. She ran all the way – past room after room after room – until she reached the main hallway, then threw the door open and raced round the house to the back.

She looked around wildly. Rigby and Mrs Fishwife were, thankfully, nowhere to be seen. Isobel's blood was thumping in her ears but she forced herself to be very still. That was the only way she'd see the boy again.

For a few seconds, nothing moved. Then something wavered at the edge of her vision. Isobel's head jerked towards it and she saw the boy, very clearly, opening the gate and running into the gardens. Isobel was sure he was heading for the air-raid shelter.

'Wait!'

Isobel glanced behind her. Flora had made it to the back of the house too. But Isobel didn't wait as she tore off after the boy. She ran faster than she ever had in her life, but Flora still caught up with her.

'It's the boy,' Isobel panted.

'I know,' Flora said, sounding out of breath herself. 'I saw him too.'

They were nearly at the air-raid shelter now. Isobel's breath felt hard in her chest and her legs were on fire, but she forced herself to keep running. They ran past the rose bushes, past the summerhouse, past the hazelnut tree on their right—

Then Isobel was flying through the air, and then she was on the ground. As if from far away, she heard Flora gasp. Her breath was knocked out of her completely and her stomach and chest hurt. She rolled on to her side, coming face-to-face with a clump of buttercups. Then she saw a pair of skinny grey woollen legs, with shiny black shoes on the end, coming to a stop about a foot away from her face.

'What did you trip her up for? You could have really hurt her!'

For a second, Isobel thought Flora was shouting at her. But then she realised she was the one Flora was talking about, the one who could have been hurt. Plus, when she looked up Flora wasn't looking at her, she was looking at someone else. Isobel turned. A pair of dirty brown shoes entered her vision.

Close up, she realised that the boy was older than her, perhaps older than Flora, even. He was skinny with long arms and was wearing a dark grey flannel shirt and blue trousers, patched at the knees. A flat cap perched on his head. It was slightly too big for him and the boy pushed it up, letting Isobel see his face properly. She sat up, surprised. His cheeks were red, his eyes were wide and he was breathing heavily through his mouth. He looked absolutely furious.

'Serves her right for following me!' he said.

Flora put her hands on her hips, outraged. 'That's rubbish!' she said. 'Why shouldn't she follow you? This is our home. You're the one who shouldn't be here.' She looked him up and down, a haughty expression on her face. 'You're the one who's a thief.'

The boy's bottom lip jutted out. 'I'm not a thief!' he yelled.

'Could have fooled me,' Flora said. 'What are you doing heading for the air-raid shelter if you don't want those dresses?'

The boy opened his mouth to yell again, but then shut it again, confused. 'Dresses? What dresses?'

Flora rolled her eyes. 'The ones in the air-raid shelter. Don't play dumb.'

The boy looked at her incredulously. 'What would I want with dresses?'

'To sell them,' Isobel explained. 'Not to wear.'

The boy looked down at Isobel, like he'd forgotten she was there. He held out a hand to her grudgingly and she took it. 'Sorry,' he said when she was upright. 'I didn't mean to hurt you. But I don't want anything to do with any dresses. And you've got to stop following me, all right?' He looked around warily. 'I don't want that gardener finding me. He came after me with a spade last time.'

Flora pulled Isobel back by her shoulders, so they were standing next to each other, both facing the boy. 'We'll only stop following you if you tell us what you're doing here,' she said.

The boy's face darkened. 'It's none of your business.'

'We'll keep following you then!'

They stared at each other angrily for a few seconds. Then the boy looked away. He scratched at a livid red scab on his elbow, then started biting his thumbnail, his face troubled. 'You can't,' he said, sounding desperate.

'Why can't we?' Isobel asked.

'I can't tell you.' The boy stopped biting his nail and looked up, furious again. 'This is all your fault, anyway! Well, not your fault but your grandpa's. If he hadn't died then none of this would have happened.' The words were pouring out of him, like he couldn't stop them.

'That Mr Godfrey would never have come and he wouldn't have let my dad go cos he thought he was stealing, though he *wasn't*. Dad would still be the gamekeeper and Pat and I would help him and we could do what we've always done, and everything would be all right.'

'What do you mean?' Isobel asked. 'What have you always done?'

The boy didn't reply. He started chewing his nail again. 'Dad'll have to come here,' he said, as if to himself. 'He'll have to convince Mr Godfrey to take us back.'

'He's not going to do that,' Flora said. 'He thinks you're all thieves. He told us that the next time you come here he's going to call the police. He doesn't like you at all.' Flora folded her arms. 'I don't blame him. Snooping round the bushes, tripping up my sister . . . I don't think I like you either. Plus, you can't blame my grandpa. It's not his fault he died, is it?'

'It's his fault for not telling anyone!' the boy shouted.

'Telling anyone what?' Flora shouted back. 'Stop speaking in riddles!'

'Oi!'

The three children froze. The last shout hadn't come from any of them. It was much louder and deeper, the voice of a man rather than a child, and it sounded like it was coming from the rose garden. Then they heard the sound of a dog yapping. Quick as a flash, the boy crouched down below the bushes.

'It's Rigby!' Isobel whispered. 'He's heard us.'

'You see!' the boy said unhappily. 'This is why you've got to stop following me.' He raised his head slowly. Rigby was walking down the path towards them with Jake at his side, about fifty feet away. The boy hesitated, indecision crossing his face. He picked something up next to him that Isobel hadn't noticed before, something heavy. It was a white sack with a reddish-brown stain on the bottom. She just had time to think that it looked like blood before the boy leaped upwards, still holding the bag, and dashed into the open.

'Stop!' Rigby roared, breaking into a run. 'I'll have you, you little runt!'

Flora and Isobel ran out too and saw the boy swing into the shelter with one smooth movement.

'What's he doing?' Isobel said, turning to Flora in alarm. 'Why's he gone in there? He's going to get caught!'

Flora sniffed, like there was nothing she could do about it. 'He must be stupid as well as rude.'

It took Rigby about twenty seconds to reach the air-raid shelter. He shot the girls a look that said he'd deal with them later, then went to the entrance and peered inside. 'You'd better come out,' he called. 'You got nowhere to go.'

There was no reply. Sighing and muttering under his breath, Rigby got a box of matches out of his pocket. He reached up for the lantern that hung near the door, swung the glass front open and lit the candle inside. Then, awkwardly, he lowered himself into the shelter. Jake stood on the stone ledge, yapping into the darkness.

Next, the girls heard crashes and thuds. It sounded like Rigby was overturning all of the boxes and suitcases in the shelter in his quest to find the boy. There was nothing they could do but wait.

After a few minutes, Rigby's head appeared in the entrance. Isobel flinched, expecting to see him pulling the boy behind him. But when he'd dragged himself up, she saw his hands were empty. Jake whined as Rigby got to his feet, brushing the dust off his trousers. He shook his head, mystified, then straightened up and caught Isobel's eye.

'The little blighter's got away. I dunno how, but he has.' Rigby shook his head again. Isobel felt a pang of relief, which disappeared as she saw Rigby's mouth widen into a horrible leer. 'You haven't, though,' he said, sounding pleased with himself. 'I'm sure the Master will want to hear all about your little chat with the thief. I'm sure he'll know just what to do with you.'

CHAPTER NINE

$\mathcal{T}$he corridor that snaked behind the staircase and led to Mr Godfrey's study felt like the longest corridor in the world. It was dark, with sombre portraits of people Isobel didn't know above the wood panelling. She felt like they were looking disapprovingly at her. She looked straight ahead, staring at the back of Rigby's jacket, so she didn't have to look at them. The back of her throat burned.

She glanced at Flora, who was biting her lip. She didn't look particularly scared though. It was more through concentration, like she was thinking about something tricky. She noticed Isobel staring and leaned over.

'How did he get out of the air-raid shelter?' she whispered.

The same question had been hovering in Isobel's mind. 'He must have hidden in a suitcase,' she whispered back. 'One of the big ones.'

'I suppose,' Flora said, looking unconvinced. 'Did you see the sack he was carrying? That would have been hard to hide.'

'I'd stop your little whispers when you see the Master,' Rigby said cheerfully from his position in front of them. 'You're in enough hot water as it is.'

The girls fell silent as they continued on. Eventually, they got to a huge, heavy oak door. Rigby turned to look at them with a look of triumph, then knocked twice and swung the door open.

'I've got some troublemakers for you, Mr Go—' Rigby stopped. 'Oh,' he said, nervously.

It took Isobel a bit of time to understand what was happening. First, she was aware of a strong, sharp smell, a mixture of old tea and leather. On a big, heavy-looking desk were teetering piles of papers. They were covered with drawings of planes and tanks. Next to them was a glass containing some amber liquid, and next to that was a plate which had cheese and sausage on it. Isobel blinked, because she'd never seen such thick slices of either, and certainly not both together. Then she noticed a brown paper bag, the same one that Rigby had taken into the house a week or so before.

It was only after she had noticed all of these things that she saw Mr Godfrey. He was sitting to the side of the desk, his trousers down to his knees. Isobel gulped, then looked away as she saw his left leg. It was skinnier than his right one and his thigh went inwards, like something big had taken a bite out of it. The skin was different too: red and shiny, crinkled in places like when Mum was sewing and pulled the thread too tight. There was a pot of cold cream on the desk and Mr Godfrey was rubbing this into his leg using a white handkerchief.

When he saw Rigby and the girls, a look of absolute horror crossed his face. Isobel found she was staring at his leg. She tried to drag her eyes away, but she couldn't.

There was a moment of awful silence. Then Rigby cleared his throat. 'I'm sorry, Master—'

'Get out!' Godfrey roared, flinging the cloth at him. 'Get out, get out, get out!'

Rigby pushed the girls roughly out of the room and shut the door behind him. Not looking at them, he barged past and strode down the corridor, the thud of his hobnail boots gradually fading as he got further away.

Isobel turned to Flora, wide-eyed. They stood, frozen, for a few moments in the corridor. Then they heard something from inside Mr Godfrey's study – a thunk, perhaps of someone getting up – and they turned and ran.

In the main hallway they nearly collided with their mother, who was coming out of the Drawing Room and holding a letter out in front of her to help the ink dry.

'Girls, stop running!' she said, pulling Isobel to a stop. 'You know you're not meant to run in the house.' Then Mum saw the expression on their faces. 'What's the matter?' she asked, her voice turning higher with worry. 'Has something happened?'

Isobel felt her cheeks burn. She looked at the floor quickly, so she didn't have to look at Mum. She found that she didn't want to tell her what had happened in Mr Godfrey's study. An image of Mr Godfrey's leg flashed into her mind and she shut her eyes tight, willing it to go away.

It seemed that Flora felt the same way. She just mumbled, 'Nothing's happened,' then looked at the floor too.

Mum straightened up, her brow still furrowed like she didn't quite believe them. 'Well, you're supposed to be doing your sums,' she said. 'Have you finished?'

Isobel shook her head. Mum checked her watch. 'Go on, then,' she said. 'Back to the library with you. You've only got half an hour before lunch.'

White-hot panic sliced through Isobel at the thought. Mr

Godfrey hadn't joined them for lunch for nearly a week, but there was always a chance he might be there. The burning at the back of her throat came back.

'Go on,' Mum said again, giving Flora a little push. 'I'll be there to check what you've done in twenty minutes.'

Back in the library, Isobel's unsharpened pencil was left on the table, just where she had left it. She sat down but when she stared at the sheet of sums, she couldn't make sense of them. She looked up at her sister, who was staring into space, her arms folded in front of her.

'Did you notice the bag?' Flora said. 'It was the one the man in the car brought. There was a jar of jam inside. As well as the sausage and cheese.' She shook her head. 'I think Mr Godfrey's using the black market. I think that's what those sacks are all about, and the people coming in the night.'

Isobel nodded. Mum had explained what the black market was at home. Isobel knew that even with rationing, you could get hold of nicer food, if you had the money and knew the right people. Mum said it was wrong. But Isobel couldn't think about that now. 'But Flora, did you see . . .' She stopped, unable to put it into words.

Flora bit her lip. 'Aunty Bea said he got hit by shrapnel in the first War. It wasn't our fault,' she said after a while. 'We didn't mean to see it.'

Isobel knew they hadn't meant to. It was Rigby's fault, if it was anyone's. But she also knew something else, as solid as a stone in your hand. She knew that just by being there, just by seeing what they had seen, they had done something very, very bad.

*

Isobel spent the first few minutes of lunch jerking in alarm every time the door opened, but first it was Aunty Bea, then Mrs Fishwife with the meal. Mr Godfrey didn't appear.

Aunty Bea waited for Mrs Fishwife to finish serving the boiled potatoes before she got to her feet. 'Is there a plate for Mr Godfrey?' she said, hesitantly. 'I thought I could take him his.'

Mrs Fishwife handed her a plate, Isobel thought a little reluctantly. 'Of course, Ma'am.'

Aunty Bea smiled tightly, then left the room.

Mum cleared her throat. 'Well, there's no use us letting ours get cold,' she said, lifting her knife and fork. 'Come on, girls, eat up. Miss Stewart, thank you. You can go.'

'I'll just wait on Mrs Godfrey, Ma'am,' Mrs Fishwife said firmly, putting the lid back on the vegetable pot. 'Just in case Mr Godfrey needs anything else.'

Mum and Mrs Fishwife shared a look that Isobel didn't quite understand. Then Mum nodded.

It was a quiet lunch. The cabbage tasted mushy in Isobel's mouth and she found she didn't really want to eat it.

After a few minutes, Aunty Bea returned. She was still holding Mr Godfrey's plate of food. She gave them a small, defeated smile.

'He said he's not hungry.'

Flora and Isobel looked at each other. Isobel thought it wasn't surprising Mr Godfrey wasn't hungry, with all of that sausage and cheese she'd seen on his plate. But she didn't say anything.

'I'll keep it hot for him, Ma'am, just in case,' Mrs Fishwife said. She balanced it neatly in the crook of her arm, picked up the vegetable pot and – with her customary nod – swept out of the room.

Aunty Bea sat down heavily and started picking at her own meal. Mum looked at her like she wanted to say something, but she didn't. No one said anything until lunch was over. Mum was just ringing the bell for Mrs Fishwife to come back when there was another sound – a huge clanging that filled up Isobel's ears.

'What's that?' Flora said, looking around to see where it was coming from.

'It's the doorbell,' Aunty Bea said. 'But I don't . . . I mean, who would be coming to visit us?'

Mum got up from the table, looking cheerful at the interruption. 'There's only one way to find out!' she said. 'Come on.'

When they got into the main hallway, Mrs Fishwife was already opening the door. Isobel thought it might be some more men delivering sacks, but it wasn't. This was someone else, someone standing on the steps, leaning heavily on two crutches with muscular arms. He wore a white shirt with braces, and a flat cap, which he took off when he saw Mum. A smile spread across his face as he nodded to her.

'Mr Ward!' Mum said, her voice lighting up with pleasure. 'James! It's been an age since . . . And who's this with you?'

Isobel knew exactly who it was, even before James pushed the boy in front of him into the hallway. 'This is my son, Simon,' James said, a note of pride entering his voice. 'Go on then, Son, say hello.'

'How d'you do,' Simon said politely.

The boy was wearing the same clothes as he had been only hours before in the air-raid shelter. However, when he took his cap off, Isobel saw that someone had clearly tried to flatten his red hair into a respectable style. He noticed Isobel staring and stared back, his expression unrepentant.

'What's he doing here?' Flora hissed into Isobel's ear. 'He'll only get us in trouble again.'

'You must come in for tea,' Mum said, beckoning Simon and James inside. 'Please.'

Aunty Bea had hung back by the stairs, like she was shy. When James and Simon came into the hallway, they saw her. James hesitated, a cloud passing over his face. 'I don't want to cause any trouble,' he said. 'I know I'm not welcome here.'

'Don't be ridiculous,' Mum said. 'The Ward family has worked as gamekeepers in Splint Hall for generations, further back than anyone can remember. Of course you're welcome.' She looked at Aunty Bea. 'Aren't they?'

Aunty Bea coloured, then looked away as she folded her arms. 'Of course,' she said quietly, stepping towards the Drawing Room. 'I suppose we could have some tea. Could we, Miss Stewart?'

Miss Stewart nodded, then headed for the kitchen.

As James went into the Drawing Room, Isobel noticed the reason he was using crutches. His left leg had been amputated just below his knee. His trouser leg flapped as he sat down and Isobel couldn't help staring.

'Don't mind this,' James said, tapping his leg. Isobel looked away, swallowing.

'Where were you stationed during the War?' Mum asked.

'Made it to Italy,' James said. 'I got injured in 1943 and I got sent home. That was the end of active service for me.' He sighed. 'I reckon I would have liked to make it to D-Day. Must have been something to see.'

'Does it hurt?' Isobel blurted out, still looking at his leg.

Flora gave her a particularly piercing version of the Look, but James didn't seem to mind. 'On and off,' he said. 'Gets worse in damp weather. The boys laugh at me – say I'm more reliable than the BBC, knowing when it's going to rain. It bothers me more how I can't get out and about. I can't do the things I used to do.' After he'd said that, he looked at Simon, almost guiltily. Then he looked back at Isobel and the moment passed. The door opened and Mrs Fishwife came in with the tea. When everyone had a cup, Mum took a sip and then put hers back into the saucer with a clink. 'Are you still living in the village?' she asked.

A shadow passed across James' face. 'Yes, Ma'am,' he said, 'though our house got bombed during the Blitz. You probably heard about it.'

'Oh,' Mum said. 'Of course. Your family's always lived in the cottages on the edge of the grounds,' She shook her head. 'I couldn't believe it when I saw them.'

'We were lucky we were in the shelter. I'm pleased the wife didn't see what happened, though. She loved that cottage to bits. But she'd already passed,' James explained.

'I'm sorry,' Mum said.

James shrugged. 'It was a long time ago. Anyway, we're staying with my sister till they clear the rubble. They're sending bulldozers tomorrow, as it happens. All the way from Aldrington.' He looked quickly at Aunty Bea, then looked back. 'Though we haven't heard if the cottages will be rebuilt, as yet.'

Aunty Bea went pink again.

'Of course they'll be rebuilt,' Mum said. 'They're part of the Burlington estate. Mr Godfrey will see to it.'

There was a silence, in which Aunty Bea looked down at her lap. Then James smiled. 'You hear that, Son?' he said, touching Simon's shoulder. 'We'll be back in our own place in no time.'

He reached out for his cup on the table in front of him, and as he did so the cuff on his sleeve rode up. Isobel saw a long black, snake-like neck tattooed on his wrist. Before she could see exactly what it was, James put his cup to his lips and the tattoo disappeared under his sleeve again.

'Dad,' Simon said.

James looked at his son, then sighed. He put his cup back in his saucer. 'All right,' he said. 'Though I don't know it'll do any good.' He looked at Aunty Bea. 'The reason I've come is to ask for my old job back. *Our* old job back. I'll need Simon and Pat – he's my eldest – to help, especially now I've got this.' He gestured at his leg. 'I don't want much money and I'll apologise for . . .' He took a deep breath. 'For what Mr Godfrey thinks I did.'

'What does he think you did?' Mum said, looking at Aunty Bea.

'He didn't do anything,' Simon said.

'Sshh, Son, there's no point hashing over all that again,' James said.

'They stole,' Aunty Bea whispered, fiddling with her hair. 'Mr Godfrey saw them putting pork chops in their bag.'

'What?' Mum said, surprise written all over her face.

James' nostrils flared. 'It wasn't stealing,' he said. 'It was an arrangement we had. With Lord Burlington, when he was still here. Your dad.'

'Hang on . . .' Mum said, her forehead crinkling as she thought. 'Rigby talked about thieves when we were on the drive here. Thieves that used to work for Splint Hall. He didn't mean you, did he?' She looked at James, who looked awkwardly at Aunty Bea. Aunty Bea said nothing.

'But that's ridiculous!' Mum said. 'You would never steal. We know that! It must just be some misunderstanding.'

James sighed again, suddenly looking years older. He looked from Aunty Bea to Mum, then back to Aunty Bea. She was playing with a loose thread on her lap, her hair falling over her face. 'It doesn't matter about that now,' James said, leaning forwards. 'Look, before he died, did your dad tell you anything? Anything out of the ordinary, about this place? Or about what happened after the last war?'

'The last war?' Mum said. 'No, I don't think so. Well, he told us about the people we lost, like your poor brother, but other than that . . .'

Isobel looked up quickly at James, shocked to hear his brother had died in the last war. Her eyes darted to Flora, who was sitting on the edge of her seat, looking expectantly at James. It would be like losing her, which was unthinkable, like Isobel no longer having her right ankle. She looked back at James, not sure how he could bear it, but he seemed to be thinking about something else.

'I don't mean what happened during that war, I mean what happened after,' he said.

Mum frowned. 'What do you mean, after?'

'When me and him went—' James stopped abruptly, like he'd said too much. 'Did he leave you any letters?'

'No,' Mum said. 'It all happened so suddenly. Well, he left his will, of course—'

'I'm not talking about his will,' James said. 'This would be . . . private. Not for any old lawyer to see.'

'James, what are you getting at?' Mum asked, mystified.

James rubbed his eyes. Then he put his hand down again and Isobel saw another glimpse of the black tattoo. She saw long jaws with flames licking out and she knew exactly what it was.

It was a dragon.

'The thing is,' James began, 'after the first war, your dad and I—'

But before he could say anything else, the door flew open. It was Mr Godfrey. Everyone stiffened as he looked around the room, not blinking. It was clear he was very angry but there was something else in his expression too, something written in the quiver of his mouth. It was the satisfaction of having been proved right.

James got to his feet quickly. 'I don't mean to cause any trouble—' he began.

'Don't mind me,' Mr Godfrey said. 'I'm only the head of this household. Why should I have any say over who comes into my home? Why should I be given that little shred of respect?' He spat this last bit, and Aunty Bea jerked, as if in pain.

'Charles, I think we should listen to what they have to say,' she said, but Mr Godfrey held up a hand to silence her.

'You will leave this house,' he said to James. 'You will take your son with you. I never reported the crime originally, if you remember, as my wife begged me not to. But if you come back, I will call the constabulary and tell them about the whole sordid affair.'

'For goodness' sake!' Mum said. 'James, don't leave. I'm sure this is all just a silly mix-up.'

But James' face had set like stone. He nodded, once, then made to leave. 'Come on, Son,' he said, his voice gruff. 'There's nothing we can do.'

Simon's eyes had turned bright green with rage. He was so angry that Isobel thought steam might start coming out of his nostrils. But he bit his lip and got up to follow his father. James manoeuvred his way around the chairs and headed for the door, Mr Godfrey standing aside to let them pass. Isobel heard the door close with a soft click as they left. She swivelled her head to look out of the window and saw James going down the stairs slowly, Simon giving him his arm, their backs small and hunched in the huge driveway. Suddenly, she couldn't bear it.

'You can't let them go!' she shouted, leaping to her feet. 'It's important, I know it is!'

Mr Godfrey gave her a look so twisted with dislike that Isobel looked away in spite of herself. 'You had better hold your tongue,' he said. 'Rigby has told me all about your little meeting with that boy. You girls deliberately disobeyed me, and there will be consequences. I've told Miss Stewart that you will be having nothing but bread to eat until I say otherwise.'

'Charles,' Aunty Bea gasped.

'You can't do that!' Mum said.

'We weren't meeting with him!' Flora shouted. 'It's not our fault he was in the garden.'

Mr Godfrey ignored her, turning to Aunty Bea. 'As for you,' he said quietly, 'Rigby has informed me what is in the air-raid shelter.'

Aunty Bea breathed in sharply.

When Mr Godfrey spoke again, he no longer sounded angry.

Isobel thought he sounded a little sad, even. 'I thought you were going to get rid of them,' he said. 'I thought we agreed that they were unsuitable, now that you are married. And do you really think it's right to keep such frivolous things, when people across the country are struggling to clothe themselves properly? When there's still rationing?' He gave a tiny, disappointed shake of his head.

'Most of the dresses were given to me by my mother,' Aunty Bea said quietly. 'Surely, you must understand . . .' She looked up at her husband, then looked away. 'But, no. I mean, I suppose you're right. It is rather . . . vain.'

Mum looked horrified. 'Bea—'

'Good. Then Rigby shall burn them,' Mr Godfrey said.

'No, he can't!' Mum said, looking from Mr Godfrey to Aunty Bea, then back again. 'Bea, you can't let him. For goodness' sake!'

Aunty Bea lowered her eyes. The silence stretched on.

'This is madness!' Mum cried. 'How will burning them help anyone?'

'My dear *sister*,' Mr Godfrey said, 'if you don't like it, then you can leave.'

Then he turned and left the room.

CHAPTER TEN

The next day, Flora and Isobel didn't go down for breakfast. They didn't talk about this but agreed silently like sisters do sometimes, even ones that don't always get on. They didn't talk about Mr Godfrey either, or what had happened, just as they hadn't talked about it yesterday evening when they'd been sent up to their room with just a slice of bread. Isobel was trying her best not to think about it.

She stood on her bed and peered out of the small, round window. It looked different in the daylight. The sky wasn't sunny today but cloudy, like an old grey sheet. The kind of sky that Isobel used to see all the time, after a raid, when you weren't sure what was a cloud and what was just dust.

Flora was playing with a hatpin. Mum had left it on the table when she'd come to say goodnight one evening. Flora was bending it into a hook, then straight again, then back to a hook. Bored, she hooked it round the neck of her dragon and jerked it upwards. The dragon swung from side to side in its noose.

'Don't do that!' Isobel said.

'You're so funny about them,' Flora said, shaking her head. But she took the hook off and put the dragon back on the table.

Then she went still as she looked at the hook, something seeming to strike her.

'Izzy,' she said, growing excitement in her tone, 'do you think we could use this to pick the lock of the little door?' She held up the twisted pin.

Isobel looked down at her. 'I don't know,' she said, shrugging. 'I've never picked a lock before.'

'Neither have I,' Flora said. 'But it's worth a try!'

She forced Isobel to help her move the chest of drawers again. Then Flora spent ages fiddling with the lock, using the hatpin.

'What are you even trying to do?' Isobel said, after a few minutes.

'I've read about it in books,' Flora said. 'You just have to find the bit that sticks up and push it down, then the door will open.'

It sounded easy enough, but clearly it wasn't. After a few minutes, Flora flung the hatpin down and grunted with exasperation. 'It doesn't work,' she said. 'I don't know why. In stories, it's always easy.'

Isobel picked the hatpin up, so that no one would tread on it later. 'We should move the chest of drawers back. In case anyone comes up here.'

As soon as she'd said it, they heard the steady tread of someone coming up the stairs.

Flora's eyes widened. 'Quickly!' she mouthed, flapping at the drawers.

They only just had time to push the chest back to its normal position and fling themselves down on their beds before the door opened. Luckily it was only Mum.

'What were you up to?' she said, standing in the doorway.

'I heard some thumps and creaks, like you were moving furniture around.'

Isobel shook her head at exactly the same time as Flora lied, 'One of the dragons got stuck behind the chest of drawers.'

Mum looked at them suspiciously, but let it go. That was when Isobel realised she was wearing her hat and coat. In her right hand she was carrying something small, square and cream. A letter. In her left, she had a paper bag.

'Are you going out?' Isobel said, her voice coming out squeaky. Worms slithered in her tummy at the thought of being left alone in Splint Hall.

'*We're* going out,' Mum said firmly.

'Where are we going?' Flora said.

'We're going to post a letter.'

'But doesn't Rigby post the letters?'

'I want to do this one myself.'

Isobel swung her legs down to the floor. As she did so, the room spun a little. Her mouth felt dry. 'Mum, I'm hungry,' she whispered. 'Can we really only eat bread?'

Mum's lips tightened. For a second she looked really angry and Isobel was worried she'd said the wrong thing. But when Mum spoke, her voice was soft. 'Of course not,' she said, fiddling with her glove. She put the letter in the pocket of her grey coat, then looked up and saw they were standing there, still in their night clothes. 'Well, what are you waiting for? Come on, slow coaches!'

In less than five minutes, Isobel and Flora were fully dressed and sneaking down the stairs. Well, they weren't exactly sneaking, Mum whispered as she went down on her tiptoes, so that her heels wouldn't clop against the wood. They just didn't want anyone to hear them, which wasn't quite the same thing.

The house was quiet and still, and the three of them managed to not-exactly-sneak all the way out of the front door. When they got to the woodland path, Mum stopped for a minute and breathed out a big, long sigh.

'That's better,' she said.

'What's better?' Isobel asked.

Mum looked at her and grinned suddenly. 'Nothing. It's just lovely to be out in the fresh air, isn't it?' She grabbed Isobel's hand. 'Come on!'

At the potato field, Mum stopped again. 'Now, I think someone said that they were hungry, didn't they? Let's sit on this wall so we can have some breakfast.'

Isobel's stomach growled as Mum reached inside the paper bag.

'Scones!' Flora said, in disbelief.

'With cheese in,' Isobel said, inspecting one. Then she added, without thinking, 'Did Mrs Fishwife make them?'

Mum had been reaching inside the bag again. She stopped, an apple in her hand. 'Mrs Fishwife?' she said, looking confused. 'Who's . . . Oh,' she said, understanding spreading over her face. 'You mean Miss Stewart?'

Isobel felt her face burn up as Flora shook her head at her. 'That's not very nice, girls,' Mum continued, frowning.

'I don't call her that, Mum,' Flora said. 'Isobel's just being childish.'

'Yes, you do!' Isobel said, outraged. 'And I'm not!'

'Girls, enough,' Mum said. 'I won't have any quarrelling. There's enough of it in the house without us joining in.'

Everyone fell silent.

'Miss Stewart did make the scones,' Mum said after a little while. 'I gave her the recipe a couple of days ago.'

'But Mr Godfrey said we weren't allowed to have anything other than bread,' Flora pointed out. 'Won't she get in trouble?'

'Not if we don't tell him. Or that snake, Rigby.' Mum's eyes flashed and suddenly she looked younger, almost like a girl their age. 'Anyway, Miss Stewart made me take the scones. She took them to my room this morning and said she wasn't in the habit of starving children.' She looked sideways at Isobel. 'She's not as bad as you think, you know. It's not easy for her, looking after this big house all on her own.'

Isobel looked down at her scone, ashamed.

A sudden gust of wind tugged the empty bag out of Mum's hands. 'Whoops!' she said, making a grab for it, and missing. It fluttered on the breeze like it was playing a game, staying still for just long enough for Mum or Flora to try to snatch it back, then darting out of reach. 'You get it, Izzy!' Mum said, as it floated away from them.

It was hovering just above the green tops of the potatoes when Isobel got to it. She stamped her foot to pin it in place, then reached down to pick it up.

'Hurrah!' Mum cheered, clapping her hands.

But when Isobel closed her fist around the bag, something made her pause. She straightened up, looking perplexed, then bent down again.

'What is it?' Flora said.

Isobel put her hand flat down on the earth. 'It's warm,' she said.

'What's warm?'

'The ground.'

Mum laughed, like they were still playing a game. 'What do you mean, Isobel?'

Isobel put her other hand down to make sure. The paper bag danced away again, forgotten. 'The ground's warm,' she repeated.

'But it can't be,' Mum said, coming over to kneel beside Isobel. She put her hands down on the ground, so close they were nearly touching her daughter's, and her smile faded away. 'How strange,' she said.

Isobel looked up at the cloudy grey sky, the sun nowhere to be seen. Flora, who had crouched down too as she never wanted to be left out of anything, was clearly thinking the same thing.

'There's no sunshine today,' Flora said. 'What's making the ground feel warm?'

She turned to Mum, confident that she would be able to explain. But Mum looked confused and gave her head a little shake. 'I'm sure it's just something to do with this late summer we're having.' She smiled as she brushed a crumb off Flora's cardigan. 'You must be enjoying it. We all know how you love to be warm!'

Flora smiled back but it was a small smile, and Isobel didn't smile at all as she took her hand off the ground. It did feel nice. But Isobel also thought it felt strange, like it would if it snowed in June. Even if you had a snowball fight and had the best time in the world, it just wouldn't feel right. It also reminded her of something. Isobel realised, with a jolt, what it was. It was the same kind of skin-prickling warmth that was in the tunnels underground, just before she'd seen the creature with the claws.

Mum took both of them by the hand and they continued on

their journey without speaking. Isobel tried to dislodge thoughts of the ground heating up and terrible claws, slashing in the darkness.

They were just about to cross the road when Mum pulled them back. There was a low, whiny, growling sound, spooling out like a coil of ribbon. Isobel stiffened. It sounded a bit like the planes that used to drop bombs. But this sound was lower to the ground, somehow.

'It's all right,' Mum said, nudging her gently. 'It's just some cars.'

They watched as the cars came over the hill, following the road as it wound around a farmhouse. Mum wasn't completely correct. They were too big to be cars. One of them had a big wooden crate on the back. Lots of men were sitting inside, wearing overalls and thick black gloves. They grinned and tipped their caps as they went past. Some of them were holding huge spades, others had hammers.

'Of course,' Mum said as it went past. 'James said they were clearing the bombsite today.'

Isobel felt a shudder go through her. 'Is it dangerous?' she whispered.

'I'm sure they know what they're doing,' Mum said.

'But what if there's an unexploded bomb?'

Mum gave Isobel's arm a squeeze. 'That would be very unlucky.'

'Mum,' Flora said, in that tone she had when she wanted everyone to know that she was about to say something important, 'do you think James really stole those pork chops? Because if he did, I don't think he should be allowed to work at the house either.' She folded her arms. 'Stealing's wrong. Isn't it?'

Mum looked at Flora like she wasn't quite sure who she was for a second. 'Of course stealing's wrong, sweetheart,' she said, a little impatiently. 'But it's a bit more complicated than that. James is right that when he used to work here, my father always used to give him bits of meat to take home.' She sighed. 'He was a very generous man. My mother used to raise her eyebrows, but he'd just say James needed it more than we did. I think that James probably just thought Mr Godfrey would do the same.'

'He didn't know Mr Godfrey very well, then,' Isobel mumbled.

'That's true,' Mum admitted. 'But even if it hadn't been Mr Godfrey, I don't think most people are in the habit of giving meat every day to their servants.' She shook her head. 'It was like they were friends, sort of. Daddy used to say the Wards did the most important job out of everyone, including him.'

'Wait a minute,' Flora said, uncomprehending. 'He gave James meat *every day*?'

Mum nodded. 'I could never work out how he got through it all, to be honest.'

'What do you think James meant, when he asked if Grandpa told you anything?' Isobel asked.

Mum fiddled with her hair, and Isobel thought she wasn't going to answer the question. But then she said, 'I don't know. I've been thinking about it all night.' She looked at her daughters. 'The thing is . . .'

'What?' Isobel asked.

Mum looked at her, like she wasn't sure whether to say anything. 'He meant to tell me something, I'm sure of it,' she said suddenly. 'I mean, I've always known there was something going on in this house. Things were always happening. There was the meat, that was strange, but other things were odd too. James would disappear for hours at a time, sometimes even days, and

111

come back with terrible injuries. Once he had an awful burn on his shoulder, I remember. Daddy got Mrs Potts – our old housekeeper – to dress it for him. I remember asking how he'd got it and Daddy saying it was a secret, but that he'd tell me when I was older. And then . . .'

'And then what?' Flora said, as Mum stopped.

Mum smiled, a little sheepishly. 'Well, then I was nineteen and I went to London to stay with Aunt Mary. And soon after that, I met your father, and we got married. And then—' Here, she gave Flora a little nudge, 'you were born. And Daddy – Grandpa, I mean – died not long after. His heart gave out, just like Mum always said it would.'

'But what was the secret?' Flora said, her forehead puckered as she thought.

'I never found out,' Mum said, shaking her head. 'I've thought and thought, but I don't know. But what James said made me remember something.'

'What?'

'Something did happen after the first war. I haven't thought about it for years, but shortly after that war finished Grandpa went away again. He wasn't gone for very long, only a couple of days, but when he came back he was . . .' She struggled to find the word. 'Different.'

'Different how?' Flora said.

'It's hard to explain,' Mum said. 'Quieter. And after that he and James were much closer. I used to see them out of my bedroom window when it was dark, walking the grounds for hours. Well,' she said, smiling suddenly, 'I couldn't see them, I could just see the red circles from their cigars.'

Flora let out a long, irritated sigh. 'What's the good of a secret if no one knows what it is?'

Isobel's mind raced. She didn't know what the secret was either, but suddenly a horrible suspicion was spreading through her: that it was to do with the thing she had seen in Burley Caves. That terrible clawed, hissing thing. She needed to tell her mother, she needed to make her understand. She reached up for her hand, but suddenly Mum stepped backwards, pulling the girls with her gently as the cars buzzed round the bend to the village.

'Come on, then,' Mum said when the cars had gone. 'We can't stay here yapping all day.'

'But . . .' Isobel said, falling silent as she remembered how Mum and Flora hadn't believed her when she saw the creature. She couldn't tell them, and even if she did, Mum didn't seem to be listening anyway. Instead, she was looking at her watch.

'It's nearly nine,' Mum said. 'The post office will be open soon.'

'Who's the letter for, Mum?' Flora asked.

Mum stayed silent for a while, looking straight ahead. 'It's for Uncle David,' she said finally. 'Your daddy's brother.'

'Why are you writing to him?' Isobel said.

But this time, Mum didn't answer. She straightened her hat then took Flora and Isobel by the hand again and they walked down the road. When they got to the village, it was even quieter than when they'd previously visited. Most of the shops had their shutters down, like their eyes were still closed. But the post office was open. The door was ajar, throwing a cheese-shaped wedge of light on the pavement, and from inside, Isobel could hear voices.

'Wait out here, girls,' Mum called, over her shoulder. 'I won't be long.'

Isobel and Flora stood on the pavement while Mum was posting her letter. Soon, a light went on in the grocery, and a couple of minutes later the door creaked open and a woman came out. Her hair was covered by a blue scarf and she looked older than Mum. She picked up a broom that was leaning against the wall and started sweeping the few leaves that had gathered in front of the shop. She noticed Isobel and Flora and stopped suddenly, still hunched over. She stared at them for one long moment, then went back to her sweeping, shaking her head. Her headscarf flapped with the movement.

'Why's she shaking her head at us?' Isobel whispered to Flora.

Flora shook her own head, like she didn't know.

'It's a bad business,' the woman said suddenly, making them jump. Her voice was as thin and crackly as a new fire.

'What is?' Flora said warily.

Strangely, the woman laughed. 'You being Burlingtons, and not knowing.'

'We're not Burlingtons actually, we're Johnsons,' Isobel pointed out again.

'Your mum's a Burlington, ain't she? She was born a Burlington and she's a Burlington now, inside. Just cos you get married, it don't change what you are.' The woman stopped sweeping. She shook her head again. 'Those poor boys. With *them* coming, and not getting the help they need. I try my best, but . . .'

'What boys?' Flora said, a little impatiently. 'Do you mean Simon and his brother? And who's coming?'

'The ones what always come, after wars,' the woman said. It was said matter of factly, but there was something sad and empty in her voice. Something that made Isobel's neck prickle. 'The ones what must be stopped. Though I don't know how they can be, this time.'

Isobel shivered. She wanted to ask the woman *who* was coming again, she wanted to tug her arm to make her tell them, but then there was a clang and she turned to see Mum coming out of the post office.

'Miss Joyce,' Mum said. 'It's me, Julia! I don't know if you remember me.' Her smile wobbled as Miss Joyce looked at her silently. 'These are my daughters. Flora and Isobel. We've come back to live at Splint Hall.'

Miss Joyce smiled sadly. 'I know who you are,' she said. Then she walked back into the shop, the door banging shut behind her.

'What was all that about?' Flora whispered as they walked away.

'I'm afraid we're not very popular at the moment,' Mum said. 'Mr Godfrey isn't well-liked in the village. People are angry that the house wasn't requisitioned during the War. They don't see why he shouldn't have sacrificed something, when they've sacrificed so much. And I've heard that he keeps raising the rents,' she added, lowering her voice.

'But that's not our fault,' Flora pointed out. 'We don't like him either. Especially since we found out he's using the black market.'

Mum looked at her, shocked. 'What makes you say that?'

As Flora told her about the sacks stacked up in Rigby's shed, and the men coming in the night to collect them, and the sausage and cheese they'd seen in the study (though she left out the bit about Mr Godfrey's leg), Mum's lips pressed together tighter and tighter. 'I'm sure there's another explanation,' she said, when Flora was finished, but she didn't look sure at all.

115

'Well, even if there is, I still don't like him,' Flora said.

'Flora, you shouldn't say that,' Mum said, but from the tone of her voice Isobel knew she wasn't really cross. 'Mr Godfrey just likes to do things a certain way. An old-fashioned way. He doesn't think people like us should mix with people who live in the village.'

'Why not?' Isobel said.

'Just because,' Mum said. 'Lots of people used to think that way. It was the way things were, not very long ago. Many people who lived in villages worked for rich families as servants, and you weren't supposed to mix.'

'Did you have lots of servants?' Flora asked. 'When you grew up, I mean?'

'Oh yes,' Mum said. 'We used to have five indoors. A cook-housekeeper, like Miss Stewart, a butler, a kitchen-maid, a parlour-maid and a footman. I never really liked it, though. It felt strange to me, having people help you with your clothes and bringing you everything you needed. To be honest, it meant there wasn't very much to do.'

'Is that why we only had Sally?' Flora asked.

Mum smiled. 'I'm surprised you even remember her. She was a great help, but she went off to the Wrens and never came back. The last I heard was that she was working in a chemist's in town.' Mum sighed. 'That's the thing, you see. The War changed it all, but some people just want to go back to the way it was before.'

'Like when Grandpa was alive?' Isobel said.

'Well, actually Grandpa wasn't really like other lords. He had lots of friends in the village, including Miss Joyce, the woman you saw in the shop. He was a generous man. People were always coming to stay,' Mum said, her eyes growing sad. 'There was always laughter and dancing.'

Isobel felt her legs get heavier and heavier as they got closer to Splint Hall, though they hadn't walked that far. She thought it was the house itself. Isobel couldn't imagine anyone laughing or dancing in it. Splint Hall wasn't a place you could be happy in. It was the opposite – it made everyone feel tired and sad and strange, like it had this special power. The others could feel it too. Everyone got quieter and Mum kept biting her lip. Isobel had never felt like this at home. She wondered whether it was just because of Mr Godfrey, or whether there was something inside the house – something mean crouching between the walls, or even hidden in the spaces between the bricks.

'You're awfully quiet,' Mum said, looking at Isobel with that funny expression she sometimes had. 'What are you thinking about?'

'Mr Godfrey,' Isobel answered, truthfully.

Mum sighed. She itched her right eye like she was tired. They were walking in the sunshine and it was so bright that Isobel could see the lines at the corners of her eyes – there were more of them than she remembered.

'You mustn't worry about him,' Mum said, but she wasn't looking at Isobel, she was looking at Flora, who had gone ahead and was about twenty feet in front of them. Her head was bent down so she was looking at the floor and Isobel could see from the way her back was moving that she was fiddling with a daisy chain.

'I don't like him,' Isobel whispered.

'He's not my favourite person either,' Mum said. 'But there's not a lot we can do about it.'

That was what Mum always used to say about the War. Not

about it not being her favourite – that was obvious, the War wasn't anyone's favourite – but that there wasn't a lot they could do about it. She used to say that they couldn't help the hand they had been dealt, they just had to get on with things.

'We could go home,' Isobel said.

Mum stopped walking. She turned to Isobel, worry scratching a deep groove in her forehead. 'We can't go home, Isobel,' she said softly. 'You know that. You know what happened to our house.'

'But maybe we could get another one . . .' Isobel said, knowing in her heart it was impossible.

Mum looked at her for ages. Flora was far away now, nearly at the end of the path and on to the grounds, but Mum didn't seem in a hurry to catch up. She sighed, and suddenly Isobel felt bad for saying she wanted to go home. She wanted to say something else, about how she was sorry that Grandpa wasn't there any more and that she wished she could have met him, and she wished Splint Hall was how it used to be. She opened her mouth to speak, but the words didn't come. Instead she had a vision of the letter in the post office waiting to be put in a bag and then in a van and then taken to somewhere far away. She thought of all the letters and cards that went out like this, weaving invisible threads across the country. It was like people were holding hands across hundreds of miles. But then she thought of the telegrams – the ones that cut these threads as easy as kitchen scissors. The ones that made people bend right over as if they were going to be sick.

'I wish Daddy was here.'

Mum's face kept looking in front, but her hand squeezed Isobel's tighter. 'So do I, darling,' she said. 'So do I.'

CHAPTER ELEVEN

Back at Splint Hall, they were just about to go up the thick stone steps when they heard a noise from the gardens. It was a scraping, thudding sort of noise, and it was coming from the air-raid shelter. As they looked towards it, a suitcase emerged from the entrance. It stood upright for a second, then toppled over to the ground with a bang.

'The dresses!' Flora cried. 'Rigby must be moving them.' She turned to her mother and pulled her sleeve desperately. 'Mum, you can't let him. They're so beautiful. He can't burn them, he can't!'

Mum's face grew grim as she listened to the noises. She half turned, undecided, then there came an especially big clunk and her face set like stone. 'You're right,' she said. 'You both stay here. I'll deal with this.'

Holding on to her hat with one hand, she marched down the steps and on to the gravel driveway.

Flora turned and marched down the steps after her.

'Flora, Mum said not to!' Isobel said.

Flora turned round. 'What if Rigby's mean to her? You can stay here if you want.' She gave Isobel a condescending look. 'But I'm not letting her go there by herself.'

Isobel clenched her fingers into fists and followed. Mum was walking very fast. Both the girls broke into a run and had just caught up with her when she reached the air-raid shelter. She put one gloved hand firmly on the wall and leaned over the suitcase into the darkness.

'Stop what you're doing, right now!' she called. 'These aren't Mr Godfrey's property. They are the personal items of my sister that predate her marriage, and as such they are hers to do what she wants with. And I can assure you, she doesn't want them burned!'

There was a silence. Inside the air-raid shelter, nothing moved.

'Come out, you coward!' Flora shouted.

'Flora!' Mum said. She turned to the girls, her hands on her hips. 'I thought I told you two to stay where you were?'

Isobel and Flora looked guiltily at each other, but before they could reply, there was a noise of footsteps from the air-raid shelter. It sounded like whoever was inside was making their way to the entrance. There was a pause, as if they were deciding where to put their foot next, then there was a sudden crash.

'Oof!' someone said. It didn't sound like Rigby though. It sounded more like—

'Miss Stewart!' Mum said, her voice high with surprise. 'What on earth are you doing?'

Miss Stewart peered up at them, shielding her eyes from the light. There were wisps coming out of her normal neat bun and a black smudge on her wrist. 'What's it look like I'm doing?' she snapped, looking half guilty, half cross. She inspected her hand and, seeing a graze, blew on it. Then she folded her arms and said, 'I'm moving these dresses to somewhere Rigby can't get his fat hands on them.'

Mum stared for a moment, astonished. Then, unexpectedly, she started to laugh.

'It's nothing to laugh about, Ma'am,' Miss Stewart said. 'There's no sense in burning such lovely things, that's why I'm doing it. But if I don't get these dresses out before Rigby and Mr Godfrey get back from their drive, they'll still be cinders by tonight, and I'll be out of a job.' She looked around her. 'Some of these suitcases are big as tanks. They aren't half heavy.'

Mum pursed her lips to stop herself from laughing. 'I'm sorry, Miss Stewart,' she said. 'I was just surprised, that's all.' She hesitated for a second. 'Where's my sister? Does she know anything about this?'

'Course not,' Miss Stewart sniffed. 'Go against Mr Godfrey's wishes like that? You must be joking. She's in the car with Mr Godfrey. They've gone for a drive. He always insists she goes on his drives.'

Mum nodded. 'How will we explain that they're missing, then?'

Miss Stewart pointed behind them. They turned and saw smoke curling up into the sky, from somewhere past the greenhouse.

'I'll say I burned them already, to save him the trouble,' Miss Stewart said, looking proud of herself. 'I already burned an old dress of Ma'am's, one she doesn't wear any more. I'll show them the scraps.'

'That's clever,' Flora said admiringly.

But Miss Stewart looked worried. 'It won't be if half of these cases are still in the air-raid shelter when they get back,' she said. 'Then we'll all be for it, I can tell you.'

Mum was already rolling up her sleeves. 'We'll help move

121

them, won't we, girls? You pass them up to us. Let's get them all out first, then Flora and Isobel can take the smaller ones and we'll take the bigger ones. Where were you going to put them?'

'Coal cellar,' Miss Stewart said. 'Rigby never goes in there, on account of the coal being too heavy for his bad back.'

Over the next half an hour, Flora and Isobel ferried the smaller cases from the air-raid shelter to the coal cellar. It was a walk of about 200 feet, which doesn't sound like very far, but when you're holding onto a heavy suitcase – and your sister keeps walking too fast, and nearly pulling it out of your grasp – it feels like forever.

'Slow down!' Isobel said, for what seemed the fiftieth time.

'No, you speed up!' Flora retorted. 'Mr Godfrey'll be back any second.'

Isobel bit her lip and did her best to move her legs, which felt like lead, a little faster. She had red grooves and scrapes all over her, but she wouldn't stop. None of them would. Even Mum, who had to take the bigger suitcases with Miss Stewart, and had to pause more than once to rub her hip.

The portmanteau Isobel and Flora were currently carrying was turtle green and as hard as wood, with huge gold buckles that were rubbing against Isobel's tummy. Finally, they got to the coal cellar. Mum and Miss Stewart were right behind them. They lifted both cases down to hide in the inky blackness among the dark lumps of coal.

'Nearly there, girls!' Mum gasped as she straightened up. 'Only one more each.'

Isobel lifted her sleeve to wipe off the sweat that was gathering under her eyebrows. Then she ran back to the air-raid shelter. There were only two cases left, one big and one small. They picked up the smaller one and Mum and Miss Stewart picked up the big one, and they raced back to the coal cellar.

'They can hardly fit!' Miss Stewart said, looking down. 'We'll have to rearrange them a bit, I reckon.'

'We can do that,' Mum said, already sitting down and lowering herself into the cellar. 'Girls, you go back to the shelter and check we haven't left anything behind. Go on, hurry!'

Back at the shelter, Flora swung herself confidently down on the swing. Isobel stayed where she was as her sister inched round the four walls, putting her arms out in front to check.

'It's empty!' she called in triumph. 'We did it!'

Isobel felt something soar in her chest. She thought of the dresses, safe in the coal cellar, and grinned to herself.

'Wait . . .' Flora said curiously.

From inside the shelter, there was a scraping sound.

'Ugh, I think there might be rats!' Flora cried. Then she squealed in shock. 'Oh! Get off me!' She scrambled to the entrance and pulled herself up, her cheeks pink and her breath coming in short bursts. 'There's someone there!' she said. 'There's someone in the air-raid shelter!'

'But there can't be,' Isobel said. 'We've been here the whole time and no one's gone in. We'd have seen them!'

Flora took a few steps away and pointed fearfully. 'There is! They were grabbing my arm!'

Isobel opened her mouth to argue, but suddenly a face appeared in the opening. She jumped back with fright, but then she saw who it was.

'I wasn't grabbing your arm!' Simon said, looking at Flora. 'You were grabbing mine!'

'Oh, it's you,' Flora said, her fear instantly turning to anger. 'How did you get in without us seeing?'

'None of your business,' Simon said automatically. He threw something out on to the grass, then pulled himself up, swinging his legs out from under him and standing up in one swift movement. Then he picked up what he had thrown. Isobel saw it was a stick, with one end sharpened into a point. She looked Simon up and down. He had black smudges all over his legs and arms, and part of his shirt was missing. The edges of it were charred and blackened, like it had been burned. But that wasn't the strangest thing. Simon's hands were covered in a mysterious, silvery substance, like he had dipped his hands in a pond shining with moonlight.

'What on earth have you been doing?' Flora said, sounding very much like Mum. 'What's that stuff on your hands?'

'None of your business,' Simon said again.

'But it *is* our business.'

'No, it isn't,' Simon said cheerfully. 'Thanks for moving those suitcases, though. It makes it a lot easier.'

Flora folded her arms. 'Makes what easier?'

'Going in and out.'

'But why are you going in and out?'

Simon didn't reply, which made Flora clench her arms even tighter, something Isobel knew she only did when she was really angry. 'Anyway, we didn't move the suitcases for you. We did it for our aunty, if you must know.'

Simon was inspecting his cap. He shook it and some powdery black stuff fell out onto the ground. Satisfied there was no more in there, he shoved it on his head. Then he looked at Flora, as if he was already bored of the conversation. 'What was in those cases, then?'

'We told you before,' Flora said. 'Dresses.'

'Oh yeah,' Simon said. 'The ones you thought I was stealing.'

Flora ignored him. 'We moved them all to the coal cellar. If we didn't get them out, Rigby was going to burn them. It would have been a catastrophe!'

Simon looked at her for a second. Then he started to laugh.

'I don't see what's funny,' Flora exploded. 'They were very expensive.'

This just made Simon laugh louder. Still holding the stick, he flopped down on to the ground and rolled about, clutching his sides.

'It is NOT funny!' Flora stamped her foot in anger. 'I'm going to tell Mr Godfrey that you were here. Then he'll call the police and you and that stupid father of yours will get locked up. It won't be funny then, will it?'

Simon stopped laughing as quickly as if a switch had been flicked. He looked up at Flora in shock.

'Flora, you wouldn't,' Isobel said.

'Yes, I would!' Flora looked at Simon sneeringly. 'They're just thieves, after all.'

Simon turned the bright red shade he had done in the Drawing Room, when Mr Godfrey had said the same thing. He clenched the stick so tightly that Isobel thought it would break in half. 'Don't you dare call us that!' he bellowed, leaping to his feet. 'Dad's not a thief and neither am I.' He moved suddenly towards Flora and she took a step back, but all he did was pull up his cuff. Isobel felt her breath catch in her throat. Like James, Simon had a dragon snaking up his arm.

'We're not thieves, we're keepers,' Simon yelled, still furious. 'But it's all gone wrong because of your grandpa dying too soon and Mr Godfrey laying off my dad.' He dragged his hands through his red hair like he was going to pull it out. 'You're Burlingtons and you don't even know!'

'Don't know what?' Isobel said, but Simon just shook his head.

'It's all gone wrong and they're coming, don't you see? You're busy worrying about saving stupid dresses but they're *coming*. And we've got to protect people but we can't!'

'Who are coming?' Flora said. 'Miss Joyce said the same thing earlier. That they're coming. But no one will tell us *who*.' She didn't look angry any more. In fact, she looked a little afraid.

'Them,' Simon spat. 'The splints.'

When he said the word 'splints' something cold pooled in Isobel's tummy. 'But what are—'

Simon was still talking. 'The Hellborn. Creepers. The Bone Army. Whatever you want to call them. They've got a thousand names but they're one and the same.' He shoved the stick into the ground beside him, its sharpened point sticking up like a spear. Isobel felt her spine tingle as he said, 'People think the War's over, but it's not. They're coming. The splints are coming and this time they won't be stopped.'

There was a silence, in which Isobel could hear the birds singing and Simon's voice coming in great, raggedy gasps. Isobel felt like she'd been drenched in a bucket of icy water. *Splints*, she thought, trying out the word in her mind against the creature

126

with the bone-thin arm and terrible claws. Was that what she had seen?

She looked at her sister. Flora had unfolded her arms and was playing with the sleeve of her cardigan, scrunching it in her fist and then unscrunching it again.

'The War is over,' she whispered. 'You're just trying to scare us. It *is*.'

Simon looked like he was going to say something, but then they heard Mum call, 'Girls!' They looked up and saw Mum coming towards them, and when she caught sight of Simon she hesitated a little, not looking angry, just puzzled. Isobel turned to see Simon, who didn't look angry either, or even scared. Instead, a wave of absolute exhaustion crossed his face. He started to get to his feet, wearily, and Isobel moved towards him, thinking she had to tell him what she'd seen—

But then Isobel heard a crack like a bone breaking, like a peal of thunder cut off after it had just begun. Suddenly Simon was on his belly, sprawled on the ground, and Isobel couldn't make sense of it except that she was on the ground too and she didn't know how she had got there. As if from far away she heard a long, echoey boom and then her mother cry out. She knew she should get up, they should go to the air-raid shelter, it was happening again. Simon was right, the War wasn't over, and there would be more bombs, there were always more, but the ground was shaking and it was all Isobel could do to hold on to it. She curled herself into a ball and put her hands over her ears, waiting for it to stop.

CHAPTER TWELVE

The next thing Isobel felt was someone putting their arms round her.

'It's all right, darling,' Mum whispered closer to her ear, her voice sounding thicker than normal. 'It's all right.'

'But the War's come back,' Isobel choked, finding that she was crying.

'No, no it hasn't,' Mum said, stroking her hair. 'It must have been an unexploded bomb, that's all. They must have triggered it when they were clearing the rubble. It's just one. That's it. It's over.'

Suddenly Flora was there too and they were all on their knees hugging, wet faces against each other's shoulders, arms around each other's backs. Isobel could smell Mum's soap-and-lilies smell and she breathed out shakily.

When they pulled apart, Isobel saw Simon. Or, rather, Simon's back. He had got to his feet and was standing looking towards the village, where a mushroom of smoke was hovering like an evil cloud.

Simon turned, his face as white as snow. 'My brother,' he said, his eyes wide. 'Pat. He was helping . . .'

He tore off up the garden, towards the gate.

'Wait!' Mum shouted, but he didn't.

Miss Stewart had been staring at the cloud too. 'We've got to help,' she said, half to Mum, half to herself. 'They'll be needing us. What if they're—' She swallowed the last word, so Isobel only caught the 'B' of it, but she knew immediately what it was. Buried. That was what happened to people when bombs went off. Sometimes people weren't found for days.

Mum nodded. She dropped to her knees. 'Girls, I've got to go and help.' She looked back anxiously at Simon, who was now nearly at the edge of the grounds. 'You stay here, you'll be perfectly safe.'

'But can't we come with you?' Isobel said.

A shadow crossed over Mum's face. 'No, darling. You just go inside and read, or play, or do anything. Anything you like. We'll be back as soon as we can, I promise.'

Mum gave them one last anxious look. She kissed each of them on their foreheads, then got to her feet and started running. Her hat began flapping and she pulled it off and threw it on the ground. Miss Stewart ran beside her, holding up her black skirt so she could go faster. Flora and Isobel watched as they got further and further away, before they turned off on to the path and they couldn't see them any more.

'What if there's another one?' Isobel whispered, not looking at Flora.

'There won't be,' Flora said, putting her arm around her. 'And even if there is, we're all the way over here. It can't hurt us.'

That made Isobel feel a little better, until she thought of all the people who were over there, or who soon would be, who could be hurt. James. Simon's brother, Pat. Simon. Miss Stewart. Mum.

'There won't be another one,' Flora said, as if she could read her thoughts. 'Come on, let's go inside until they get back.'

She held out a hand to pull Isobel up. As Isobel got to her feet, she saw her sister see something. Something that made her eyes widen. 'Oh,' she said.

'What is it?' Isobel asked, swerving round to see.

There, on the grass, was Miss Stewart's apron, flung off in the rush to get into the village. And there, hanging off the cord, was her huge bunch of keys, sparkling in the sunshine.

'I don't think we should be doing this,' Isobel said.

It was ten minutes later. As soon as she'd noticed the keys, Flora had snatched them up without a word and run straight towards the house. Isobel had followed her, growing increasingly nervous as she ran up the stone steps, then up the wooden staircase in the main hall, then finally up the two flights of stairs to their room.

Flora pulled the chest of drawers back, a little violently.

'Careful!' Isobel said.

But Flora was already crouching on the floor, trying the different keys in the lock of the small wooden door.

'Flora, I said I don't think we should do it.'

'Why?'

'Because . . .' Isobel searched her mind for a reason. 'Because if it's locked, it's locked for a reason. And Miss Stewart is nice. She helped us save Aunty Bea's dresses! We shouldn't be stealing her keys.'

'We're not stealing,' Flora said. 'We're just borrowing. Besides, she'll never know. Unless you tell her, which you won't.' She looked threateningly up at Isobel, her blue eyes narrowed. 'Will you?'

Isobel tried to hold her gaze, but eventually she looked away. 'No.'

Flora went back to trying each key. Most of them were far too big – Isobel could see that from here – but she tried them anyway, going through them one by one. Isobel sat back on her bed, feeling like she might cry. It seemed like Flora had forgotten it completely, but she could still hear the crack of the bomb going off, and the echoey boom that followed it. She wondered if Mum had got there yet, and if so, what she had found. Then she shut her eyes tight to make the thought go away.

'These are all too big,' Flora said. 'I'm going to go from the other end.'

She tried smaller keys until a tiny copper key gave a satisfying click. The word 'splint' popped into Isobel's head – sharp and pointed like Simon's stick. Suddenly she really didn't want Flora to open the door.

'Flora, don't!'

But it was already swinging forwards. There was a musty smell, like old leaves and mice. Inside the light was pale and grey and it was difficult to make out anything other than gloomy shapes.

'Flora!' Isobel said, to her sister's lower half. Because Flora had disappeared through the door. Only her grey-stockinged legs could be seen, then they were gone too.

Isobel breathed in deeply, then followed.

The room was bigger than she had imagined, she realised as she straightened up. It was about the same size as their bedroom, but the ceiling sloped sharply downwards, so that Isobel had to bend her head if she wanted to walk anywhere. Her knees were covered in dust. In fact, there was a thick grey layer of dust everywhere – on the floor, on the windowsill and on the wall of boxes that were stacked up on top of each other in front of them. Flora was brushing some off the one on the top. She turned her head to the side to avoid the cloud that rose up into the air and sneezed. When the dust had settled, she tried to tug the box down.

'It's too heavy,' she said to Isobel. 'Help me.'

'Wait. Flora, look at this!'

On the other side of the room, Isobel had noticed a wooden door. Unlike the door from their bedroom, this was a normal-sized one that any adult would be able to go through.

'Is there another room as well as this one?' Flora said, surprised.

Isobel went over and tried the handle. 'It's not locked,' she said.

'Go on, then.'

When Isobel pushed the door open, light flooded into the room, along with a gust of wind that blew the dust into swirls. When Isobel's eyes adjusted, she was amazed to see blue sky and green trees in front of her. She looked down and immediately wished she hadn't. There was an iron platform with railings attached, but the bottom of it was made of spirals and curls welded close together. You couldn't fall – the gaps were too small for that – but you could see all the way down to the ground below. And it was a long way.

Flora leaned out past Isobel. 'It's the staircase down to the garden!' she said. 'The one we saw when we were looking for Simon. It doesn't go to Mr Godfrey's room at all. It goes here.'

Isobel nodded, gripping hard on to the railing. 'Do you want to go down?' she asked, dreading the answer.

But Flora shook her head. 'I want to see what's in these boxes first.'

Between them, they managed to half pull, half topple the first box onto the floor. Flora opened it excitedly, then her face fell when she saw what was inside. She pulled out pages and pages of paper, covered in small, neat sums.

'Miscellaneous household items March 1931,' she read. 'Shoe polish, two pennies. Petroleum, four shillings. Candle wax, five pennies.' She turned the sheet over. 'Butcher's bill. Steak, one shilling. Chickens (fifteen), one pound two pence. This is just a list of how much money they've spent on things!' She put the sheet down and searched through the box then sat back on her heels, disappointed. 'They're all the same! How boring.'

Isobel had picked up the yellowed piece of paper and was reading it for herself. 'Fifteen chickens,' she said, in disbelief. '*Fifteen?*'

'So?'

'Don't you think that's a lot?'

Flora shrugged. 'It wasn't the War then, was it? There wasn't any rationing. Besides, Mum said that Grandpa used to have a lot of guests.'

Isobel stared at the piece of paper, not quite convinced, but Flora was already pulling down another box. 'Maybe there'll be something more interesting in here . . .' she said.

But there wasn't. That one turned out to be records of what the staff had been paid. Flora put it back immediately, saying it didn't feel right to snoop. The next box, surprisingly, was full of shoes – thick, sturdy boots of all shapes and sizes.

'Look, Izzy, I think these might fit you,' Flora said, pulling out a dark green pair.

The box after that was full of scarves, and the box after that was books, and the one after that was letters. Isobel was interested in those for a bit but then quickly got bored. They were all from Grandma's sister, a Lady Ethel Woldringham, and were mostly about which pigs had done well at the latest county fair. She seemed to be particularly interested in Gloucester Old Spots.

'I can't believe it,' Flora said, looking around despondently. 'We waited for so long to get in here, and it's just boxes full of old rubbish.'

Isobel wanted to say, 'I told you so,' but – nobly – she didn't. Instead, she said, 'We haven't tried any of the boxes on the other side.' They had got about two thirds of the way through the boxes, but all of the ones they had opened were on the left. The ones on the right, near the wooden door that led to the staircase, remained untouched. She got to her feet and, crouching so she didn't hit her head, walked to the other side of the room.

'It's no use,' Flora said.

Isobel pulled a box down. It was heavier than she thought it would be and it slipped out of her grasp, tumbling to the floor.

'Careful!' Flora said.

Isobel reached down to rub her foot, as the edge of the box had caught it. Then something made her look up again, and she paused, trying to make sense of what she was seeing.

She was looking at a chair. The chair was behind a desk, and on the wall around the desk was pinned lots of sheets of paper with scribbled black drawings on them. Isobel couldn't quite make out what they were of.

'Flora, there's a desk!' she said. 'Behind these boxes. Help me move them!'

It only took the girls a few minutes to move enough boxes for them to slip through and stand in front of the desk. They stood for a few moments not saying anything, just looking.

'My goodness,' Flora said eventually. 'I know Mum said Grandpa liked dragons, but I didn't think she meant *this* much.'

The whole back of the wall was papered with sketches of dragons, held up with straggly bits of string. There were dragons standing upright, their huge, heavy wings dragging on the ground like curtains. Isobel had always imagined the wings of dragons to be like those of birds, but these were more like the leathery wings of bats – folding up neatly into their sides as they slept. There were dragons on their bellies, crouching as they surveyed unseen prey. There were dragons roaring showers of sparks, dragons lunging with outstretched claws and dragons resting, one huge eye open as they slept. But that wasn't the most astonishing thing. As Isobel gazed, she saw that there were people among the dragons. One was pulling what looked like a huge splinter from a dragon's scaly tail. Another was feeding a smaller dragon. Its head was bent back and its jaws open, a hunk of meat hanging tantalisingly above it.

Suddenly, Isobel thought about a number of things one after the other, but so quickly it was like she had thought of them all at once. The black tattoos on Simon and James' arms. Simon's singed shirt. The meat that Grandpa used to give James, and how Mum didn't know how they got through so much. Simon bright red with anger, saying they weren't thieves, they were . . .

'Keepers,' she whispered.

'What?' Flora said, frowning as she peered closer at the drawings.

'They're keepers!' Isobel said, her voice becoming stronger

with excitement. 'Don't you see? Simon and James aren't gamekeepers, they're dragon keepers!'

Flora turned to look at her, her face completely blank. She stared at her sister for a few moments. Then she dissolved into laughter.

'Dragon keepers!' she choked. 'What exactly is a dragon keeper?'

'Someone who looks after dragons, of course.'

'Aren't you forgetting something, Izzy?' Flora said. 'Dragons aren't real!'

Isobel folded her arms obstinately. Up until a minute ago, she would have said the same as Flora. Dragons were make-believe. They belonged in storybooks. Or they had done, until she had met Simon and James and seen all of her Grandpa's drawings. Now dragons were suddenly enticingly real, from the shimmer of scales on their skin to the smoke they breathed from their nostrils. She knew it. She wasn't sure exactly how she knew it, and she certainly didn't know how to prove it, but she knew it.

'If they don't exist,' she began, 'why's Grandpa drawn all of these pictures of them?'

'I don't know. Because he liked make-believe, even though he was a grown-up, I suppose. That's what Mum said, remember? She said Grandma used to say if he loved her half as much as he loved dragons, she'd be the most beloved wife in England.'

'I know that's what she said.' Isobel stamped her foot in frustration. 'But that doesn't mean dragons aren't real!'

Flora wasn't laughing now. Instead, she was looking at Isobel with a condescending, pitying expression that made Isobel want to tumble one of the boxes down on her head. 'Of course they're not, Izzy. Everyone knows that. If they were real, someone would have seen them.'

Isobel looked up at the drawings again. 'Maybe they have. Maybe Grandpa did, and that's why he drew all of these.'

'If Grandpa saw a dragon,' Flora said, 'why didn't he tell anyone about it? Why didn't he tell Mum?'

'Maybe that's the secret.'

'And where are these dragons, anyway? They're huge! Look at the size of that one, next to the man. If they were just walking around, everyone would know about it.'

'I *said*, maybe that's the secret. They're not just walking around! They're hidden somewhere.'

Flora made the *tsk* sound she always made when she thought Isobel was being childish. 'Where on earth would you hide something that size?'

Isobel thought about it. 'I don't know,' she admitted.

'Exactly!' Flora said triumphantly. 'It's impossible.' She shuddered. 'Anyway, they're terrifying. Look at their jaws and the spikes on their tails. No one in their right mind would want to be a dragon keeper. Why would you want to help those things?'

Isobel thought about that, too. She realised, with a dreadful sense of foreboding, that she knew the answer. It was shadowy and ill-formed, like the shape she had spied in Burley Caves, but it was there.

'What's wrong?' Flora asked, her expression half worried, half irritated. 'Why have you gone all pale? There's no need to be scared of them, Izzy. I told you, they don't exist.'

'I'm not scared of *them*,' she whispered. 'I'm scared of something else. I'm scared of what they're fighting. Because that's what they do. That's what Simon meant. That's why his family look after the dragons. They have to protect us.'

'Protect us from what?'

Isobel didn't answer. Instead she looked again at the pictures, searching for something she didn't want to name yet, though that name was already needle-sharp in her mind. She went to the desk, which had piles of papers on it. As she rifled through them she found letters, more dragon sketches, a matchbox with a bicycle engraved on the front.

'What are you doing?' Flora asked.

Isobel noticed that the desk had a drawer. She pulled at it, but it was locked. 'Where are the keys?' she said. Not waiting for an answer, she climbed back through the boxes and into their bedroom, then came back holding them in her hands. She tried the smallest key of all – a slender black one – and it fitted. She pulled the drawer open triumphantly.

'What are you looking for?' Flora asked, a little more impatiently this time.

But Isobel didn't reply, because she had found it, and it had made her fingers start to shake.

It was a drawing, but this time it wasn't of a dragon. This was a smaller creature. It was humanlike but too long, too thin and with tiny slits for eyes and a mouth that wasn't really a mouth at all. At the end of its long, skeletal arms, its hands were hung with claws.

Flora's eyes widened in shock.

'This is what I saw,' Isobel said. 'I didn't see all of it, I just saw the claws. But it was real. You and Mum and Aunty Bea didn't believe me, but it was there. It was a splint,' she whispered.

'A Hellborn. A Creeper. Simon just talked about them, before the bomb went off.'

For one tiny fraction of a second, Flora looked scared. Then she started shaking her head. 'It's only a story,' she said. 'It's not real. For goodness' sake, Isobel, you're too old to believe these silly things. It's like you're getting younger, not older,' she added, a little spitefully. 'Sometimes I honestly think you're going backwards.'

'No, I'm not, Flora!' Isobel insisted. 'I saw it! Don't believe me if you want, but I'm telling the truth. Mum said no one knows why it's called Splint Hall, but I think Grandpa knew. It's because of these things, I'm sure of it.'

Flora's face clouded with anger. She tried to grab the paper, but Isobel darted out of reach. She turned the paper over. 'There's something written here. Something about the splints. I think it's a poem.'

'It's only a story,' Flora said stubbornly. 'Mum said the dragons weren't real. You shouldn't even read it. It'll just give you nightmares. That's what happened in the caves. You had a nightmare, even though you were awake. That happens sometimes. You don't need to read that stupid poem.'

When Isobel didn't answer, Flora bit her lip. 'Oh, go on then,' she said, suddenly sounding desperate to know. 'What does it say?'

'It's called "The Song of the Splints".' Isobel cleared her throat and began to read the spidery black writing.

Cursed to live away from light
we take revenge in earth's dark night.
When sharp-toothed monsters fill your sleep
we'll stir awake and start to creep.

Up through tunnels, burrows, holes,
we'll come to feast upon your souls.
Our bones are thin, our hearts no more.
We feed on pain and gorge on war.
We'll come for all that you hold dear.
There's no escape. We'll come. We're here.

CHAPTER THIRTEEN

'It's not real,' Flora said, her words echoing in the silence of the room.

Isobel put the paper carefully back into the desk and shut the drawer. The key made a small grating sound as it turned in the lock. Flora held out her hand and Isobel put the keys into it.

For a couple of moments, neither of them said anything.

'It can't be real,' Flora said again, but her voice went up at the end of the sentence, making it sound like a question.

Isobel was starting to get a tickly feeling behind her knees, like she wanted to stretch them out, or run, or do anything but stand still. She clenched her toes tightly, hoping that would make it go away. 'We have to tell Simon,' she said. 'About what I saw in the caves. He can tell us what's going on.'

'Simon?' Flora said. 'He won't tell us anything.'

'He will if we tell him about what I saw,' Isobel said.

Flora chewed her bottom lip as she thought about it. 'Maybe. Or he'll just laugh like he did about the dresses and say we're crazy.'

Isobel shook her head. 'He won't. Anyway, who else can we

talk to about this? Mum won't believe us. None of the grown-ups will.'

'Well maybe that's because it's not real!' Flora shouted.

From outside, there came a low, growling noise, like the drone of a bee. Isobel and Flora went to the window. Isobel half expected to see a dragon, its scales gleaming in the sunshine, but the lawn was green and empty. It looked tiny from up here, like a toy garden attached to a doll's house.

'What's that noise?' Flora said.

Then Mr Godfrey's bottle-green-and-cream car swerved into the driveway. It slowly crunched through the gravel closer to the house, stopping in front of the steps. The driver's door swung open and Rigby got out, wearing the dark uniform and peaked hat he had worn when he'd picked them up from the station.

He opened the passenger door. With difficulty, and leaning on Rigby's outstretched arm, Mr Godfrey got out.

'Do you think they even know about the bomb?' Flora said, a note of disgust in her voice.

But then the other passenger door opened and Aunty Bea got out. Mum followed close behind, swerving round Aunty Bea in her haste to get up the steps.

'It's Mum!' Isobel cried.

Flora and Isobel slipped past the boxes and crawled through the small doorway as fast as they could. Soon, they were hurtling down the wooden stairs, forgetting all about Mr Godfrey's rule that they shouldn't run. They met Mum on the first-floor landing and she flew onto her knees so she could hold them tightly.

'What happened?' Flora said, her voice muffled by Mum's coat. 'Was anyone hurt?'

Mum squeezed them even more tightly before she replied. 'It happened when they were moving the truck. The bomb was buried eight feet down, they think, but they backed over an old bit of roofing and the movement must have triggered it, somehow. No one died, thank goodness. But a couple of other houses were damaged and James' cousin Stuart was badly injured. He was the one driving,' she explained. 'They've taken him to the hospital in Aldrington.' She sighed. 'That poor family. They don't seem to have much luck.'

Isobel twisted out of her mother's grasp, suddenly angry. 'You said there wouldn't be one.'

'One what?'

'An unexploded bomb!'

Mum's face softened. 'I know, darling. I'm sorry. I didn't think there would be. It really was very unlucky.'

Isobel bit her lip, hard. If Mum hadn't thought there would be one, but there was, perhaps there were more than they all thought. Perhaps there were hundreds, waiting under the surface for people to step on them or drive over them, or even dig them up by accident when they were planting seeds.

'Was Pat all right?' she asked. 'Simon's brother?'

'Yes,' Mum said. 'He was fine. Walked away without a scratch.' She looked at the girls, her gaze becoming questioning. 'What was Simon doing here, before the bomb went off?' she said. 'You really shouldn't encourage him to come, you know. If Mr Godfrey sees him, he'll be angry.'

'We didn't encourage him!' Flora protested. 'He just turned up. He *always* just turns up. Anyway, look Mum, Miss Stewart left her keys behind.'

Mum looked a little suspicious, but then she shook her head

and the moment passed. 'Thank you for looking after them,' she said, letting the keys fall heavily into her palm.

'Why were you in the car with him?' Isobel said.

'With who, Simon?' Mum said, sounding confused.

'No. *Him*. Mr Godfrey.'

'Oh, he arrived in the village soon after we did. Apparently they heard the explosion from five miles away and Mr Godfrey asked Rigby to go straight there.' Mum straightened out her skirt. 'He wasn't best pleased. He roared at the poor men who had been trying to clear the site.'

'But . . . but it's not their fault, is it?' Isobel said.

'No, of course not, darling. War doesn't always bring out the best in people, I'm afraid.'

A door slammed downstairs. Soon afterwards, they heard the murmuring of voices.

Mum's face tightened imperceptibly. 'You stay here,' she said. 'In fact, go up to your room. I'll be back up in a mo.'

With a final squeeze, she turned and walked along the corridor. Flora and Isobel heard the squeak of her footsteps as she went down the wooden stairs.

'Let's go and listen,' Flora whispered.

'No! You heard Mum say Mr Godfrey was in a bad mood.'

'Yes, but we might hear something about Simon and James. You were the one who said we needed to talk to Simon. They might talk about where they're staying.'

Flora snuck down the corridor, taking care to only tread on the red and purple patterned rug, and waited at the top of the stairs. She turned and beckoned her sister closer. 'Come on!' she mouthed.

When Isobel got there, she realised it was no use anyway. The voices were too quiet.

'We need to get to the next landing,' Flora whispered. 'Then we'll be able to hear.'

'But they might see us!'

'No, they won't.'

Treading as softly as possible, the girls inched down the staircase until they got to the landing halfway down, stopping on the step before. From the landing, the stairs swerved down in the opposite direction, so from here they couldn't be seen by anyone looking up the staircase. But through the wooden bars of the landing, they could see the tops of the grown-ups' heads. Aunty Bea was helping Mr Godfrey out of his coat. She turned to put it on the rack and Isobel saw her face: her lips were pressed firmly together, and her eyes were glowing. She was furious.

Aunty Bea turned to her husband. 'What were you thinking, talking to those poor men like that?' she said.

Isobel was so shocked, she nearly fell off her step. She'd never seen Aunty Bea get angry with Mr Godfrey before.

'What on earth do you mean?' Mr Godfrey said.

'They'd just had a bomb go off underneath them!' Aunty Bea shouted. 'A bomb, Charles. One of them went to hospital. He might lose his arm! And all you could think about was the loss of rent!'

'Well perhaps you'd think about that too,' Mr Godfrey replied, 'if you bothered to take any interest in the running of this estate, that is.'

Aunty Bea stared at Mr Godfrey, disbelieving. Isobel half thought she was going to say sorry, but instead she laughed. It was the kind of laugh people make when they hear a joke that is so terrible it is ridiculous. 'You don't let me anywhere near the running of this estate,' she said.

'We can write to the War Damages Commission,' Mum said. 'They give money to repair bombed buildings. We won't even have to pay for the repairs ourselves! Surely we can stand a bit of loss of rent—'

'The War Damages Commission are concentrating on rebuilding half of London,' Mr Godfrey snapped. 'They're hardly going to bother with a few cottages.'

'How do you know?'

'Because I've already written to them and that was their reply.'

'Even so,' Mum said. 'We should be helping our tenants. We could sell one of the Gainsboroughs; we'd hardly miss it. Then we could rebuild the cottages. That's what Father would have done.'

Mr Godfrey clenched his stick tightly. 'I'm well aware it's what your precious father would have done,' he said. 'I know all about him and his ways. Who do you think sorted out this place and the mess he left it in?' He shook his head. 'I've never known a man so terrible with money.'

'That's not true!' Mum said.

'How would you know?' Mr Godfrey said. 'Have you gone through the years and years of accounts as I have? Have you seen the costs going up and the rents going down, while your beloved father was off drawing pictures of his beloved dragons, like a child at play? Have you seen how this place nearly went bankrupt after his death? Well, have you?'

He spluttered this last bit so loudly that a tiny pearl of spit landed on Mum's sleeve. She didn't flinch. 'No,' she said.

'Of course, you haven't. I doubt you have the brains, and even if you did I am quite sure you wouldn't have the patience.'

'Charles, really!' Aunty Bea cried.

'What you two don't seem to understand is that this house is perilously close to collapse,' Mr Godfrey said through gritted teeth. 'We can't get the staff to run it properly. The rents are dwindling as people move to the cities to work. And this government seems determined to take whatever money we do make in tax!'

'But what about your *work*?' Mum said, saying the last word slowly and deliberately, and looking Mr Godfrey straight in the eye. 'The men coming to the house in the night, things being delivered and taken away? Isn't money coming in from that?'

Mr Godfrey started, then recovered quickly. 'I would remind you that my work is for the government. It is not of your concern. And besides, the money isn't nearly enough to save this house.'

'So, sell something, like my sister says!' Aunty Bea pleaded. 'We have so much already.'

'I will do no such thing!' Mr Godfrey roared. 'Why should I? These treasures don't belong in some poxy museum or, God forbid, tradesman's living room! They belong to this house. They belong to *me*.' He stopped to take a breath. 'It seems I understand my duty to Splint Hall better than you two ever did.'

'I doubt that,' Mum said quietly.

'I will write a formal notice to the Wards,' Mr Godfrey continued, as if she hadn't spoken, 'to tell them that the cottages are not to be rebuilt and that they are to be evicted.'

'Charles, you're not being fair,' Aunty Bea cried. 'Where will they go?'

'They shall have to move. Plenty of people are doing it. There is no reason why they can't set up somewhere new. They will have to work hard, of course, but that will be good for them and good for the country.'

'But they work hard enough as it is!'

'Rubbish!' Mr Godfrey roared. 'They don't even know the meaning of the word "work". Keeping the lawn trimmed? Digging up some potatoes? Hah! They should try spending hours at a desk while their leg is throbbing so much that they can hardly think. They should try ignoring the pain for years, keeping on with their projects, never letting anyone down, never missing a deadline. That's work! That—' he said, practically spitting the words out, 'is the war effort.'

There was another horrible silence. Isobel and Flora heard the clock strike four. As the last chime rang out into the emptiness, Aunty Bea approached Mr Godfrey. 'No one's saying you haven't worked hard, Charles,' she said. She put a hand on his arm but he jerked away as if her touch burned him.

'I don't have any more to say on the matter,' he said, his voice low. 'I'll be in my study and I do not want to be disturbed.'

Isobel and Flora heard the thumps of his stick as he made his way across the hallway and down the corridor towards his study. It seemed to take forever. Then Rigby cleared his throat, a low, grating sound. 'Ma'am, Mrs Johnson,' he said, tipping his hat. He followed Mr Godfrey down the corridor.

'Bea . . .' Mum said, turning towards her sister.

'Don't, Julia,' Aunty Bea said, sounding impossibly tired. She crossed the hallway too but went into the Drawing Room. After a few seconds, Mum followed, closing the door with a soft click.

The girls were left sitting on the stairs, looking down at the empty hall.

The next morning, Isobel sat upright, suddenly wide awake. Something had woken her. It wasn't hunger, though she could feel that buzzing away in her stomach like a wasp. It was something else. She had been dreaming about splints. She had been running away, hearing their horrible gasp behind her, and Simon had been there . . . he had grabbed her hand and pulled her towards the air-raid shelter—

Up through tunnels, burrows, holes,
we'll come to feast upon your souls.

Suddenly, Isobel knew exactly what had woken her up.

She sprang out of bed and started pulling her clothes on. She did it so fast that her socks got twisted and she had to force herself to slow down and put them on properly. She pulled on her dress and then her cardigan – it was inside out but she didn't care – then grabbed her shoes from under her bed.

'What is it?' Flora asked. She sat up in a muddle of blankets, her eyes red and bleary. 'What are you doing?'

'I'm going to the air-raid shelter.'

'Why?'

Isobel finished buckling her shoes before she answered. 'Because there's something there. No, not something,' she corrected. 'There's some*where* there. Somewhere else.'

'What do you mean, somewhere else?' Flora said. 'Izzy, stop. You're not making any sense.'

But Isobel didn't wait to explain. She stood up and rushed out of the door, ignoring Flora's cry of 'Wait!' behind her.

The house was quiet and still. It was so early that Miss Stewart hadn't even got up yet to light the fires. Isobel tiptoed down the first staircase, holding her breath as she reached the landing where Mr Godfrey's bedroom was, then tiptoed down the second staircase, crossed the hall and opened the door.

Outside, the sun had just risen. The sky was turning pink and the lawns were still the dark blue-green they are at dusk and dawn. Isobel felt the dew wet her ankles as she raced for the air-raid shelter. Her breath sounded too loud and her legs were going too fast, like they might trip over themselves.

At the shelter she held on to the side and peered into the darkness. It was hard to see anything and suddenly Isobel felt very stupid that she hadn't brought a torch.

She reached out for the rope and missed. She tried again and grabbed hold of it, the fibres satisfyingly rough against her hands. A noise came from the direction of the house and Isobel turned to see her sister, hair flying out behind her and white socks bright against the grass as she ran.

'I told you to wait!' Flora said when she arrived a few seconds later. Her collar wasn't done up properly and she hadn't tied the ribbon in her hair like normal. 'You can't go in there when it's so dark. You'll break your ankle. What on earth are you doing?'

Isobel suddenly hated that she was the youngest. She hated having an older sister who thought she knew better than her all the time, even if she didn't. Even if she didn't know anything.

'Well?' Flora said, her hands on her hips.

150

'I'm finding the answer!' Isobel blurted out, kicking off the ledge.

It was only when she'd dropped to the floor, steadying the swing with her hand, that she realised quite how dark it was.

'For goodness' sake, Izzy, I bet you can't see a thing.' Flora disappeared from the doorway. 'I'm going to light the lamp. There's matches here.'

As Isobel's eyes got used to the darkness, she began to see the outline of the walls. She scoured them for any sign of a door or an opening. She knew that there must be one. One that led to a tunnel. That was what Simon meant about going in and out. That was how he had appeared, as if out of nowhere, yesterday when they'd been moving the dresses. That was how he had hidden from Rigby. This wasn't just an air-raid shelter. It was the entrance to somewhere else. Isobel was sure of it.

Then she noticed that there was a small section of dark at the back which seemed softer and blacker than the rest. It was only about a foot high. As she walked towards it, the darkness moved, took shape. Isobel saw something long and thin unfurl from the bottom of it. Her heart jumped and for a second, she forgot to breathe.

'Look, now we can see,' Flora said triumphantly, holding up the lamp in the doorway.

In the orangey glow, the dark shape scuttled towards the corner.

'What's that?' Flora said.

Isobel took a step forwards. The thing was cowering against the wall, its tiny wings spread over its head like it was shielding itself. It was a creature, black or dark brown – Isobel couldn't be sure in the half-light. Its claws clicked on the floor as it moved sideways, trying to put as much distance between Isobel and itself as possible.

'What is it?' Flora said, sounding more fascinated than afraid. She balanced the lantern on the ledge then lowered herself into the air-raid shelter. The two sisters stared at the creature together. Underneath the wings, it had a small, leathery body, at the bottom of which was a long tail. Its skin was covered in scales but not like those of a fish. This was more how Isobel imagined the tough skin of an alligator, but pewter-coloured instead of green.

'It's a dragon,' Isobel breathed. 'A baby dragon.'

CHAPTER FOURTEEN

Isobel wasn't sure how long she and Flora stood staring at the dragon. It was still shielding its head with its wings and it didn't move, except for the rise and fall of its chest, which seemed to be getting faster and faster. Soon, it started making little gulping sounds, like it couldn't catch its breath.

'We're not going to hurt you,' Isobel said softly.

Suddenly the air-raid shelter darkened as a figure appeared in the doorway. It crouched down to grab the rope, then stopped. The figure shook its head.

'Why are you two here *again*?' Simon said, sounding cross.

At the sound of his voice, the thing moved. Its wings went down and its head turned sideways. Isobel saw long jaws and tiny, pincer-like teeth. Simon's jaw dropped open. He leaped down into the air-raid shelter at exactly the same time as the thing ran past Isobel and Flora on small, unsteady legs, wobbling from side to side like it didn't quite know how to run yet. When it reached Simon it jumped a foot into the air and he caught it, snuggling it into his chest.

'It can't be a dragon,' Flora said, shaking her head in disbelief. 'It's not.'

'It is,' Isobel said. 'Isn't it?' she added, eagerly, to Simon.

Simon opened his mouth, then shut it again. 'I guess we can't hide it now,' he said, grudgingly, stroking the top of the creature's head. 'Yeah, it's a dragon.' He glanced at them, his eyes narrowing. 'I don't know what he's doing here though. What did you do?'

'We didn't do anything!' Flora said, outraged.

'We just found it,' Isobel added.

Simon looked down at the dragon again, biting his lip in worry. 'She'd never have let him go,' he said, almost to himself. 'Something must have happened.'

'Who's she?' Flora said.

'His mother, of course.'

Isobel's heartbeat quickened as she thought of what the baby dragon's mother might look like.

'I saw him get hatched yesterday,' Simon said, his expression proud as he looked down at the baby. Isobel thought back to his charred shirt and the silvery substance on his arms. 'That's why I'm here, to check on him. It took ages for him to fight his way out – dragon eggs are thick as anything – but he did it. His mother cleaned him up and everything was normal.' His expression slid into a frown. 'It must be something to do with the bomb. Maybe it hurt her, somehow, and she's sent him to get us. Maybe she's trapped. I'll need to go down there . . .'

'Down where?' Isobel said, realising she'd forgotten all about what she'd originally been looking for. From what Simon said, she'd been right. There was a door to another place.

But Simon just looked away furtively. 'Nowhere,' he said.

Flora folded her arms. 'All right. You're not going anywhere before you tell us *exactly* what's going on.'

Simon tutted in exasperation. 'I've already told you what's going on! You just didn't listen.'

'Tell us again. Tell us about the keeper . . . thingy.'

'It's not a *thingy*,' Simon said, his eyes flashing. 'It's a job. A very important job, as it happens.'

The dragon squawked as if to say that he agreed. He dug his claws into Simon's chest and turned his head sideways to look at Flora and Isobel. He eyed them suspiciously for a couple of seconds then hissed like a cat, but louder.

'Why's he making that noise?' Flora said warily.

'He doesn't like humans,' Simon said.

'How come he likes you then?'

'Because I'm a keeper,' Simon explained. 'I'm not like other people. He knows that. Dad said we smell different – there's something in our blood that they can sense, or something. We're not really sure, but they know us. They know we look after them. Plus, I was the second thing he saw after he was born, wasn't I?'

Simon crouched down low. The dragon squawked again as he carefully put him on the ground, but he stopped immediately when Simon got something out of his pocket. It was a thin piece of bacon. Isobel just caught a glimpse of the fat glowing palely before the dragon tore it from Simon's fingers.

'We feed them,' Simon said. 'They can get by, sort of, by eating bats and lost rabbits and, well, anything else that lives underground. But we give them what we can too. Your grandpa used to help us. He knew all about the dragons, that's why he gave us all the meat.' Simon's eyes flashed again angrily as he spoke. 'We didn't steal it! We didn't even eat any of it.'

'All right, all right,' Flora said, holding her hands up in surrender. 'So you're not thieves.'

'That's right, we're not,' Simon said instantly. 'Everything we got, it was for the dragons. Though it's been hard to get food for them since . . . well . . . since I can remember. Cos of the War and everything. And Lord Burlington dying and that Mr Godfrey taking his place.' His voice tightened with anger as he looked down at the dragon. 'They've had to go without. He's smaller than he should be. Babies are normally the size of dogs. He's not even as big as a cat yet.'

He stroked the back of the dragon's head gently and the dragon closed its eyes with pleasure. Isobel smiled. Even though she knew he would grow into something huge, something possibly even terrifying, she couldn't help finding him rather sweet.

Flora tapped her foot impatiently. 'So, you feed the dragons. What else do keepers do?'

'We help them if they're hurt,' Simon replied. 'We dress their wounds, give them medicine, that sort of thing. That's what being a keeper is. It's our job to keep them healthy, so they can do *their* job.'

'What's *their* job?' Isobel asked, foreboding twisting inside her.

'Killing splints,' Simon said flatly.

When he said 'splints' the little dragon hissed again and pawed the ground like a tiger waiting to pounce.

'And what exactly are splints?' Flora asked. She sounded like she didn't care at all about the answer, except for the way her voice shook slightly on the last word.

Simon's face darkened. 'Some say they're from hell, but only

156

the Devil knows for sure. They come from down there—' he pointed to the ground with his thumb. 'Deep down, down so far that nothing good lives, nothing *can* live cos it's so molten hot. It's where volcanoes are made, Dad says. Splints are evil, twisted things with long claws and mouths that don't close, like black holes. They're always hungry.'

There was a silence.

'I don't believe you,' Flora said. 'You're just trying to scare us.'

'I wish.'

'*I* believe you. I saw one,' Isobel said, before she even knew she was going to say it. 'In Burley Caves.'

Simon's head snapped up so fast Isobel was worried for his neck. 'What do you mean, you saw one?' he said. 'You can't have!'

'She didn't,' Flora said stubbornly. 'She's just imagining it. She gets nightmares all the time.'

Isobel glared at her. 'I *did* see one. You know I did.' She turned back to Simon. 'I only saw its arm, which was grey and thin, much thinner than a human's. And I saw the claws on its hand. It made this strange hissing noise when it breathed.'

Simon's face had turned as white as Miss Stewart's apron. 'That's the noise they make,' he whispered. 'I didn't tell you about that. How would you know about it?'

'Because I saw it!' Isobel said. 'Why does no one believe me?'

Simon didn't answer. Thoughts were travelling over his face like clouds flitting across the sky before a storm. 'If you saw it, that means they're already on the move . . .' His attention snapped back to Isobel. 'Where exactly did you see it? What happened?'

Isobel told him the story, starting with getting separated from the others and ending with her escaping from the caves.

'You're lucky to be alive,' Simon said, shaking his head in wonder. 'You throwing that candle was the best thing you could have done. They don't like fire, you see. It reminds them of where they've come from. And they know it's the only thing that kills them.'

'But you said the dragons kill them,' Flora said.

'Of course, because the dragons breathe fire,' Simon said, his tone matter-of-fact once again. 'That's what stops them getting to the surface. Always has done, for years. Hundreds of years. Thousands, far as we know.'

'See?' Isobel said, looking at Flora. She turned back to Simon. 'That's why it's called Splint Hall, isn't it?'

Simon nodded. 'Course. It's named after them, so we never forget, about them or the dragons.' He gave a short laugh. 'Not that we ever could.'

'So there's more than one dragon? How many are there?' Isobel asked.

'We look after two,' Simon replied. 'Now three,' he said, looking down at the baby dragon, who had Simon's shoelace in his teeth and was pulling hard. 'Stop that!' he said, pushing him away. 'But there are more,' he said, turning back to Isobel. 'Not many. The earth's thick, you know, and there's miles and miles of it before you get to the splints. Dad says there are ancient cracks, caused by earthquakes. They're like tunnels and they're big enough for the splints to get out. But there are only a few of them. There's another place we know of in Wales and another one in China, but that's it. When this dragon's older, he'll go to Wales to meet other dragons like him. He'll choose a mate, then he'll come back here, to do the job his parents do right now.'

'But *how* can there be dragons?' Flora said, shaking her head. 'Mum and Aunty Bea grew up here. They've never seen them!'

'Cos they live underground, of course,' Simon said, looking at her like she was a fool. 'That's where the splints come from, so that's where they've got to be. Haven't you got any brains in that head of yours?'

Flora would normally be furious when someone said something like that to her, but this time she wasn't. She looked like she was too busy thinking, turning something over and over in her mind. 'So the dragons protect us from those . . . things,' she said, looking at Simon for confirmation. 'That's good, isn't it? That means we don't need to worry. There's no chance of those—' She swallowed. '. . . Splints getting up here.'

'I said *normally* they protect us.'

'What do you mean, normally?'

Simon sighed. 'The thing you've got to know about splints is that when anything bad happens in the world, they get stronger. It's like they can feel it, somehow. All that suffering, anger, pain. They lap it up like warm milk.'

'The War!' Isobel said, suddenly understanding. 'In Grandpa's desk we found something, some sort of poem about the splints. It was written like they were speaking, and it said, '*We feed on pain and gorge on war.*' The War made the splints stronger!'

Simon nodded grimly. 'Much stronger. It happened after the last war too, the one before this one. Dad said splints came for three days, they just kept coming and coming and coming. And that wasn't the worst thing.'

'What was?' Isobel said, not sure she wanted to know, but fascinated at the same time.

'One of the dragons got a bone stuck in his foot. Dad had to pull it out and then stop the bleeding, right before the splints reached the cavern.'

'The cavern?'

'Where the dragons live,' Simon said impatiently. 'Do you know how you stop a wound bleeding? You wash it, then you get a poker and you put it in the fire and then—'

'Stop,' Flora said, shaking her head.

'I bet the dragon didn't like that,' Isobel said.

'It didn't,' Simon said, a note of pride in his voice. 'But Dad had to do it. Otherwise the dragon would have been injured and how can it fight splints like that?' A shadow passed across his face. 'Though now it's even worse. The dragons haven't been eating like they should, cos of all this rationing. It's getting better now the War's ended and Miss Joyce can help out again. She's been giving us meat from her farm.'

'The bag you were carrying,' Isobel remembered, thinking of the red stain. 'The day we met you.'

'Piglet,' Simon said, with absolutely no guilt in his face. 'The dragons are getting stronger, but they're still weaker than normal.' He shook his head, looking down at the little creature, which was nuzzling his leg. 'It's not a good time for a baby to be hatched.'

Isobel looked at the dragon resting its tiny head on Simon's knee. A pang went through her at the thought of a splint getting hold of him. 'Can't you keep him up here, where he's safe?'

Simon shook his head. 'His mum'll be going spare, looking for him. She won't be able to fight the splints if she's doing that, will she?' He ran his hand through his hair quickly, his face troubled. 'Anyway, I'm worried something's happened to her. Something bad. Underground, there are caves with rocks hanging down as big as me and you, even. Huge, pointed ones. What if the bomb shook one, and it fell down to the ground, and . . .' he trailed off, unable to finish the sentence. 'Or what if she's buried under rocks and she can't get out? She'd never let her baby out of her sight, unless she had to. Unless she wanted him to get help. Something must be wrong. And the splints are coming.' He looked up at them, terror making his eyebrows twitch. 'Dad and Pat already thought they were. It's autumn but it's getting hotter and hotter. That's always the sign they're on the move. They bring the heat with them, you see, all the way from the centre of the earth. But now you've seen one, they must already be here . . .' He sat back against the wall in despair. 'What are we going to do?'

Isobel imagined the dragon's mother, collapsed under rocks like a bird with a broken wing. Then she imagined the splints and their steady march up, up, up . . . up twisting tunnels and mine shafts, up rabbit burrows and through air-raid shelters and out.

We'll come for all that you hold dear.
There's no escape. We'll come. We're here.

Flora sniffed decisively into the silence. 'Well, it's obvious, isn't it?'

'What's obvious?'

She flapped a hand at Simon. 'What we're going to do. You're not strong enough to dig out a dragon by yourself. So we'll have to help.'

Simon stared at Flora like she'd suggested they fly to the

moon. 'You two, go down there?' he said, jerking his thumb down again. 'Are you mad?'

'Why not?'

'Why not?' Simon spluttered. 'You don't know the first thing about being underground, that's why not. You've got no idea how dangerous it is.'

'More dangerous than the splints coming, and there being no dragons to protect us?' Flora said, raising her eyebrows and sounding like Mum. 'More dangerous than that?'

That made Simon pause for a second. But then he thought of something, and his face set with determination again. 'You don't need to come,' he said. 'I'll tell my brother Pat, and we'll go together. He's older. He'll be able to lift heavy rocks.'

Flora folded her arms. 'We're coming, and that's that.'

'No, you're not!'

'Says who?'

'Says me,' Simon said, puffing out his chest in an attempt to look bigger. 'I'm one of the keepers in this village, and I say!'

'Stop it!' Isobel said as Flora started to laugh. 'Stop fighting.'

'You don't understand,' Simon said, shaking his head. 'There are things down there, not just dragons and splints but other things. Dangerous things. I don't want anyone to get hurt.'

'We'll all get hurt if the splints come!' Flora pointed out. 'Everyone will.'

'I said no!'

'Stop fighting!' Isobel said again, louder this time. 'You said they get stronger when people are angry. You're making it worse!'

Simon and Flora fell silent. For a while, the only sound that

162

could be heard was the baby dragon's tiny snuffles as he slept on Simon's lap.

'If you want to help, get food,' Simon said, looking down at him, then looking back up at the girls. 'That's what you can do. I bet there's loads of meat in that fancy house of yours.'

'There isn't, actually,' Flora said. 'Rationing's for everyone.'

'We can hide some of our food in our pockets at lunchtime,' Isobel said. 'It won't be much, but it'll be something.'

Flora looked sharply at her but said nothing.

'That won't be enough,' Simon said. 'You'll need to go to the kitchens, take something proper.' His eyebrows were raised, like he was daring them to say no.

'All right,' Flora said instantly.

'I'm talking about stealing.'

'I know what you're talking about. And we'll do it. We want to help,' Flora added, pointedly.

Simon nodded. 'All right. We'll meet back here, after lunch.'

'But someone will see us!' Isobel protested. 'We should wait till dark.'

'We can't,' Simon said, shaking his head. 'We've got to get down there. The dragons might be hurt, or . . .' He trailed off, unable to complete his thought. 'It's got to be as soon as possible. You'll give us the meat you've got, then me and Pat'll take him back.' He looked up at them, his face serious. 'Agreed?'

Isobel and Flora nodded. 'So what happens to him now?' Flora said, pointing at the dragon. 'Is he just going to stay here? What if Rigby comes?'

Simon shrugged. 'Where else can he go? I can't take him into the village, can I?'

163

'We could hide him in our bedroom . . .' Isobel said, thinking it over. 'He's asleep now, so we can move him.' She stepped towards the dragon, but even though she was careful to tread lightly, the dragon's red eyes snapped open instantly. He bared his teeth at Isobel and hissed again loudly, flexing his little feet. Isobel swallowed down the sudden hurt she felt as Simon laughed.

'It's nothing personal,' he said.

'Fine,' Flora said, already moving to the entrance. 'He'll just have to stay hidden, then. Come on, Izzy.'

Simon carefully put the dragon down in the corner, making soothing clicking noises as he did so. Then one by one the three children pulled themselves up, out of the air-raid shelter and into the morning.

'See you after lunch, then,' Flora said, turning to go, but Simon pulled her back suddenly.

'Wait,' he said. 'You won't tell, will you? You mustn't tell anyone about him. I mean it. It's important. Do you promise?'

Flora looked at him like he was something she'd found on the bottom of her shoe. 'Course we won't tell,' she said tightly. 'We're not tattletales.' She grabbed Isobel's hand and started marching back to the house. Isobel twisted round to wave goodbye at Simon. He gave her a very small wave back, then darted off into the bushes, his grey jumper and shorts quickly disappearing into the green.

'I can't believe him,' Flora whispered, not very quietly. 'Who does he think he is, telling us we can't go underground with him?'

'He is a keeper,' Isobel pointed out.

'So?' Flora bristled. 'I bet I could be one too, given the chance. Why does he get to go and see the grown-up dragons and we're not allowed? It's not fair. And telling us not to tell anyone. As if we would!'

Isobel said nothing, because deep in her mind – down where her most secret, hidden thoughts swirled – she was relieved not to be going underground. She wanted to see the grown-up dragons, of course. This morning, she'd even been ready to find the hidden door and go down herself. But that was before Simon had talked about how far down the dragons were. It wasn't even the molten heat or the splints or the terrible dangers that Simon had mentioned that Isobel was most scared of. It was simply thinking of being that far underground, with the huge weight of earth on top of you, that made her feel like all the air in her chest was being squeezed out. Like there had been a bomb and she was buried, and no one knew where, so no one could help. Like she had felt in the air-raid shelter, on the night of the bomb.

Blinking hard, Isobel looked up at Splint Hall. The sun, which had now risen fully, was making the windows sparkle. The red bricks looked warmer and friendlier than normal. A blackbird chirped as it flew up, landing to perch on the iron staircase that Isobel now knew led up to their secret attic room. Luckily, apart from the birdsong, the house seemed completely silent.

'I don't think anyone's up yet,' Flora said, echoing her thoughts. 'That's lucky.'

They slipped through the heavy oak door into the hallway. Noiselessly, they tiptoed across the black-and-white tiles and up the heavy oak stairs. They were about halfway down the first-floor hallway when they heard a cough from the bedroom on their right.

The girls stopped immediately. Someone inside the room – which Isobel realised was the pink room where they'd found the toy dragons – cleared their throat quietly. Then they said something, but it was too quiet for them to hear.

'It's Mum,' Flora breathed into Isobel's ear.

Before Isobel could say anything back, Flora stole towards the door. It was open just a crack and she peered through the gap.

Not wanting to be left out, Isobel crossed the corridor and joined her sister. In her haste she slipped slightly and her shoe made a small thud. Flora raised her eyebrows and put her finger to her lips, but Mum didn't seem to hear.

'I keep thinking about when this was our room,' she said, softly.

Isobel looked through the gap and saw Aunty Bea. She was sitting on the pink coverlet in her white nightie, her back against the headboard and her knees tucked up so she could rest her chin on them. At Mum's question, she lifted her chin and nodded. 'I do, too.'

Mum was sitting cross-legged in front of her, leaning forward, her back to Flora and Isobel. Her hands were clasped in her lap tightly. 'When the light comes through the window like that, it feels like nothing has changed, doesn't it? Like if we went downstairs we'd find Mum going over the menus with Mrs Potts, tutting at us for being up so early.'

Aunty Bea smiled. 'And Betty doing the fires.'

'Then later, Daddy would come downstairs, all bleary-eyed, and take fifteen minutes to put his boots on.'

'And Mum would say if he wasn't so partial to Cook's sponge pudding he'd be able to reach over his belly more easily.'

Aunty Bea laughed then put her hand to her mouth, as if the sound was too loud.

Mum leaned further forward, her manner suddenly urgent. She said, 'Bea, we must talk,' at exactly the same time as Aunty Bea said, 'I found a letter.'

'What?' Mum said. 'What do you mean, a letter?'

'From the War Damages Commission. When you said it last night, it jogged something in my memory. I knew I'd heard that name before. So when Charles was having his bath, I looked in his study. And I found a letter from them.'

'Go on.'

Aunty Bea took a deep breath. 'Charles had written to them, like he said. But he . . . he lied when he said they wouldn't give him the money. They did, Julia.' She held something up, something that crackled slightly. 'Look.'

Mum took it out of her hands. She didn't say anything for a few seconds. 'Bea, that's a cheque. For a lot of money.'

'I know.'

'But this is serious. If he's taking the money from the government but not using it to rebuild the cottages, it's fraud.'

'I *know*,' Aunty Bea said, wiping her eyes angrily.

'But this changes everything,' Mum said, and there was a note of joy in her voice that Isobel didn't understand.

'Whatever do you mean?'

'I've suspected he's been using the black market, seeing what he eats at breakfast. The girls have told me about the deliveries and pick-ups in the night. I'm going to take a look at Rigby's shed, the first chance I get, but I'm quite sure he's not just buying extras, Bea. He's trading. And now this! You can go to the police and—'

Isobel felt Aunty Bea draw back before she saw it. 'I couldn't,' she said.

'But you can't let him get away with it! I know it would be hard—'

'I'm married, Julia,' Aunty Bea said, the anger in her voice surprising Isobel. 'He's my husband. I couldn't betray him like that!'

Mum was silent for a few moments. 'Bea, the way he treats you . . .'

'Well, not every marriage can be like yours,' Aunty Bea said bitterly. Immediately, she looked at Mum, a little ashamed. 'I didn't mean . . . I'm sorry, I know it's been hard for you, with Peter . . .'

Mum squeezed her hand.

'I know you've never liked Charles.' Mum started to say something, but Aunty Bea cut her off. 'That was obvious when you came to visit, after you'd had Isobel. When there was that awful argument. I know that he can be . . . difficult. But you've got to understand. I was so jealous of you, when you left for your new life and your head-over-heels romance. I had to be the one who stayed, hearing Mum and Daddy talking about when you were next going to be home and what you were up to. And then they died, and Mr Granger told me how much money we owed . . . And Charles was there, and he had a good job in the government, which would give Splint Hall money that we needed, and he liked me . . . what was I supposed to do?

'He helped me, Julia. When you weren't there. He got everything straightened out. He's not as bad as you think. He's doing his best. I . . . I've seen the deliveries too, and I don't like it, but if he *is* doing the black market, then he's doing it for us. You heard what he said, about us being close to ruin.'

Isobel had never heard her aunt speak so much at once. It seemed that Mum needed some time to take it in as well. Eventually, she cleared her throat. 'But it's wrong, Bea. And the way he speaks to you—'

'There are people who put up with worse. And what about Splint Hall?' Aunty Bea looked at Mum, suddenly angry again. 'What if we do lose this house? You know what Daddy said.' She lowered her voice, so much that Isobel had to struggle to make out the next words. 'About the secret.'

Mum let out a long breath. 'Bea, he never told us. We can't live our lives because of it, when we don't even know what it is, or if it's important. Knowing Daddy, it was all some silly game, anyway!'

Aunty Bea shook her head. 'It wasn't. You know it wasn't. And it's my job to keep Splint Hall in the family. I'm the one who inherited it. Why can't you see that?'

'What I can see is that I shouldn't have left you here,' Mum said, moving closer to her sister. 'And I'm sorry for that, really I am. You're right, I was selfish, going off to London. I hate that I let us grow apart before the War. I was always the selfish one; you've always been kind and loyal and faithful. And it's wonderful, you're wonderful – really you are – but you can't . . .' Mum broke off, struggling to find the words. 'You can't live like this. It's not right.' Mum took Bea's hand in hers again. 'Yesterday I went to the post office to send a letter. It was to Peter's brother, David. I asked him if we can go and live with him in Norfolk. I think he'll say yes. You should come too, Bea. You can start again.'

Aunty Bea didn't say anything. She reached up to dab at her eyes once more, and Isobel noticed her hand was shaking.

'Please, Bea,' Mum said. 'I can't bear to see you so unhappy. *Please.*'

Aunty Bea shook her head, tears finally springing from her eyes. 'I can't,' she whispered.

Mum's back tightened. After a few moments, she reached out to take Aunty Bea into her arms. Aunty Bea didn't make any sound as they embraced, but Isobel could see from the rising and falling of her shoulders that she was crying. Then she felt herself being pulled away by Flora.

The girls tiptoed softly down the corridor and up the wooden stairs that led to their room. Without saying anything, they got into their cold beds, still in their outdoor clothes, and looked up at the sun streaming through the round window.

'We shouldn't tell Mum that we saw that,' Flora said into the silence. 'She wouldn't have wanted us to see it. So don't go blurting it out like you normally do.'

Isobel nodded, her throat tight. After a while, Flora turned on to her side and her breathing became long and even, but Isobel knew that she'd never get to sleep herself. So she looked up at the light dancing on the ceiling, thinking of Aunty Bea's chest rising and falling. It had reminded her of the baby dragon and the way his chest had moved up and down when he was scared.

CHAPTER FIFTEEN

When they went downstairs a couple of hours later, Isobel saw something that made her feel a strange mixture of relief and terror. They had gone outside to check where Miss Stewart was. Through the tiny window at the back and right at the bottom of Splint Hall, Isobel saw her arm moving round and round as she turned the mangle. It was wash day.

Wash day used to be Mum's worst day of the week and Isobel imagined this was true for Miss Stewart too. First the clothes had to be put in an enormous wooden tub with many buckets of hot water and sprinklings of white powder. Then you had to stir the clothes with a wooden stick. Mum always gritted her teeth when she did this, both hands holding the stick, her skin shiny with steam and effort. Once the clothes had been scrubbed on the draining board, they had to be fed through the mangle to squeeze the water out. Both Isobel and Flora had tried to turn the handle of the mangle once but the only way they could was if they both did it together, and even then it was hard work. When all the water was out of the clothes, then – and only then – could they be hung out to dry. It had always taken Mum the best part of a day, and she was only washing three people's clothes. Miss Stewart had to wash hers, Flora's, Mum's, Aunty Bea's, Mr Godfrey and Rigby's. That was six people.

'It's going to take her hours,' Flora said, echoing Isobel's thoughts. 'That means . . .'

Isobel was thinking it too. The scullery was a tiny room off the kitchen. Isobel knew that Miss Stewart would keep the door closed though, so the steam didn't come in and warm the food. So that meant she'd be out of the kitchen nearly all day.

'Come on!' Flora said. 'We couldn't have asked for better luck.'

'The door will probably be locked,' Isobel said, a part of her hoping that would be the case.

But it wasn't. As soon as they tiptoed through the back door, waving to Miss Stewart through the window (Isobel ignoring her flash of guilt as she did so), they saw that the heavy black kitchen door was ajar.

'Come *on*,' Flora hissed, moving towards it. 'Do you want to help the dragon, or not?'

The kitchen was darker and hotter than Isobel was expecting. There was a big oak table, mottled with years of stains and burns, in front of the black stove which stretched along the wall to their left. Isobel could feel the heat coming off it already. Hanging above the stove were a number of iron hooks with every tool you could ever need to cook a meal. Another smaller wooden table was wedged between the stove and the window. A bowl covered with a white tea cloth and some onions were resting on it.

Flora was prowling around as softly and stealthily as a cat. 'Where would she keep the meat?' she whispered. She lifted the

172

tea cloth and let it drop back down again when she saw what was inside.

'Somewhere cold?' Isobel whispered back.

Flora looked round the room, her forehead furrowed with concentration. Then her expression cleared. She was looking at two wooden doors on the back wall.

'Wait!' Isobel said, grabbing her sister's arm. 'One of them will be the door to the scullery, where Miss Stewart's doing the washing!'

Flora shrugged her off. She tiptoed to the doors and put her ear up against the one on the left. She listened for a few seconds, then went to the other. She only listened for a couple of seconds before lifting her head up. 'She's in there,' she mouthed, pointing at the door.

'Are you sure?'

Flora went to the other door and turned the handle. Isobel shut her eyes for a second, expecting a shout at any moment. But when she opened them, she saw the inside of a cupboard. Flora was holding up something wrapped in white paper, a triumphant grin on her face.

'Chops!' she whispered. 'There's more. *Much* more. Izzy, come and look.'

The pantry was stacked high with parcels. The bigger ones turned out to be chicken. Flora was right, there was a whole shelf stuffed full of chops, while another smaller shelf was given over to bacon. Isobel's stomach clenched, remembering the salty stew Miss Stewart had made for them.

'There's so much,' she breathed. 'Who's it all for?'

'You heard Mum. He's a trader. He'll sell it to whoever gives him the best price.' Flora's voice was spiked with anger. 'He's no better than one of those spivs we used to see at home, hanging around the market.'

Isobel picked up a smaller bag. The meat inside was slimy and heavy in the bottom of the paper.

'I think it's liver,' Flora said, grimacing. 'Never mind, the dragon won't know the difference, and it won't be missed like a chicken would. Let's take that, some of those chops and a couple of bags of sausages.'

'Don't you think we'll get in trouble?' Isobel said, hating herself for caring.

'We can't help that, can we? We've got to feed the dragons.'

Isobel nodded. There was a scraping noise from behind the door on the left. It could have just been Miss Stewart getting up to collect the next wet piece of clothing, but the girls weren't taking any chances. Grabbing the meat and stuffing it into their pockets, they left the kitchen as quickly as they could, Flora shutting the door carefully behind them.

They hurried up the stairs and on to the hallway.

'We did it!' Flora whispered, her face glowing as she grabbed Isobel's hand. 'Come on, let's hide it in our room.'

Then they heard a single, dry cough behind them. Isobel and Flora froze. They turned very slowly, Isobel praying that it wasn't who they thought, but knowing in her heart that it was.

It was a shame that the kitchen door was so thick, Isobel thought, and that they had shut it when they were inside. Perhaps if they hadn't they would have heard Mr Godfrey leaving his study and coming down the corridor. Because here he was, his moustache bristling as he looked them up and down with his cold blue eyes.

'Before you go,' he said, 'would you mind telling me exactly why you were in the kitchen, and what you have in your pockets?'

The seconds ticked by. No one spoke. Mr Godfrey's vein bulged unpleasantly on his forehead.

'I asked you what was in your pockets,' he said, so quietly it was almost a whisper.

Isobel felt hot, then icy all over. It was exactly like when she was ill with scarlet fever. She could feel Flora beside her, starting to seethe.

'Nothing,' Flora said.

Mr Godfrey's bottom lip quivered. He fixed his gaze on Isobel. 'You will give me what you have taken, right now. Or I promise the consequences will be severe.' His pale eyes seemed to bore right into Isobel's soul. Her hand shook as she reached into her pocket.

'Isobel, don't!' Flora cried.

But Mr Godfrey snatched the paper-wrapped chops out of Isobel's hands before she could change her mind.

He balanced his elbow on his stick and opened the paper. When he saw the meat inside he looked at it silently for a couple of seconds. Then he looked up, and though his skin was glowing red with anger, Isobel saw a glint of triumph in his eyes.

'Beatrice!' he roared, so loudly that Flora and Isobel stepped backwards.

Immediately they heard the sound of a door being opened, then hasty footsteps. Aunty Bea arrived at the same time as the door to the kitchen opened and Miss Stewart came up the stairs, her fringe plastered to her head and her face nearly as red as Mr Godfrey's. Her quick eyes ran over Flora and Isobel, then settled on Mr Godfrey and the parcel in his hand. She looked questioningly at Isobel and Isobel looked away, flooded with shame.

'Whatever's the matter, Charles?' Aunty Bea said, trying to keep her voice bright.

Then there were footsteps coming from above. Mum reached the hallway and strode towards them, clenching her fists tight.

'Charles, what is it?' Aunty Bea asked again.

Mr Godfrey drew himself up to his full height. 'These girls have been found stealing from the kitchen.'

Mum looked at Flora and Isobel in disbelief. 'I'm sure they haven't,' she said. 'They would never do such a thing.'

'I'm afraid the evidence is irrefutable. I heard them come out of the kitchen myself. Then I found this in Isobel's pocket.' He thrust the chops at Mum. 'No doubt there's more. Go on, turn out your pockets.' This last bit was directed at Isobel and Flora.

Flora sighed loudly, like this whole episode was beneath her, but Isobel could see that her eyes were scared. There was nothing they could do. Slowly, they each reached into their pockets and drew out their bloody parcels. Isobel stared at them in her hands, not wanting to look up and see Mum's disappointment. Then the meat was gently taken out of her hands. Miss Stewart bobbed a curtsey in Mr Godfrey's direction, then disappeared back into the kitchen.

Mum stared at the closed door, mystified. 'I'm sure this must just all be a mistake. Or a misunderstanding. Why on earth would they take raw meat?'

'Because they're giving it to those criminals, that's why!'

Mr Godfrey said. 'James and his son. They're clearly in league with them.'

'Charles, please,' Aunty Bea tried.

He held up a hand to silence her, then turned back to Mum. 'This has gone on far too long. I will not have thieves living under my roof—'

'You're the thief!' Flora shouted.

Mr Godfrey's mouth fell open. Red patches appeared on his neck. 'What did you say?'

'There's loads of meat in there,' Flora cried, turning to Mum. 'He's been starving us all this time while he's been hoarding everything, just so he can sell it on the black market—'

'Flora, stop!' Aunty Bea said, appalled.

'But it's true!'

Mum looked at Aunty Bea, who looked back at her pleadingly. Her lips tightened, and she reached out for Flora and Isobel's hands, but she said nothing.

When Mr Godfrey spoke again, his voice was steady. 'This is the last straw. You clearly have no discipline over them. They run in the corridors, they enter rooms they've been forbidden to enter, see things they're not meant to see . . .' He stopped to steady his hand, which was shaking, on his stick. 'They talk back, and now this . . . this terrible accusation! I will not have it. I tell you, I will not have it!'

'Charles, please don't over-excite yourself,' Aunty Bea said, putting a hand on his shoulder.

'Don't you start!' Mr Godfrey shouted. 'I should have known you'd take their side.'

'I'm not taking anyone's side!'

As he did so often, Mr Godfrey ignored her. 'You and your daughters will have to leave,' he said to Mum. 'Right away.'

Mum stiffened. Isobel expected her to shout – to scream, even – but she didn't. Instead, she went very calm and still. She looked Mr Godfrey straight in the eye. 'Fine, if that's what you want.'

'It is,' Mr Godfrey said, not missing a beat.

Mum's gaze travelled to Aunty Bea. 'Is it what you want, Bea?' she asked.

'Of course it's what she wants,' Mr Godfrey snapped.

'I was talking to my sister!' Mum said, her eyes flashing like diamonds. 'And she is perfectly capable of speaking for herself.'

'Fine,' Mr Godfrey said, turning to his wife with mock civility. 'Tell them, Beatrice. I'm only your husband, after all. How should I know what you do or don't want? If you want them to stay, then say so.'

Aunty Bea looked desperately from her husband to her sister. Her cheeks flushed red as the seconds ticked on, slowly. She scrunched the sleeve of her shirt into her fist, then let go. 'I . . . I have a headache,' she said, looking at the floor.

Mum looked at Aunty Bea, and in that look, Isobel thought she saw her heart break, just a little. 'Bea—'

But Aunty Bea had run from the corridor, almost tripping over the rug in her haste to get away. Isobel heard her feet on the stairs, then the sound of a door shutting.

Mr Godfrey looked at Mum, his eyes triumphant. 'Then that's settled,' he said. 'You can leave first thing in the morning. I'll have Rigby drive you to the station.'

'How courteous of you,' Mum murmured.

If Mr Godfrey noticed her sarcasm, he didn't show it. 'I'm sure you'd like to spend your remaining day in your rooms, packing your belongings,' he said. He waved his hand, as if to dismiss them.

Mum gave the smallest of nods. Then with her head held high, she led Isobel and Flora down the corridor and up the stairs.

Mum was silent as she helped the girls put their clothes into the brown suitcase under their bed. It didn't take long. Then she sat on Flora's bed and put one arm around Flora, one around Isobel.

'Where are we going to go?' Flora said.

Isobel glanced up. Mum looked tired. There were red, puffy bits underneath her eyes. Isobel would have thought she'd been crying but she knew that Mum didn't cry.

'I've been thinking we might go and live with Daddy's brother, Uncle David. He lives a long way from here, in Norfolk. By the seaside.' Mum forced her lips into a smile. 'Won't that be nice? We'll be able to go for long walks on the beach and even build sandcastles. And have fish and chips! How about that?'

Isobel looked to her sister but for once, Flora was silent. Maybe – like Isobel – she was thinking of Mum telling Aunty Bea the same thing this morning, and how she mustn't find out that they saw.

'Well?' Mum pressed. 'What do you think? I know it's not been easy, being here. This would be a New Start by the sea.'

An image popped up in Isobel's mind – of Mum saying the same words, *a New Start*, in the tiny room they all shared at Mrs Dooley's. Suddenly, Isobel wanted to cry. Words bubbled up from inside her, angry, complaining words that said *this* was meant to be their new start, they were here right now. She pressed her lips together to stop them coming out.

'What about Aunty Bea?' she managed, finally.

'Well, I was hoping she might come too,' Mum said, avoiding Isobel's eyes. Isobel thought of Aunty Bea's back rising and falling. Of her saying, *'I can't.'*

'Why didn't she say she wanted us to stay?' Flora said, hurt making her voice sound younger. 'Doesn't she want us here?'

Mum sighed and kissed her forehead. 'Of course she does. It's just difficult.'

'It's only difficult because of *him*,' Isobel said.

Mum sighed again but didn't disagree. 'What were you doing, taking the meat anyway? What on earth did you want with it?' she asked, but she didn't sound cross.

Isobel stole a glance at her sister, who gave a tiny shake of her head.

'Well? Is it a stray dog or cat?' Mum said.

'Something like that,' Flora mumbled.

Mum pulled them even closer. 'I know how you two love animals, but there is rationing on, you know. You can't feed every poor creature that comes your way. There's not enough to go round as it is.'

'There'd be more if Mr Godfrey wasn't doing what he's doing!' Flora pointed out.

'Well, two wrongs don't make a right.'

'Sorry,' Isobel said, her face burning. 'Sorry that we made Mr Godfrey angry. Sorry that we have to leave.'

'It's not your fault and I don't want you ever to think so,' Mum said, lowering her head to look Isobel in the eye. 'The way he . . . well, the way things are around here, we would have left sooner or later.' She sighed. 'Perhaps it's better that it's sooner.'

They stayed sitting on the bed for a long time – so long that the sun crept high enough in the sky that it shone through their round window. Isobel knew it must be nearly lunchtime. She kept thinking about the baby dragon, waiting in the air-raid shelter, curling himself around his hungry belly. She thought of Simon and his brother Pat, waiting for them as well, looking at their watches. But there was nothing they could do, unless they told Mum the real reason they took the meat. Unless they told her about the dragon and the splints. The idea of telling her grew more and more insistent as time ticked on. It thudded in Isobel's ears like Mum's heartbeat. But every time she opened her mouth, she remembered Flora shaking her head, and Simon begging them not to tell, and shut it again.

Eventually, Mum uncurled her arms from round her daughters and got up.

'I'll go and see Miss Stewart about something to eat for your lunch,' she said, looking very tired. 'And I suppose I'd better find my sister. You'll be all right here, won't you?'

Isobel nodded, unable to speak. Mum put her palm to both of their cheeks, then closed the door behind her as she left.

'Maybe we should tell her,' Isobel whispered, as the sound of Mum's footsteps faded. 'I know Simon said not to, but she might be able to help. She might be able to get the dragons some meat. Flora?' she said, when her sister didn't reply. 'Flora, what do you think?'

'I don't know,' Flora said, looking – strangely for her – a little lost. 'I don't know what to do about any of it.'

Isobel didn't know what to do either. Down in the air-raid shelter, there was a tiny dragon who was desperate for food but they couldn't give him any. Somewhere in the village, Pat and Simon were getting ready to go underground to help the dragons. And somewhere deep in the earth, the splints were marching. Tomorrow, Isobel, Flora and Mum would leave, but it wouldn't matter where they went. Eventually the splints would find them. If the dragons couldn't protect them, the splints would find everyone.

Isobel knew all of this, but she felt powerless to change any of it. It was like when the siren went off and, after the mad scramble to the air-raid shelter, you were shut up in the darkness, just waiting. Hoping and praying that the bomb wouldn't fall on you. What Isobel had always hated the most was that there was nothing they could do.

There was a knock on the door. Miss Stewart entered, holding a tray with two sandwiches on it.

'Mrs Johnson said you were hungry,' she said, putting the sandwiches down on the bedside table. 'It's all I've got, I'm afraid. Master said you shouldn't get it at all, but . . .' She sniffed.

'Thanks, Miss Stewart,' Isobel said gratefully, feeling her tummy clench in anticipation.

'Thank you,' Flora said as well.

Miss Stewart sniffed again. In fact, it was more of a snort. 'No child's going to go hungry on my watch, long as I can help it,' she said.

Isobel bit into her sandwich. It was slimy and almost jelly-like, the way Spam always was, but it was salty and savoury and very welcome. She looked up and saw Miss Stewart, who hadn't left but was hovering in the doorway.

'There's something else,' Miss Stewart said quickly. She reached into her apron and put what she was carrying on the chest of drawers.

Isobel's bite of sandwich nearly got stuck in her throat as she saw what it was. There were four brown-paper-wrapped packages, each looking very familiar, each holding something solid at their centre.

It was the meat they had taken from the pantry.

'People think my sort don't see things,' Miss Stewart said, as if to explain. She brushed the front of her apron, then folded her hands awkwardly in front of her, like she wasn't sure what to do with them. 'They must think we're stupid or something,' she continued, 'just cos we're servants. But I'm not. I knew what Mr Godfrey was doing as soon as Rigby asked me to store the extra meat in my pantry. I don't like it, not one bit, but what am I to do? If I told anyone, he'd just wiggle out of it somehow, same as his kind always do, and I'd be out on my ear.'

'But that's not fair!' Flora said.

'Well, it is what it is. Someone higher up than me would need to blab for Mr Godfrey to get what's coming to him. But I can help you with this.' Miss Stewart's eyes softened. 'Back when I was a kitchen maid, I saw Cook give James all that meat, day after day after day. I saw him disappearing into the shelter, not that it was a shelter back then. It was just a shed. He used to be in there for hours. I saw when he came back with his scrapes and burns. I don't know what he was up to then, and I don't know what you're up to now, but I reckon it's important.'

Isobel swallowed awkwardly. She looked over at Flora who, for once in her life, was speechless.

'Thank you,' Isobel said.

'You don't need to thank me,' Miss Stewart said immediately. She folded her arms, worry crumpling her forehead. 'Though you two just mind yourselves, and look after each other, you hear me? I know how sisters can be to each other. Me and my sister were the same. Then she moved to Scotland when she married, and I realised she was the best friend I ever had. I never knew it till she wasn't there.' Miss Stewart stopped abruptly. She looked faintly surprised, like she hadn't expected to say that much. 'What I mean is,' she added, 'whatever you're doing, wherever you're going, you'll need each other. So no more squabbling, you understand?'

Isobel felt her cheeks go hot. She glanced at Flora and saw she'd gone red too. They both looked away, Flora out of the window and Isobel down at the bedspread.

'Well?' Miss Stewart demanded.

'We understand,' Flora mumbled.

Miss Stewart turned her piercing gaze on to Isobel, who nodded. Satisfied, she turned to leave.

'But, won't you get in trouble?' Isobel said. 'If the meat's missing?'

Miss Stewart looked worried for a moment, like she hadn't thought of that. Then there was a yap from downstairs, and she pursed her lips with satisfaction. 'I'll say that I left it on the table and that little toe-rag of a dog got it, won't I?' She grinned at the thought, then disappeared down the stairs before either Isobel or Flora could say anything else.

The girls stared in silence at the door for a few moments, their sandwiches forgotten.

'You know what this means, Izzy?' Flora said, unable to keep the excitement from her voice.

'We can give the dragon the meat!' Isobel said.

Flora nodded. 'We haven't got long,' she said, looking at the clock on the mantelpiece. 'It's two o'clock already. They'll go without it if we're not there.'

'But how are we going to get out without Mr Godfrey or Rigby seeing us?'

Flora's gaze flickered to the tiny door that led to the attic. Isobel felt her tummy lurch, like the ground had wobbled beneath her. 'But . . . but it's so high—'

'We've got to,' Flora said, matter of fact. 'We don't have any other choice. You take these two.' She handed Isobel the two smaller parcels. She stuffed the others into her pockets, then pulled on a jumper over the top, and made Isobel do the same. 'Are you ready?'

Isobel grabbed her toy dragon from the table and stuffed it in her pocket, next to one of the parcels. She nodded, ignoring the fear bubbling in her chest.

They moved the chest of drawers out of the way, going as quietly as they possibly could. Then Flora opened the tiny door and kneeled down so she could go through. Isobel followed. By the time she stood up in the attic room, Flora had already got the door open. The staircase glinted as the tops of the trees rustled below them.

'Don't look down,' Flora said. 'It's like any other staircase if you don't look down.'

Isobel's hand was shaking slightly as she went through the door and grabbed the railing. It was cold and felt very thin, so she held it with her other hand too. A light breeze blew through her hair, whipping it into her eyes.

'Come on!' Flora hissed from beneath her. 'It's not too bad, honestly.'

Shaking her hair away, Isobel put one foot down onto the step, then the other. It wobbled slightly under her weight, making her breath freeze in her throat, but held. Seeing Flora about fifteen steps down, she started to hurry. It was impossible not to look down though, she thought. If she didn't look down, how would she know where to put her feet? Even if when you looked down, you saw the ground through the holes in the staircase, and it looked very far away . . .

Flora was waiting for her at the bottom. She beckoned Isobel towards her and mouthed 'Hurry up!'

Isobel took a deep breath, then started moving down the staircase again. She ignored the wobbles and moans from the metal, and the slipperiness of her palms on the railings. Soon, she was halfway down. She sped up a little with excitement and her foot slipped off the step. For a horrible second, Isobel felt herself falling through the air, but her hand on the railing soon jerked her upwards, and she landed on her bottom on one of the steps.

'Careful!' Flora hissed.

The fall had made quite a crash. Isobel went down the staircase even faster, forgetting to be scared. When she got to the bottom Flora pulled her around the side of the house. They heard a door opening. Then, a few moments later, they heard the door close again.

'Do you think it was Rigby?' Isobel said. 'Did he see us?'

'I don't know,' Flora said, her face troubled. 'Come on!'

The two girls ran as fast as they could across the gardens, not stopping until they reached the air-raid shelter. Inside, they found Simon. He was holding a lantern and looking down at the floor, where an older boy was examining the dragon.

'You're late,' Simon said.

'You're lucky we're here at all,' Flora said. 'Mr Godfrey found us taking meat from the kitchen. But anyway, we're here now. Look.'

They took the meat out from their pockets. As soon as it was unwrapped, the dragon lifted its head up from the floor. It was making a scratching, whining sound.

'Give it here, then,' the older boy said, his voice gruff.

Flora gave him the chops. He put the parcel down on the floor and the baby dragon stuck its snout into it immediately, making greedy, snuffling sounds.

'That's better, isn't it?' the boy said, stroking the dragon's head. Isobel realised he looked almost exactly the same as Simon, except a few years older. He had the same dark red hair, and the same green eyes. His jaw was the only thing that was different – it was softer and less pointed than his little brother's. But he had the same distrust in his eyes and the same mouth, one that looked like it would be quick to shout if he was angry. 'You can leave the other meat there,' he said, pointing at the floor.

'You're welcome,' Flora said sarcastically. 'It was no trouble at all getting it for you. It's not like there's rationing or anything.'

'Why should we say thank you?' Simon said, his eyes flashing with anger. 'Your family's the one that's got us into this mess. It's your job to provide for them, and it's ours to look after them. That's how it's always been.'

'How were we supposed to know that?' Flora shot back.

'Stop shouting,' Pat said, watching as the dragon licked the paper clean. 'We don't want anyone to hear us.'

Simon fell silent. From outside, a dog barked.

'What was that?' Pat said.

For a second, no one moved. Then they heard the dog bark again.

'It must be Jake and Mr Rigby!' Flora said.

'It didn't sound like Jake,' Isobel said. 'It's too loud.'

'Si, go and look,' Pat said, as the dog barked again. But Isobel was already at the entrance of the shelter. She stuck her head out and immediately drew it back in again, her heart racing.

'What is it?' Flora said in alarm.

'It is Rigby, but he's got Mr Godfrey with him!' Isobel said. 'And there's someone else. I think it's a policeman!'

Pat and Simon were on their feet immediately. 'Come on, Si,' Pat said, his face twisting with worry. 'We can't have anyone finding the dragon.'

'Where are you going?' Flora said.

'You need to leave,' Simon said, ignoring her question. 'Right now.'

Isobel risked another look outside. The group were halfway down the lawn. The policeman was holding the leash of a large dog, which was barking and pulling frantically.

'We can't leave!' Flora said. 'They'll catch us.'

'So?'

'So?!' Flora said with astonishment. 'Have you met Mr Godfrey?'

The dog barked again, closer this time. Isobel looked out and this time, Mr Godfrey looked right at her. His eyes were burning with anger and his lips were pressed together in a grim line.

'Please!' Isobel said. 'Please take us with you. We know there's a secret door in here. Show us. Mr Godfrey's really angry. I don't know what he'll do.'

'No!' Pat said. 'It's too dangerous. Believe me, you wouldn't want to come if you knew what was down there. There's no way you're coming. Absolutely no way.'

'Pat,' Simon said quietly.

'What?'

'What if they tell them? About him.' Simon pointed at the dragon in Pat's arms.

'We wouldn't!' Isobel said immediately, shocked at the thought. But her sister looked at Pat, a glint in her eye.

'We *might*,' Flora said.

Pat looked at her with disgust.

'We wouldn't,' Isobel said again. 'She's just saying that because she's cross.' Flora started to speak, but Isobel raised her voice over her. 'We've never said anything, and we know all about it – that you're keepers, and there's splints coming for us and dragons who protect us, and even though it's got us in trouble we've never said. We didn't tell Rigby or Mr Godfrey any of the times when Simon came to the air-raid shelter. We never would. We're just trying to help. That's why we brought the dragon meat.'

Pat stood where he was, still holding the dragon. Indecision flickered across his face.

'Please!' Isobel begged. 'You can't let Mr Godfrey catch us. It's not fair. We're only in trouble because we helped you.'

The dog barked again, savagely this time, and Pat made his mind up.

'All right,' he said. 'Hurry up, Si!'

'Take this!' Simon said, shoving a sack at Flora. Then he ran to the back of the shelter. He counted three bricks from the bottom and seven bricks from the right, then ran his hands along the wall as if he were feeling for something.

'Hurry up!' Pat said again.

Simon didn't reply, but suddenly pushed his fingers in deep. There was a click, and a door sprang open. It was about the same size as the secret door in their room, Isobel realised, and though it had been painted with bricks to look like it was part of the wall, it was made of wood. She had been right, she realised. The air-raid shelter *was* the entrance to somewhere else. But there wasn't time to think about that now.

Inside the door, it was pitch-black. Simon grabbed the sack back off Flora and some pointed sticks from the floor, then disappeared into the opening. Flora followed him immediately.

'Go on, then,' Pat said impatiently, gesturing at the door.

Isobel knew she needed to go too. She certainly didn't want to face Mr Godfrey. But suddenly her legs wouldn't obey her when she told them to move. They were remembering the last time she had been underground. The prickling heat and the sound of her breath in the silence. And then that other sound, the hissing that wasn't quite a whistle. And then she was thinking about the raid, and the juddering of the ground—

'You will take the boys to the station,' she heard someone say, as if from very far away. It sounded like Mr Godfrey. 'I will deal with the girls myself,' he continued.

'What are you doing?' Pat said urgently. 'Go on!'

They must only be a few feet away by now, but Isobel was still frozen to the spot. They were going to catch her, she thought dully, because she was scared of the dark, just like Flora said she was. But then she felt something round her waist. Pat was pulling her with his free arm and bundling her into the doorway. She fell into the tunnel, landing heavily on her hands. Simon pulled her out of Pat's way as he barged through with the dragon, which squawked in protest as the door shut behind them with a thud.

The door was thick but Pat still held up one finger for them to be quiet. In the next few minutes, they heard some muffled sounds. Some bangs, crashes and yells – Isobel was sure the yells were made by Mr Godfrey – as the adults realised that the children had, somehow, got away.

After that, there was silence.

PART TWO: THE JOURNEY

CHAPTER ONE

At first, all of Isobel's nightmares seemed to come true.

The darkness of underground was like nothing she had experienced before. During the War, there had always been lights. Lanterns that cast oblong shadows on Mum and Flora's faces as they waited in the air-raid shelter, or bobbed up the garden path on their way back to bed after the All Clear. Even when she had got lost in Burley Caves, she had had a candle.

But as she sat on the other side of the wall, listening to the silence, the darkness was absolute. Isobel held a hand a couple of inches away from her face and couldn't see it. For a single, heart-stopping moment she wondered if she was still actually there. The darkness seemed to be a living, breathing thing, more alive than Isobel herself and more than capable of swallowing her up.

'Have they gone?' Flora whispered.

'Ssshhhhh!' Simon replied.

Isobel hugged her knees as the silence crept back. How long it lasted was impossible to tell. She reached into her pocket and clutched the toy dragon in her hand. It felt slightly warmer than normal and made her feel a little bit better, but not much.

'They must have gone now,' Flora said, a note of impatience in her voice.

Pat made a small, disgruntled noise in the back of his throat. 'It never hurts to be careful,' he said. 'Especially down here.'

Isobel felt, rather than saw Pat shift his weight to the left. She thought he might be putting his ear to the wall. After a few moments, he moved back.

'Sounds like they've gone,' he finally agreed. 'Si, the lantern.'

A few moments later, there was the flare of a match, then the beautiful, flickering light of a candle. Simon carefully shut the door of the glass lantern he was holding. There was a hook above his head and Isobel realised it must have been hanging there all along.

'That's better,' Flora said, straightening her skirt over her knees.

Only the baby dragon seemed less than pleased at the light. He blinked at the brightness then hissed, turning his face away.

'Dragons can see in the dark,' Pat explained, seeing Isobel looking. 'It helps, down here.'

Isobel nodded.

'So where are we going, then?' Flora asked. Now that the threat of Mr Godfrey had passed her voice sounded bright, cheerful even. But Simon's face darkened.

'You're not going anywhere,' he said stiffly, folding his arms so his elbows made sharp points. 'It's too dangerous.'

'What?' Flora said, looking at Pat with raised eyebrows.

'He's right,' Pat said, looking at his brother. 'I let you in here cos I didn't want you to get caught. It didn't seem fair, given that you helped us with the meat. But now Mr Godfrey's gone, you can go back in the air-raid shelter. They'll have gone back to the house now, so you can sneak out.'

Flora folded her arms. 'Not a chance.'

'You can't come with us,' Pat said, shaking his head. 'We can't do what we need to do here with a couple of girls hanging around. You don't know how dangerous it is.'

'However dangerous it is, it's better than facing Mr Godfrey,' Flora said. 'We're coming, and that's that.'

'No, you're not,' Simon shouted.

Pat handed the dragon to Simon, who put the lantern down on the floor to take him. Now that there was light, Isobel could see the outline of the door set into the dark wall. Pat felt his way along the top of it. 'This is for the best,' he said. 'Believe me. If you knew what was down here, you wouldn't want to come.'

'How would you know?' Flora shot back. 'You don't even know us.'

Pat didn't reply. His face creased into a frown as his fingers continued to travel along the top ledge of the door.

'What is it?' Simon said.

'I can't find the lever – ah!' Pat said, his face clearing. 'Here it is.' Isobel saw his fist clench as he pressed down.

Nothing happened.

'That's strange,' Pat said.

'Do it again,' Simon urged.

Pat tried once more. Still nothing happened.

'You've got to pull it towards you as well as down,' Simon said.

'I know that!' Pat snapped. 'That's what I'm doing.'

197

Pat pulled the lever again, multiple times, but the door stayed resolutely shut. Eventually he sat back down. 'You try, then,' he said to his brother.

After putting the dragon carefully on the floor, Simon tried the lever himself. He didn't have any more luck than Pat. 'I think it's jammed,' he said. 'Mr Godfrey and the others must have done it when they were crashing around, looking for us.'

Isobel swallowed painfully. 'You mean we can't get out?'

Pat and Simon shared a worried look.

'Just push it,' Flora said. 'If we all push, it might open.'

'It won't,' Pat said.

'Have you got any better ideas?' Flora crawled over to the door and put her hands on its surface. 'Come on!'

As soon as Isobel pushed, she knew it was useless. Even when Simon and Pat grudgingly joined them, there was no way the door was budging. It felt like they were pushing against a mountain. Eventually even Flora had to admit the truth. They were trapped.

'Great hiding place this is,' Flora said.

'We told you not to come,' Simon said. 'Maybe you should listen next time.'

Isobel bit her lip nervously. 'So, what do we do now?'

Pat seized the lantern. 'Looks like you got your wish,' he said. His words were light but his face was worried. 'You'll have to come with us.'

The tunnel they were in was very small, Isobel realised. There was no possibility of standing up as it was only three or four feet high. If you were on your knees and reached your hand up, you'd find the ceiling straight away. It meant that the only way to move through the tunnel was to crawl, which Pat did, holding the baby dragon and not looking back.

With a dirty look at Flora and Isobel, Simon followed. As they got further away, the light went with them, leaving the close, inky darkness. Flora and Isobel crawled after them, not wanting to be left behind.

'What's in this sack, anyway?' Flora grunted, pulling it behind her. 'It's heavy.'

'Give it here,' Simon said. 'It's just a few rabbits and pheasants. But it's for the adults, not you. You've already had those chops.' This last bit was directed at the baby dragon, who was whining like a puppy in Pat's arms.

'There's another way out, isn't there?' Flora said, as she handed over the bag. 'There must be,' she added, a little less confidently.

'We can get out through Burley Caves,' Pat said. 'It's just more dangerous. It's easier to get spotted.'

Panic bubbled queasily in Isobel's tummy. 'We can't go out through Burley Caves,' she said. 'That's where I saw the splint.'

'Yeah, Simon told me,' Pat said. 'Don't worry, it'll be long gone by now.'

'How do you know?'

'It was a scout,' Simon said. 'One of them always goes ahead, then goes back to tell the others what they've seen. Which if you were a keeper, you'd know. And you'd know that if it is still around, it's not good to talk. They can't see much but they can hear for miles.'

After that, everyone fell silent. Isobel concentrated on putting one knee in front of the other. Her kneecaps and the palms of her hands were starting to feel sore, but she didn't dare stop.

She was already in danger of being left behind. Pat and Simon were at least twenty feet ahead (perhaps their kneecaps had got used to it, Isobel thought). This meant that the tunnel was getting darker, which made Isobel's heart beat faster with fear. To stay calm, she fixed her gaze on Flora's socks, which flashed white as her legs moved forwards – disappearing under her black leather shoes, then appearing again. She realised after a while that Flora was going faster than her too. There was now a two-person space between her and the socks. Biting her lip, she forced her legs to go faster, then immediately banged her knee painfully on a waiting rock. When she had rubbed it better, Flora's socks had disappeared completely.

'Flora?' Isobel called, hating the way her voice was wobbling.

'We're through here,' the reply came immediately. 'Just keep going.'

The tunnel sloped sharply downwards then round to the left. Isobel could see the hazy light from the lantern again, but she still couldn't see the others. Then Flora's hand was in front of her face. Isobel grabbed it and Flora pulled her out of the tunnel and into a larger one, where Simon and Pat were waiting. The dragon, which had its claws firmly wedged into Pat's shirt, cocked its head at her and hissed.

'You shouldn't go last,' Pat said to Isobel, making it sound like an accusation. He pointed at Flora. 'You should go after her, so she doesn't get left behind.'

'We have names, you know,' Flora said. She was still holding Isobel's hand.

'Oh, I'm sorry,' Pat said as he took something out of his pocket. It was a piece of paper, which he proceeded to unfold.

'I forgot to address you properly. Miss Burlington One and Miss Burlington Two. Is that right?' He looked at them with pretend politeness. 'Should I bow to you as well before I speak?'

'Don't be silly,' Flora said, as Isobel burned with embarrassment.

Pat's anger appeared to subside as he looked at the paper. It seemed to be some kind of map. He put the paper back in his pocket and reached up for the dragon, who hissed in protest as Pat put him down on the floor. 'I'm not carrying you all the way,' Pat said to him. 'You're supposed to be getting stronger. How will you do that if you don't use your muscles?'

The dragon flapped his wings and hissed again, this time so violently that sparks shot out of his mouth.

'Don't you give me cheek!' Pat said, raising his voice. He pointed down the empty tunnel. 'Go on,' he said, giving the dragon a tiny nudge with his foot.

The dragon's nostrils flared as he scuttled off, still wobbling from side to side on his little legs. Isobel had to hide a smile as she followed Pat and Simon down the tunnel.

This tunnel was much wider and taller than the other one. You could walk fairly comfortably along it, without having to crouch, even. It smelled like dark, raw earth – the kind you get when you're digging after rain. The floor was littered with stones and roots. Suddenly, Isobel felt something feather-light rush past her foot. It was a familiar feeling; something she had felt when walking past bomb sites. 'Ugh,' she said, stepping to the side. 'I think there are ra—'

Before she could finish, there was a patter of claws, a moment of silence and then a sharp, sickening crack. Simon shone the lantern at the source of the noise. The baby dragon looked up at them, a dead rat dangling from its jaws. It laid its prey carefully on the ground, then bit into it hungrily.

'That's horrible,' Flora said, turning her head away.

'Course it's not,' Simon said. 'Don't you want him to be strong for the splints? Dragons are wild creatures and they eat meat. He's only doing what's natural.'

Over the next fifteen minutes, much to Flora's disgust, the baby dragon ate four more rats. Isobel didn't mind it, though. 'He's a ratter,' she said admiringly. 'Like Percy.'

Percy was a huge black tom cat that had lived on their street and was notorious for killing mice and rats, even the horrible foot-long ones that came out of the sewers. Mum said he was the best thing that had ever happened to the neighbourhood.

'Maybe that's what we should call him,' Isobel thought out loud, as the dragon finished his last rat with a big, swallowing gulp.

'What, Percy?' Flora said.

'No, Ratter.'

'Don't be stupid,' Simon said. 'Dragons don't have names.'

'Why not?'

'They just don't.'

'All those rats will keep him going, at least,' Pat said with relief. 'I was worried about how little meat we had for the journey.'

'Where are we going, anyway?' Flora said. 'And where exactly are we now? You haven't told us anything.'

Isobel was sandwiched between Flora and Pat, so she saw how his shoulders tensed when Flora asked that question. But when Pat spoke, his voice was normal. 'This tunnel heads north from Splint Hall. It runs all the way underneath the village to Burley Caves.'

'We're underneath the village?' Isobel repeated. She imagined all the people above them, sitting in their front rooms, walking on top of their heads, none of them having any idea that there were people below them. It was a strange thought.

'That's right,' Pat said. 'But we're not going all the way to Burley Caves yet. We're turning right soon. There's another tunnel that goes deeper underground, to a cavern where the dragons live. It's the only bit big enough down here. We're taking the baby there first.'

'So we'll see the big dragons?' Flora said, unable to hide her excitement.

'You two won't,' Pat said. 'You're waiting in the tunnel.'

'We are not,' Flora said. 'We want to see them.'

'Fine,' Simon said. 'You can go into the cavern and get burned into ash by the dragons if you want. That's up to you.'

'They wouldn't do that, would they?' Isobel said.

'They would, actually,' Pat said. 'They really would.'

'But why?' Isobel said.

'It's like I said before,' Simon said impatiently. 'Why do you never listen? Dragons don't like humans. If you're a keeper, it's all right, but everyone else, they see as a threat.'

'They're right to,' Pat said grimly. 'Whenever people have seen dragons in the past, they've always said they were monsters and tried to kill them. That's why they have to live underground, in secret.' He shook his head. 'Humans are so stupid. They've got no idea how much dragons have done for us in the past. How many times they've saved us.'

'What if we make friends with Ratter?' Flora said. 'If they see that their baby likes us, they won't hurt us, will they?' She stepped towards him. 'He'll end up liking us, I'm sure of it. Won't you, Ratter?'

'Stop calling him that!' Simon said. 'I told you that dragons don't have names. And don't get too close. He won't like it.'

Simon was right, Isobel thought, as she watched Ratter snarl again, then send a shower of blue flame in Flora's direction. Her sister jumped away in time, but her skirt now had two singed patches.

'We did tell you,' Pat said, sounding slightly amused.

Flora said nothing, but Isobel could tell from the set of her sister's shoulders that the matter wasn't over. She strode down the tunnel again, going in front this time.

'Wait,' Pat called. 'We're nearly at the turning. You don't want to miss it. You won't be able to see anything without the lantern.'

Flora either didn't hear or simply ignored him. It was hard to tell. Pat looked at her retreating back with exasperation. 'Run after her, Si,' he said. 'We don't want her getting lost. I'll bring him.' He jerked his head at the dragon.

Si looked like he didn't at all care if Flora got lost, but he did as he was told. The lantern bobbed as he ran, getting further and further away, until it was as small as a firefly. Then, it was gone.

Isobel felt the darkness swoop in again. Her palms started to sweat. She felt Pat move behind her and heard a clicking noise and a squeak as he picked up Ratter. For a few seconds, neither of them moved.

'You go first,' Pat said.

Isobel suddenly wished she was someone else. Someone whose

204

hands didn't shake in the dark and whose feet moved when she told them to.

'It's all right,' Pat said unexpectedly, as if he could read her thoughts. 'This tunnel's very safe. It's been here for hundreds of years. Just keep putting one foot in front of the other.'

Isobel cleared her throat. 'But what if there's a spl—'

'There won't be,' Pat said. 'There's only ever one scout, and you saw it. It'll have gone back to the others, now. If the dragons didn't get it.'

Isobel nodded, then realised Pat couldn't see her nodding. 'All right,' she said.

As Pat had said, she put one foot in front of the other, then the other foot in front of that one. She kept doing it, and she found she was walking. She could hear Pat walking behind her. There was a question burning at the back of her throat. She desperately wanted to know the answer but was afraid to hear it, all at the same time.

'Have you seen one?' she blurted out eventually. 'A splint, I mean?'

Pat took his time before answering. 'Yes,' he said. 'Only once,' he continued, after another pause. 'It was ages ago, before the War even, back when Dad could still come down here. We were taking some food down to the dragons and checking they were all right. It was a scout too – snuck right up on us. I only saw a glimpse of its claws before one of the dragons turned it to cinders.' He hesitated. 'It was scary, though. There was something about it that was so . . . unnatural. Like it wasn't really alive.'

Isobel nodded, then realised again that Pat couldn't see her. 'I thought that, too.'

'Simon hasn't seen a splint yet,' Pat said.

Isobel absorbed this. They both fell silent as they thought about the splints. Isobel knew it was true, but she couldn't believe that somewhere below them, they were waiting. Perhaps they were already marching, their bones clunking on the floor of the tunnels, making that strange, hissing noise as they breathed. She thought of the picture she'd found in the attic, with the splint's long, shadowy claws and even longer limbs, and shuddered. What had Grandpa thought of them, she wondered, then stopped suddenly.

'Why have you stopped?' Pat said.

'Grandpa drew a picture,' Isobel said. 'Of the splints, I mean. It looked exactly like the one I saw.' She glanced sideways at Pat, but his face was in shadow and she couldn't see his expression. 'I think he saw one.'

Pat didn't answer for a little while. 'He didn't,' he said eventually. 'He can't have. No one comes down here who's not a keeper, and the splints haven't got above ground. Yet.'

'But it looked so real—'

'Dad told him about the splints, after the first war,' Pat interrupted. 'He had to, because he had to make sure the dragons got enough food. He must have just described them well, that's all. Dad's good with words.'

Isobel thought back to the picture again. Could Grandpa really have drawn the splints just by hearing about them? She supposed it was possible, but it didn't seem right.

'I shouldn't have said that, about you being Miss Burlington One and Miss Burlington Two,' Pat said, changing the subject. He sounded a little ashamed. 'I know it's not your fault. And your grandpa was all right. Not that I knew him well, he died when I was young, but he used to give me lemon drops whenever me and Dad went round.'

Isobel didn't know what to say. 'I didn't know him,' she said eventually. 'He died before I was born. But that's all right. About calling us Miss Burlington One and Two. You're not the only one. Everyone calls us Burlingtons and thinks we're mean like him . . . Mr Godfrey, I mean, but we're not. Our surname's Johnson. Like my father's.'

Pat was quiet for a bit. Ratter made that strange clicking noise again. 'Where's your dad, then?'

'He died too. In the War. He was a pilot.'

Pat paused. 'Oh, right, sorry.' Then he changed the subject. 'I reckon I would have been a pilot. I was only a couple of months away from being called up when the War ended.' There was something strange in Pat's voice, like he was talking about a dream he had once had that he knew would now never come true. Then he cleared his throat and when he spoke again, his voice was back to normal. 'If they'd have had me, I mean. I'm really sorry about your dad.'

'I don't remember him,' Isobel said, then wished she hadn't. She hadn't admitted that to anyone: not Flora, not Mum, not even really herself.

'Yeah, but still,' Pat said. 'I reckon you can still miss someone, even if you don't remember them.'

Isobel wondered if Pat was right. She thought about Mum when she had learned about Daddy not coming back, that moment where she had bent right over, like it was too painful to stand up. Isobel hadn't felt like that. She'd heard Flora crying that night in bed and Isobel hadn't cried then either, though she'd wanted to. She'd felt like she should and she'd tried to squeeze out some tears but they wouldn't come. So perhaps it wasn't true, perhaps you had to remember someone to really feel sad when they were gone. But then she thought of Daddy. She thought how if he was here they might all be living together on their own, without Mr Godfrey, and how Daddy would have looked after them and made sure they were all right – even though she didn't remember him she knew, somewhere deep inside herself, that that was true – and something surged upwards in her chest, so strong it nearly made her stop walking. Though it wasn't actually a something at all, it was a nothing, a space where Daddy should have been. Isobel realised that it had always been there, and maybe it always would be there, and she knew then that Pat was right.

'Watch out,' Pat said. 'There's a corner here. Put your hands against the wall so you can feel it going round to the left. That's it.'

They slowly turned the corner and immediately saw the lantern, about forty feet away. Flora and Simon were standing still, their backs to them, looking down the tunnel.

'They must be waiting for us before taking the turning,' Pat said. Then he frowned. 'Wait a minute . . . what's that?'

At first, Isobel couldn't make sense of what they were seeing. But as they got closer, it became horribly obvious. Flora and Simon weren't waiting. It was simply impossible for them to go any further because where there had once been a tunnel, there was now just a huge pile of rocks and earth. Pat had said the path was safe, but he had been wrong, Isobel realised. Something had caused the roof of the tunnel to fall down. Something huge, something so strong it had shattered the layers of earth and roots and rocks.

'The bomb,' Isobel whispered.

Pat nodded, his face grim.

Isobel immediately thought of being in the tunnel when it happened – the soil in your hair, your nostrils, your mouth. She shut her eyes tight against the thought. When she opened them, Simon was looking back at his brother. 'Pat?' he whispered. 'It's blocking the entrance to the other tunnel too. The one we use to get to the cavern. Look.'

He crouched down and shone the lantern at the tunnel wall on their right. Isobel could just see a tiny black gap, about the width of her forearm. The rest of the entrance to the tunnel was blocked by rubble.

Pat put Ratter down. Immediately, the baby dragon sprang towards the pile of rocks.

'Stop!' Pat shouted.

Ratter clambered with his tiny feet, using his tail for balance, as agile as a cat. In a few seconds, he had disappeared through the gap, into the tunnel that led to the cavern. He squawked from the other side, as if asking them to hurry up.

'That must be how he got through before, when he came up to the air-raid shelter. Now we'll have to try and get through,' Pat muttered. He walked over to the pile of rocks. He moved a couple of them next to the gap, trying to make it bigger, but as he did so more rocks fell down, and he had to jump backwards to avoid them hitting his feet. He tried again. This time, he moved a large rock at waist height. There was a creak and the children looked upwards. They sprinted backwards as more rocks tumbled from the broken roof of the tunnel.

'It's too dangerous,' Flora said, shaking her head. 'We'll never get through without it caving in completely.'

'What about Ratter?' Isobel said.

At that moment, Ratter slithered out from under a rock, limping slightly.

'Poor thing, he's hurt his foot,' Isobel said.

Pat checked it over. After he'd satisfied himself that it wasn't anything serious, he stayed looking at the caved-in tunnel for what felt like ages. Simon, Flora and Isobel waited quietly. He seemed to be hoping that something would occur to him, that there would be some way forward that he hadn't thought of. But there wasn't.

'We'll have to get to the cavern the other way,' he said, finally. 'Past the lake.'

Simon's eyes were as round as two pennies. He gulped and Isobel realised with a sickening lurch that he was afraid. 'But Dad said—'

'I know what he said,' Pat replied. The light threw shadows across his face and suddenly he looked tired, older. 'We don't have any other choice.'

CHAPTER TWO

Pat didn't tell them exactly what his father had said and, for once, Flora didn't ask. Isobel didn't either. It was obvious that it wasn't good.

Isobel looked up and saw Pat trudging ahead of them, his head slightly bowed. Since they'd turned around to retrace their steps, he'd hardly said a word. Simon had tried to talk to him but Pat had only grunted in response, the last time angrily, so Simon had given up.

They carried on walking for a few minutes until Pat stopped. At his feet was the entrance to the small tunnel they'd come out of. It looked barely bigger than a rabbit's burrow.

Pat gestured to them all to come closer. He was holding the map out in front of him and he asked Simon to bring the lamp closer so they could see. 'It's best you know about this bit beforehand,' he said.

'Why?' Isobel asked.

'Because I said so, that's why,' Pat said. His voice was as brittle as dead wood. 'Look, this isn't going to work if you keep questioning everything.'

'She was only asking,' Flora protested.

'We don't have time for you to ask,' Pat said. 'You've got to trust me, all right? I didn't want you two to come along in the first place. I told you not to come. That's not because I'm mean and there's a party going on down there with sweets and chocolate cake. It's because it's *dangerous*, you understand? Now you're here, you've got to do what I say, and exactly when I say it. Else we'll all be in trouble.'

Isobel's face burned. She was glad no one could see it in the darkness. 'Sorry,' she said.

Flora didn't say anything but shuffled closer to the map. It looked like someone had drawn it by hand, with wobbly brown writing.

'It's best you know what to expect,' Pat said, sounding a bit calmer. 'Look, here's the air-raid shelter.' He pointed to a box at the top-left of the map. 'We went down this narrow tunnel, and now we're here, in the main tunnel.' His finger followed a thin, spidery line down to where it joined with a much thicker one, then tapped. The thicker line cut straight across the paper to the right-hand side of the map, and up. 'The main tunnel comes out at Burley Caves,' Pat said, tapping on the paper again. 'That's the other way out. When we visit the dragons, we normally take *this* path.' His finger tapped a right-hand turning from the main tunnel, which swooped downwards sharply and eventually opened out into a wide oval. 'That's the cavern where the dragons live,' Pat explained matter-of-factly. 'As I say, that's the route we normally go down to get to it, then we just go back the way we came, to the air-raid shelter or out through Burley Caves.'

'But this time we can't, because the bomb blocked the entrance,' Simon added.

'So we have to go back down this smaller tunnel,' Pat said, his finger tracing another thin, spidery line that led down from the main tunnel, 'until it gets to here.'

'Here' was a small circle. Almost immediately below it was another, bigger one. Then there was a thin line that led from the circles to the big oval that Pat had said was the cavern where the dragons lived.

'What are those other circles?' Flora asked.

Simon glanced nervously at Pat, who seemed to be avoiding his eyes. 'The first one's the Cave of a Thousand Kni—'

'You don't have to tell them what it's called, Si,' Pat interrupted.

'The Cave of a Thousand what?' Flora said, her eyebrows raised.

'It doesn't matter,' Pat said. 'All you need to know is that it's a cave and it's full of stalactites and stalagmites. You know what those are?'

There was a pause. 'No,' Flora said eventually. Isobel knew that her sister hated to admit that she didn't know something.

'They're kind of like icicles, but made of rock,' Pat said. 'I don't know exactly how they're made but it's something to do with water. Stalactites point down from the ceiling and stalagmites point up from the ground. This cave is full of them. It's hard to get through them all, but not impossible, because keepers before us – ages ago – made a path.'

Flora nodded. 'All right,' she said. 'So that's the first cave. What's the second?'

'It starts as the Cave of Beating Wings,' Simon said. Pat shot him a look to tell him to be quiet.

'What beating wings?' Isobel said. 'Is it the dragons?'

'No, just a few bats,' Pat said. 'That's not anything to worry about. It's what's next that's a bit tricky. At the far side of the cave there's a lake.'

'The Lake of Forgotten Things,' Simon whispered.

'Si, I told you to be quiet,' Pat shouted. 'Stop using those silly names. They're just going to scare the girls.'

Simon didn't argue, he just bent his head low over the map. Isobel felt a small pang of sympathy. When they'd been talking in the tunnel she'd started to like Pat. Now she wasn't so sure.

'Why's it called the Lake of Forgotten Things?' Flora asked.

'It's just because it's old,' Pat said. 'Most people have forgotten about it. In fact, most people don't even know it exists any more.'

'So why's it dangerous then?' Flora said.

'I didn't say it was dangerous.'

Flora folded her arms and narrowed her eyes the way she always did when she thought someone wasn't telling the truth. 'You did. You keep saying everything's dangerous. You haven't stopped saying it since we came underground. And you said the lake was tricky.'

Pat rubbed his eyes with his hands. Mum did that sometimes when she was tired, Isobel thought, then immediately felt a wave of guilt so powerful it almost knocked her over. *Mum.* Perhaps Mr Godfrey had told her that they were missing. Perhaps she was looking for them right now, in the garden, or maybe she'd got Rigby to drive her round the countryside, shouting their names out of the windows. Isobel could imagine Mum doing that.

'I said it was tricky because it's a lake,' Pat was saying. 'Lakes are always dangerous. Especially if you can't swim.'

'We can swim,' Flora said. 'We learned at the pool near where we lived. Mum taught us. You don't need to worry about that.'

'Well, I can't swim,' Pat said, sounding defensive. 'Simon can't either.'

Flora snorted. 'Seems a bit silly not to teach you to swim if you've got to go through a lake. Why didn't your dad teach you?'

'Cos there's no pool near us and even if there was, we couldn't afford to go there,' Simon said immediately. 'We're not rich like you.'

'Give it a rest, Si,' Pat said. 'They don't want to hear about that sort of thing.' He turned back to Flora. 'We don't normally have to go by the lake, do we? Dad never taught us because he didn't think we'd need to know. It's just that stupid bomb. It's changed things.'

Flora didn't say anything. For once, she didn't seem to know what to say. 'I didn't know pools cost money,' she mumbled eventually.

'Everything costs money,' Simon said.

'We don't have to swim, anyway,' Pat said. 'There's a boat. It's moored at the edge of the lake.'

'Fine,' Flora said. 'You'll just have to not fall in then, won't you?'

'We'll do our best,' Pat said. He put the map back in his pocket. 'First, we've got to get through the tunnel. As you know, it's a tight squeeze. I'll go first, with the lantern. Then you go next,' he pointed at Flora, 'then you.' He pointed at Isobel. 'Simon, you go last with the dragon, so no one falls behind and if anything happens, the dragon's protected. I'll try not to go too fast but if I do, just shout, all right?'

'But I should go first with the lantern,' Simon protested. 'The dragon likes you more than me anyway.'

The dragon looked up from where he was patiently waiting at Pat's feet and hissed.

'See?' Simon said.

'I said, I'm going first,' Pat said. He nudged Ratter towards Simon with his foot. Ratter hissed again, much louder this time. Simon leaned to pick him up and Ratter darted out of reach.

'But he won't—'

'He'll just have to, won't he?' Pat shouted, seizing the lantern and hauling the bag of meat over his shoulder. 'You'll have to make him. That's what keepers do, make the dragons do things. Just get on with it, Si. We've wasted enough time as it is.'

As Pat ducked down into the tunnel, Simon bent down too. He grabbed Ratter roughly, clamping both wings down to the sides of his body, and brought him up to his chest, ignoring the angry hisses that came his way. When he was upright again, Flora was following Pat into the tunnel. The lantern had gone with Pat, so it was pitch black again. Isobel couldn't see Simon but it hardly mattered. She could feel the anger coming off him, like heat from a stove.

'Go on, then,' he said, making it sound like a challenge.

Isobel crouched down. For one horrible second she thought she might not be able to find the tunnel at all, but she put her arms out and felt the rocky ledge, then the space underneath. Once she'd crawled into it, she could see the faint glow from Pat's lantern. It was coming from the left, so that was the way Isobel turned. When she was a few feet in she heard Simon crawling in after her.

They moved forwards for a few moments. Then Isobel turned her head and whispered into the darkness. 'Flora's bossy too sometimes. I think it's just what older brothers and sisters are like.'

Simon didn't say anything for a few moments. Isobel was starting to wonder whether he'd heard her when he said, in a tone that clearly showed Isobel didn't know what she was talking about, 'Pat's not being bossy. He's just trying to make sure everyone's safe.'

Isobel swallowed. 'I didn't mean—'

'It's your fault, anyway,' Simon cut in. 'Yours and your sister's. He wouldn't be nearly so worried if you weren't here. We didn't ask you to come. I told you to stay away, I told you to stop following me, but you wouldn't listen.'

After that, they continued on silently, Isobel stinging at the unfairness of Simon's words. They hadn't asked for any of this to happen either, she thought. It wasn't like they wanted the splints to exist. No one would want that. And they couldn't help finding out about the dragons – there was one in the air-raid shelter in their house! If Simon and Pat didn't want them to know, they should have been more careful to keep the secret. Also, Simon was the one who had asked them to bring the meat for the dragon. How was that asking them to stay away?

Isobel's anger drove her onwards for a long time. But gradually, it started to fade, and she became aware of other things. How narrow the tunnel was, for instance. Isobel had no idea how a dragon could fit down it but she wasn't about to ask, with Simon in such a mood. Her hands and knees were hurting and Isobel realised that what she was crawling on was changing – instead of the soft earth it had been outside the air-raid shelter, it was now hard, smooth rock. Every time Isobel reached out, her hand would meet with air, the bottom of the tunnel always lower than she thought, and she realised that the tunnel was sloping downwards steeply. And it was getting warmer. Isobel reached up and wiped the pinpricks of sweat off her forehead with her sleeve. And perhaps it was the heat, perhaps it was the darkness, perhaps it was the anger she felt towards Simon . . . whatever it was, Isobel was getting a headache, and one of the worst kinds. It was a slow slither of pain, like a small snake uncoiling inside her temple.

A few minutes later, the tunnel opened out into a cave. Isobel heard Simon's sharp intake of breath, which mirrored her own shock as she saw what was inside. She remembered what Simon had said, or half said before Pat had cut him off, and immediately realised what the cave's full name was.

The Cave of a Thousand Knives.

The cave wasn't that big, perhaps the size of the Breakfast Room in Splint Hall. But what was alarming about it was the sharp, pointed daggers of rock that hung down from every inch of the ceiling and jutted upwards from the floor. Some of them were so close they were almost touching; some overlapped. They were all a muddy, yellowish brown, like old teeth. In fact, Isobel thought with a shiver, it was like being in the mouth of a giant prehistoric beast.

'So, where's this path?' Flora said, her voice doubtful.

She was crouching to the right of Isobel. Pat was on her other side, holding the lantern in front of him as he scanned the cave. Isobel could see why Flora was worried. It didn't look like there was a path at all. There wasn't an inch of space on the ceiling of the cave that didn't have spikes sticking out of it. It looked almost impossible to get through.

'There,' Pat said suddenly, pointing. 'You see, under the really big brown stalactites? They're the ones that come from the ceiling. You see underneath them?'

'Sort of,' Flora said.

'There's a gap,' Pat said. 'Can't you see? There's a space where there aren't any stalagmites. They're the ones that poke up from the floor.'

'So?'

'So we can crawl through that gap, underneath the stalactites,' Pat explained impatiently. 'That must be the path.'

Flora let out something that was between a huff and a sigh. 'A path is supposed to be something you can walk on,' she pointed out. 'Not something you have to crawl on on your hands and knees.'

'I think we'll have to be on our bellies,' Simon said. 'There's only about two feet between the ground and the bottom of the stalactites.'

'Even better,' Flora muttered.

'Look, that's the path, and that's the only one there is, so we're taking it,' Pat said, already moving forwards. 'Unless you all want to stay here and wait for the splints to find us.'

Flora glared at his back, then shuffled forwards herself. She snapped her head back at Isobel. 'Stay really close to me,' she said. 'And don't get scared.'

'I won't,' Isobel said.

'You've got to just keep going,' Flora said. 'All right? It's important. You mustn't stop. You mustn't freeze like you normally do.'

Isobel could feel Simon next to her, hearing everything Flora was saying. Her cheeks began to feel warm. 'I said, I *won't*.'

Flora narrowed her eyes like she didn't believe her, but turned back around and followed Pat. Not looking at Simon, Isobel followed too.

As she crawled under the big stalactites, Isobel realised Simon was right. There wasn't enough room to be on your hands and knees. At first, she was grateful. Her knees were very sore, so at least they were getting a rest. But she soon discovered how difficult it was to move anywhere without them. She tried pulling herself forward, the palms of her hands flat on the floor, but that didn't work. The tin dragon was digging into her side, so she took it out of her pocket then tried moving again, this time with her elbows. It was a little better but painful and she still hardly moved. Trying to ignore the panicky feeling in her chest, she looked up and saw Flora digging her toes into the ground and pushing. Isobel tried it. Her dress snagged on a rock and it still hurt her elbows, but it worked. She moved off the ground and forwards about a foot, before slumping down on the ground again.

As Isobel moved painfully along, she was conscious of a low, screechy noise behind her.

'What's wrong with Ratter?' she asked. 'Why's he whining?'

'Stop calling him that,' Simon said, semi-automatically. 'I don't know,' he added, sounding worried. 'I don't think he likes it down here. He won't move. I have to keep pulling him, and he doesn't like that either.'

Isobel looked behind her. Ratter was crouching low to the ground under Simon's arm, his ears flattened like a cat's when it's angry. His eyes flashed red when he saw Isobel looking.

'Come on, Izzy,' Flora said from in front. 'I told you not to stop!'

'But Ratter—'

Before Isobel could explain, there was another sound. At first, Isobel thought it was a long, low boom, but as it carried on she

220

realised the boom was actually made up of lots of shorter sounds –
steady thuds, like someone was hitting a rock with another rock,
over and over again.

Pat swore under his breath.

'What is it?' Flora said. 'Is it another bomb?'

'I'm not sure,' he said, twisting round. 'It might be ...'
Hesitation flitted across his face, and he seemed to think better of
what he was about to say. 'Whatever it is, we've got to hurry. If it
carries on, some of the stalactites might start falling. Come on!'

Isobel started moving again, her knees scraping against the
rock. She could hear Ratter hissing behind her. The noise went
on and on. Ever so slightly, the floor started to shake beneath her.
Isobel looked up and saw the daggers wobbling above. Her hands
started to tremble.

'Come *on*, Izzy!' Flora said, her voice higher than normal.
'It's not far now.'

'Stop it!' Simon shouted behind her. Isobel realised he was
talking to Ratter. 'Just hold still. I'm trying to get us out!'

In front, Isobel saw Pat make it to the end of the cave. There
was a small, dark opening into another tunnel, which he scrabbled
forwards into, leaving the lantern behind him. Then he immediately
turned round to grab Flora's arm. Flora made it into the tunnel
too, then turned back to Isobel, her face a white sheet of panic.

After that, everything seemed to happen very fast. The
pounding increased. There was a crack above Isobel and she looked
up to see one of the stalactites loosen, then fall. But it wasn't
straight above her, it was behind. She didn't see where it landed
but Flora screamed, Simon cried out in pain then Ratter broke
free and shot forwards. He froze to the right of Isobel, crouched

as low to the ground as he could go. She could see his tiny chest heaving up and down as he breathed.

'Come here,' Isobel said, putting the tin dragon in her left hand and reaching out for Ratter with her right, but he snorted sparks at her and she jerked her hand back. Isobel looked up and saw a clump of needle-sharp stalactites right above him, quivering as the cave trembled. There was another crack and without thinking Isobel shot her arm out again. She felt a lick of searing pain on her wrist but then her hand closed around Ratter's body – it was rough but warm, just as she had expected – and, as Flora screamed again, she brought him to her chest then flung him in the direction of the tunnel. The last thing she saw was Pat's face. His eyes were wide open and his mouth was moving – he seemed to be shouting something, but Isobel had no idea what it was.

CHAPTER THREE

When Isobel came to, the first thing she saw was Ratter. She was lying on her side and he was a little way away from her, staring at her expectantly with his red eyes. When he saw she had her eyes open he looked away. Isobel coughed, her throat dry. Suddenly there were hands on her shoulders and in her hair.

'You're awake!' Flora said. She smiled a big, wide smile – one that showed the gap between her two front teeth, which she always tried to hide. Isobel realised she hadn't seen her sister smile like that since coming to Splint Hall. But as soon as it came, it disappeared, and Flora looked annoyed again. She shook Isobel slightly. 'I *told* you not to stop. Why did you stop?'

Isobel struggled to remember, but it was all a blur. 'I . . .'

But Flora had already turned to Pat, who was on her other side, leaning over something long and thin underneath him. 'Pat, she's awake!'

Isobel struggled up into a sitting position. She felt the wall of the tunnel on her shoulder and twisted so she could lean against it. As she did so, the back of her right hand touched the wall too and fireworks of pain exploded from it. Isobel looked and saw a livid red mark, stretching from her little finger to the underside of her wrist.

'You've got a nasty burn there,' Flora said. 'Ratter gave it to you when you grabbed him. Pat said he'll see to it, once he's sorted Simon.'

Isobel squinted, her eyes still adjusting to the darkness. After a few seconds, she realised that the long, thin shape that was stretched out by Pat was Simon.

'What happened to him?' she said, suddenly scared.

'A stalactite got his thigh,' Pat said.

'Not badly,' Simon said, from where he was lying down. 'Just a graze.' He attempted to sit up and Pat pushed him back down.

'Hold still!' he said. 'I've not finished putting the bandage on. And it's not just a graze, it's deep. It's only just stopped bleeding.'

'Could have been worse,' Simon muttered.

After a few minutes, Pat was satisfied that the bandage was on properly, and Simon was allowed to sit up. Then Pat turned to Isobel. 'Let's have a look at that hand,' he said, then tutted when he saw it. 'Are you proud of yourself?' he said sharply to Ratter. 'She saved your life. Look what you did!'

Ratter did his strange sideways walk away from Pat, his claws clicking on the floor. Then he turned round and immediately walked back again. He stopped in front of Isobel and crouched low to the floor, his tail swinging gently from side to side as he gazed at her. It almost seemed like he was sorry.

'It's not his fault,' Isobel said. 'And I don't think I saved his life.'

'You did,' Simon said. 'Look.'

He jerked his thumb back towards the entrance to the cave. Isobel looked, then blinked, then looked again.

The Cave of a Thousand Knives was unrecognisable. Nearly all of the stalactites had fallen from the rocky ceiling, leaving it strangely bare. But the bottom of the cave, where they had just been crawling, was a forest of dagger-sharp rocks, their points all buried in the floor.

'Pat only just got you and Simon out in time,' Flora said. 'If you hadn't got Ratter, he would have been killed by that spike there. Look.' She pointed to a bluey-white spike. 'It fell right where he was sitting.'

Simon was looking at Isobel intently, like she was a puzzle he was trying to solve. He shifted slightly and his lips pinched together in pain. Isobel thought Pat was right – Simon's wound clearly wasn't just a graze. 'You knew he'd burn you, but you still did it,' Simon said when he'd got comfortable, or, at least, slightly more comfortable. 'Why?'

Isobel's face suddenly felt hot. 'I didn't really think about it, it just happened,' she said. Then the burn in her hand suddenly vanished, like she had dipped it in a cooling lake. She looked down and saw Pat rubbing something on it. 'Oh,' she said.

'Tea-tree oil,' Simon explained. 'Oldest cure in the book. It's helped us more times than you've had hot dinners.'

'So you still get burned, even though you're keepers?' Flora said. 'Even though the dragons can smell you?'

''Fraid so,' Simon replied. 'Sometimes we have to do things the dragons don't like. Help them if they're hurt, look at their teeth, that sort of thing.' He shook his head. 'They really don't like having their teeth looked at. You get used to jumping out the way pretty sharpish, but sometimes you're not quick enough.' He pulled up his sleeve. 'His dad got me pretty badly here, look.'

The skin was puckered around his elbow. It made Isobel think of Mr Godfrey and she immediately looked away. But Simon didn't seem embarrassed.

'I'll just put a bandage on it, to stop it getting infected,' Pat said, when he'd finished rubbing the oil in. He reached into his pocket and got out some gauze, but when he tried to wrap it round Isobel's hand, he couldn't. Isobel realised Pat's hands were shaking. He couldn't wrap the bandage straight as the fabric kept wobbling when he tried to fasten it. It reminded Isobel of Mr Godfrey's hands shaking as he grabbed the meat and something cold crept into her heart. Pat was clearly very angry, she realised, thinking back to him saying they shouldn't have come in the first place. If it had just been him and Simon, they probably would have made it to the tunnel before the stalactites started falling. He must be furious that they were on the journey.

'What's wrong?' Flora said.

Isobel immediately wanted to tell her to be quiet. If Pat was angry, asking him about it would only make it worse. But Pat just said, 'Nothing's wrong,' gritting his teeth and trying again. Everyone fell silent. After a few more attempts, in which no one said anything, he threw the bandage down suddenly and clenched his fist.

'I'll do it,' Flora said quietly. She shuffled over, picked up a new bandage and tied it tightly around Isobel's wrist. When she was finished, Isobel stretched out her fingers. Flora had wrapped the bandage underneath Isobel's thumb, so she could use her hand as she normally did.

'Thanks,' she said.

Pat had watched as Flora put on the bandage. He didn't say anything, but nodded, then turned to pack up his things.

'What's making that noise?' Simon said.

As he said it, Isobel realised that the thudding noise hadn't actually gone away. It was simply quieter than it had been in the Cave of a Thousand Knives so she hadn't noticed it. Perhaps the thicker rock of the tunnel muffled it, or perhaps it had echoed in the larger space. But it was still there in the background, like someone drumming, far away.

'We should go,' Pat said, not answering his brother's question.

'But is it the splints?' Simon pressed.

Flora and Isobel shared a nervous look.

'The splints?' Flora asked.

'Dad said they make this noise when they start marching,' Simon said. 'It's because their bodies are so withered. They're just bone, really, but their bones aren't like ours – they're harder, twisted – so when they march you can hear them from miles away.'

Isobel remembered the clunk she had heard when she saw the splint in Burley Caves. It was like the sound of rock hitting rock. She shrank back against the wall. 'It *is* them, isn't it?' she whispered, looking at Pat.

Pat snapped the buckles shut on his bag. Avoiding their eyes, he scooped up Ratter who – for once – didn't make a sound. 'We should go. Flora, you take the lantern. Can you crawl on that leg, Simon?'

'Course. Like I said, it's just a graze.'

Pat nodded, then started crawling down the tunnel, away

227

from the Cave of a Thousand Knives. Flora gestured at Isobel to follow.

This tunnel sloped down even more steeply than the last one. It reminded Isobel of the hill in the park she and Flora used to roll down on their sides, spinning round and round until they hit the bottom, laughing so much they didn't know which way was up any more. Or at least, they had done till Flora suddenly decided it was childish. But that hill had been covered in soft grass, and this was hard rock. If you tried to roll down this slope, Isobel thought, you'd probably break your leg.

'Wait!' Flora called behind her. 'Simon can't keep up.'

Isobel looked back and saw Simon about ten feet behind. His face was pale and every time he moved his bandaged leg forwards the skin around his mouth tightened. She waited for him to catch up before moving forward again, more slowly this time.

Thankfully for Simon, it was only a few minutes before the tunnel opened out into the second cave. This one was bigger and – thank goodness – there were no sharp stalactites hanging from the ceiling or stalagmites pushing up from the floor. It didn't seem to have anything in it at all. Though Isobel only caught a glimpse before Pat took off his jumper and put it over the lantern, plunging them into darkness.

'Why did you do that?' Flora asked as Simon crawled into the cave behind them.

'It's better this way,' Pat said.

'But I can't see a thing.'

'Good. That means we can't be seen either.' Pat muttered the next bit under his breath. 'We need to get through this cave without anything seeing us.'

'The bats, you mean?' Flora said. 'But you said they weren't anything to worry about.'

'They're not, if we don't get seen.' He cut off Flora, who opened her mouth to protest. 'Keep your voice down, too. Look, all we've got to do is get across this cave and into the boat on the lake. It'll take us a minute or two, that's all, and it's straight ahead of us. We don't need the light.'

'At least we can stand up in here,' Simon whispered, struggling to his feet.

'Exactly,' Pat said. He said it a bit louder than he'd meant to and it echoed back to them. This cave was big, Isobel realised. Very big. And it wasn't quite true that they couldn't see anything. Pat's jumper must have had a hole or two in it. High above them, Isobel saw something move, like a piece of paper blown in the wind.

'What if one of us gets lost?' Isobel whispered.

'She's right,' Flora said. 'It would be easy to get separated.'

Pat grunted with exasperation. 'What do you want us to do, hold hands?'

There was a pause. 'I think that's a good idea, actually,' Simon said, sounding a little embarrassed.

Isobel expected Pat to laugh, or say that was silly, but he didn't. 'All right,' he said, handing the covered lantern to Flora. He picked up Ratter with his left arm and held out his right hand to Simon. 'Flora, you'll have to take the bag as well. Everyone hold hands till we get to the boat. And everyone stop talking!'

It was hot in the cave and Isobel realised her hands were slightly damp. Simon's hand was too, though, so perhaps it didn't matter. On her other side, Flora gave her hand a reassuring squeeze.

They stood there in a wobbly line until someone started walking (Isobel wasn't sure who it was), and then they all were. No one spoke. Isobel watched above her anxiously but she didn't see anything else move, and she started to think what she had seen earlier had just been a trick of the light. It was impossible to know how far they had gone through the cave but Isobel thought they were perhaps halfway. Hope soared in her chest. All they had to do was keep walking and keep quiet, she thought, until they got to the boat.

As soon as she'd had that thought, Ratter started growling. It was a different sound to his whining – like the purring of a cat but lower, with more of a hiss in it.

'Stop it, Ratter,' Pat whispered, forgetting that he didn't think dragons should have names.

But Ratter continued to growl. As he did, Isobel felt, rather than saw, more movement from the roof of the cave. This time it wasn't just one thing, it was lots of them, like goosebumps prickling on someone's arm in a breeze.

Ratter's growling got louder. Now it was the sound of a small plane.

'What's he growling at?' Flora said.

'Ratter, ssshhhhh!' Pat said.

As if in reply, Ratter roared. A jet of flame leaped out into the darkness. It only lasted for a second, but it was enough to light up the whole cave. Isobel was still looking up at the roof and she saw that it was studded with hundreds of tiny pinpricks of light. It took a couple of seconds for her to realise they were eyes.

'The bats!' Simon whispered.

'But bats can't hurt us, can they?' Flora said uncertainly.

Ratter roared again. This time, Isobel saw the lights begin to wobble like fireflies. The bats were starting to move.

'Run!' Pat shouted.

Flora flung the jumper off the lantern. Isobel saw the dark shadow of the lake – it was about thirty feet away – and then her hand was jerked forwards as Flora sprinted towards it. But Simon couldn't go that fast, which meant that Isobel felt like she was being torn in two.

'Stop!' she gasped. 'Simon!'

Flora whirled round, looking back at Simon in panic.

'Take Ratter,' Pat yelled, handing Ratter to Isobel. 'I'll bring Si. The boat's just to the right. Can you see it? Go! Go!'

As Pat put his arm over Simon's shoulder, Isobel and Flora ran forwards. Ratter was growling in Isobel's arms but he wasn't growling at her. His red eyes were fixed on the roof of the cave, which seemed to be lower than it was before. For a second Isobel thought the roof might be caving in but with a sickening lurch she realised it wasn't the roof at all, it was the bats, which were coming towards them in one huge wave. They were only twenty feet away from the boat but it wasn't enough. Suddenly the air was thick with wings and terrible squeaks, and needle-sharp claws were tearing at her arms.

'Get away!' Flora screamed.

Isobel couldn't keep hold of Ratter – he was scratching her too, desperate to be free, so she let go and he scrambled up her body so that his claws were resting on her shoulder. He roared and she felt the heat from the flame whoosh past her neck. Instantly, the bats fell back. Then in the next moment they were on them again, and Ratter roared again, and it went on and on – the bats swooping down, then falling back, then swooping once more.

'Look, Isobel, there's the boat,' Flora said breathlessly.

It was a simple rowing boat with two oars, the wood blackened with age. It rocked as Isobel and Flora collapsed into it. Flora breathed a deep, shuddering breath, then turned round to push away from the bank but Isobel caught her arm.

'You can't! We've got to wait for Pat and Simon.'

They were only ten feet away. Pat was half carrying his brother, Simon's arm around his shoulders and his face taut with pain as he hopped forwards. Pat was flailing the lantern around them with the other arm, trying to keep the bats at bay. From the scratches on his arms Isobel didn't think it was working very well. Ratter scuttled to the edge of the boat and sent thin jets of fire on either side of them. As the bats fell back, Pat half threw Simon into the boat, nearly causing it to capsize because of the weight.

'Careful!' Flora cried.

Pat leaped into the boat himself then pushed off the bank with his free arm. The boat surged forwards. As Flora laid Simon down, Pat grabbed the two oars and started rowing furiously. A few bats followed them. Up close, Isobel saw they had big pink ears like mice, upturned snouts like pigs and sharp little fangs, which they bared as they swooped down on their leathery wings. One of them gave Pat's wrist a nasty scratch and he cried out but kept rowing. A second later a snarling Ratter had leaped into the air and caught the bat between his jaws. Instead of eating it, as he had the rats, he snapped its neck then threw it into the murky water, looking disgusted.

They were about twenty feet away from the shore now. In

the pale glow from the lantern, Isobel could just about see the bats, circling like a huge storm cloud at the edge of the water. She gripped the side of the boat tightly, expecting another attack. But after a few seconds, the cloud moved upwards. A few stragglers zipped furiously around the cave for another few seconds, but none of them approached the boat.

Soon afterwards, the cave was completely still once more. The boat rocked gently as Pat rowed it through the black water. Isobel suddenly became aware of how eerily quiet it was. There were no screeches, no splashes from the lake, no noises from birds or bats or rats. It seemed they were completely alone.

CHAPTER FOUR

'Where have the bats gone?' Flora asked a few seconds later.

'They won't follow us onto the lake,' Pat said, grunting with the effort of rowing. He slowed, breathing heavily.

'Why not?'

'Because they won't.'

'But why not?'

Pat didn't say anything. Flora was breathing heavily too and Isobel had thought it was because they had run to get onto the boat. But now she realised, looking at her sister's narrowed eyes and tight mouth, it was because she was furious.

'You've got to tell us what's going on!' Flora exploded.

Pat still didn't reply and this seemed to enrage her further.

'It's not fair! You should have told us those bats were dangerous, just like you should have said the stalactites could have fallen on us. We need to know these things!'

'Why do you need to know?' Pat asked, his hands gripping the oars tightly. 'What difference would it make?'

'Because . . .' Flora had been leaning forward towards Pat but now, for some reason, she looked suddenly – desperately – at

Isobel. 'It makes *all* the difference. How can we protect ourselves if we don't know what we're up against?'

'You don't need to protect yourselves!' Pat roared, so loudly that Ratter shrank back against the side of the boat. '*I'm* protecting you. I got everyone out of the Cave of the Thousand Knives, didn't I? And then I got everyone away from the bats. No one's got lost. Everyone's all right, aren't they?' He looked at them fiercely, as if he was daring them to disagree. 'And everyone will be all right if you just do what I say and stop asking all these questions.'

One of Pat's hands slipped on its oar and he steadied it. Isobel realised there was blood on his knuckles.

'I'm protecting you,' Pat said again, this time quietly, almost like it was to himself.

Isobel looked at the blood that was running down Pat's arms from his scratches. Then she looked at Simon, who was bending over his bandaged leg, and then at Flora, who also had scratches on her arms and her face, though they weren't as bad as Pat's. She wanted to tell Pat he wasn't doing a very good job of protecting them, but something stopped her. Perhaps he *was*. They had got a few scratches and burns along the way, but – after all – everyone was all right. Everyone was here, at least. They could have been struck by the falling knives, but Pat had got them out. They could have never made it to the boat, but they did, because Pat went back for Simon. In all the stories that Isobel had read, none of the children ever got hurt, not even a scratch. But maybe that was what they didn't tell you in storybooks. That in places like this, it was impossible not to get hurt. It was like the War. If you did get hurt, you were lucky, because at least you were still here.

235

She wanted to say thank you to Pat, but the air felt heavy and thick, like it would swallow any words that were spoken. Simon was still examining his bandage, not looking at his brother. It was impossible to see what he was thinking because his head was bent over his leg but Isobel didn't think he was going to say anything. Perhaps Flora was, but at the moment she was staring at the bottom of the boat. No, Isobel realised as she looked closer, she was staring at Pat's hands, which were clenching the oars. As Isobel looked too she saw that they were shaking again. She swallowed, trying to get rid of the hard lump in her throat. It was no wonder he was angry. They had come on this journey, in spite of what he and Simon had said, and they had put everyone in danger, and now they were arguing with him.

Though Flora wasn't arguing with Pat any more. Instead, she looked away, out to the dark expanse of the lake. 'You should put something on those cuts,' she said quietly.

Pat sniffed instead of replying and carried on rowing.

Isobel still wanted to say thank you, but the moments ticked by and the words didn't come. She knew she should, but she was scared of saying the wrong thing and making Pat angrier, which was the last thing she wanted to do. She cleared her throat nervously and Flora looked at her sharply and said, 'What?' Isobel just shook her head and looked around the cave.

That was when she realised that they had rowed so far, and the light from the lantern in the boat was so faint, that she could no longer see the shore. She twisted to look in the other direction and couldn't see the shore that side either, just dark, still water, rippling slightly in the movement of the boat. Hot, itchy panic crawled on the back of her neck.

'It's all right,' Pat said, seeing her looking. 'I know where I'm going. It's a big lake, but we'll be on the other side in a few minutes.'

Isobel nodded, feeling slightly ashamed for doubting him again. She looked at Pat's cuts. Flora was right, they should clean them. Everyone knew that if cuts got infected that was Bad News. Isobel had once overheard Mrs Dooley talking about her cousin, who had slipped when fixing his roof and got a rusty nail in his thigh. She had told Mum, with a sort of dreadful excitement, how the wound had gone green – a detail that had made Isobel feel like she was going to be sick.

Pat had a particularly deep cut on his right shoulder – Isobel could tell it was deep because of how dark the blood was. It was almost black where it had seeped into his shirt, though maybe that was because the light was so poor.

'Do you have a bandage?' Isobel heard herself say.

'A bandage?' Pat repeated.

'She means for your cuts,' Flora said, glancing at her sister. 'She's right. You shouldn't leave them all out in the open like that.'

'Dad says fresh air's the best thing for cuts,' Simon said. Then he frowned. 'Though I don't think the air's exactly fresh down here.' He rummaged in his pocket and brought out a thick wad. 'Here you go.'

Isobel took it. She tore off a bit of the cloth then leaned over the side of the boat. 'We can wash away the blood first,' she said, about to dip the piece of cloth into the lake.

'Don't touch the water,' Pat said, and something in his tone made Isobel stop immediately.

'Why not?' Flora said.

237

'Don't worry about my cuts,' Pat said, not answering her question. 'I'll sort them out on the other side, all right?'

'But what's wrong with the water?' Flora demanded. 'Is it poisonous?'

'No,' Pat said, a little reluctantly. 'It's just that there are things in there.'

'What kind of things?' Flora said. 'Things like bats that want to scratch you, or knives that want to fall on you?'

'I don't know,' Pat said, and the way he said it made Isobel think he was telling the truth. 'No one's been on the lake for years. Hundreds of years, probably. That's why it's called the Lake of Forgotten Things. There might be dangerous things in there, or it might just be fish, or maybe there's nothing even in there any more. Dad said no one knows. But the best thing we can do is just try to keep as quiet as possible and get to the other side.'

Flora didn't look particularly happy, but she nodded. Isobel turned around and kneeled on her seat, peering over the edge to look down into the water. It was black and looked strangely thick, gleaming in the lantern-light. She wasn't at all sure that if she put her hand in (not that she would, after what Pat had said), the water would be clear like normal water. Perhaps it would be dirty, like water from a puddle. But the way the water moved didn't make her think of mud. It was more like oil, like something that would cling to your fingers.

Isobel heard something moving in the boat and in the next moment, Ratter was beside her. He put his claws on the edge of the boat and stretched his long neck down towards the water.

'Don't go in,' Isobel told him.

Ratter turned his head slowly towards her, then blinked and flared his nostrils. Then he turned his head back and snorted, like he was affronted she would think he would be that stupid. Tiny sparks came out of his nostrils and Isobel realised the water wasn't actually black. It was midnight blue. Ratter pulled his head backwards so that he was perched upwards. Then he shuffled very slowly right, his claws clicking on the side of the boat, until there was barely an inch between him and Isobel's arm.

'What are you doing?' she whispered, very keen to avoid getting a burn on her other hand as well.

Ratter gently nudged her arm with his head, like a cat does sometimes if it wants you to stroke it. Isobel was so shocked that she didn't respond. A few seconds later, he did it again. Very slowly, Isobel raised her arm, then placed her hand on his head. It was covered in spikes but in the middle these spikes were tiny, and all pointing backwards. It was almost like touching a hedgehog. Ratter let her hand sit there for a few seconds, then shook it off.

'Wow!' Simon said from behind them. 'Did he just let you touch him?'

Isobel turned round and nodded.

'He can't have,' Pat said, his voice strained with the effort of rowing. 'Dragons don't ever let normal humans touch them.'

'He did!' Simon said. 'I saw it with my own eyes. Isobel put her hand on his head, and he didn't mind.'

Isobel felt a small glow of pride, but then Flora pulled at the back of her dress. 'Izzy, get down from there,' she said. 'You shouldn't be touching him. He's dangerous.'

Isobel was about to tell her to get off when Ratter turned round and hissed at Flora. Not enough to make sparks, but enough to show his needle-sharp teeth. Flora drew her hand back immediately.

'How strange,' Simon said, with wonder. 'It's like he's protecting her.'

'He doesn't need to protect her from me,' Flora said, sounding put out. 'I'm her sister.'

'Maybe it's because she saved his life,' Simon said. 'Do you think that's what it is, Pat?'

'Could be,' Pat said.

'I still think you should get down, Izzy,' Flora said. 'He might like you at the moment but he's an animal and animals are unpredictable. You don't know what he's going to do next.'

'You're just jealous,' Isobel said.

'No, I'm not,' Flora replied instantly, but Isobel knew she was because of the disgruntled way she said it. 'Fine,' she said, after another few moments, sitting back against the side of the boat. 'But don't come crying to me if you get another burn.'

Isobel stayed sitting next to Ratter. After a few moments, Ratter rested his head on her arm, and this made Isobel proud – prouder, in fact, than she'd ever been of anything in her life. They looked down into the dark water together. It was so dark that it was impossible to see anything at all, Isobel thought. Even if there were creatures in the lake, they would never know.

But the second she'd had that thought, she saw something. It didn't look like a fish, though. It was thin and about a foot long, moving through the water like a stray ribbon carried by the wind. The strangest thing about it was its colour: a bright, almost electric blue. Then there was another one, but this one was the colour of sunlight, and then there was another the colour of a poppy, and another, and another, all moving together in one sparkling shoal. Isobel had never seen anything so bright or beautiful before. She didn't feel remotely afraid. Instead, as she watched them glide through the water, coming closer to the boat, she felt very peaceful.

She glanced at Ratter, wondering if he was going to start growling again or – worse – try to eat them. But he was staring down at the water too, totally mesmerised. The creatures, whatever they were, had lit up the whole lake. Isobel realised that the water was clearer than she thought but it was also far, far deeper – it was impossible to see the bottom below them.

Isobel turned back to the others to tell them about the strange creatures, but realised that they were having an argument. Flora had somehow snatched the map from Pat's pocket and was holding it high above her head. Pat had stopped rowing and was awkwardly trying to hold both oars with one hand, so he could try to get the map back. Simon was looking fearfully between the two of them.

'Look, if you want to be in charge, that's fine,' Flora said. 'I won't ask any more questions, I promise, and I'll give you your map back.'

'You better,' Pat warned, his voice like thunder.

'I will! But there's just one thing I have to know.' Flora took a deep breath. 'You normally go in and out through the air-raid shelter, right?'

Pat gave up trying to hold the oars with one hand. He put them back into their correct position and nodded grudgingly.

'But we can't, because the lever's broken,' Flora said. 'The door won't open. Then you said there's another way out, through the main tunnel, which leads to Burley Caves.'

Pat nodded, slowly this time, like he knew what was coming next and didn't want Flora to say it.

'But we can't get out that way because the main tunnel's blocked by the bomb rubble,' Flora said. 'If we couldn't get into the tunnel you normally use earlier, we won't be able to get out of it, either. So what's this tunnel?'

She pointed at the huge black line that went straight down from Burley Caves to the cavern where the dragons lived. It was so thick it wasn't really a line. It reminded Isobel of the coal chute they used to have at home.

'Can we use this one to get back above ground?' Flora pressed.

'I know what that is,' Simon said, peering at it closely. 'That's on the north side of the cavern. It's more of a shaft than a tunnel. Even when you're standing at the bottom, on the other side of the gates, you can see daylight. It's vertical, pretty much, all the way up. It would be like climbing up a cliff. I don't think we could ever get up there.'

He stopped, realising what he was saying. Everyone turned to Pat, who shifted awkwardly where he was sitting. He leaned against the back of the boat, like he was very tired. 'It's vertical to stop the splints, if the dragons . . .' He trailed off, unable to say the words. 'They *can* climb up rock faces, but it takes them longer. It's to slow them down. To give us humans a chance to be ready for them.'

'Be ready for them how?' Isobel said.

Pat shook his head. 'I don't know,' he admitted. 'It hasn't ever happened. That's why we've got to help the dragons. They're the ones with the best chance of beating the splints. Not us.'

'Hang on,' Flora said, her forehead wrinkled into a frown. 'Forget about the splints for a minute. Even if we do beat them, you just said that the shaft behind the gates is impossible to climb.'

Isobel swallowed painfully as she realised what her sister was saying.

'The air-raid shelter door is broken and the other exit is blocked,' Flora continued. 'So how are we going to get out? After we've been to the cavern, I mean?'

Pat was silent for a long time. 'I don't know that either,' he said.

Everyone fell quiet. No one said anything, but Isobel knew they were all thinking the same thing. There were two ways up to the surface, and both of those were blocked. Even if they did manage to beat the splints, there was no way out. They were trapped.

CHAPTER FIVE

*B*efore the journey, if anyone had ever asked Isobel how she would feel about being trapped underground, she would have replied that it was the worst thing she could imagine. Worse than being shot, worse than drowning, worse even than being eaten by a lion at London Zoo. It was the nightmare that woke her up most often. That feeling of being shut up, the night of the bomb. Or worse, thinking about being trapped in rubble, unable to see the sunlight, calling out but no one hearing.

But even though Isobel knew they were trapped, she felt strangely calm. Perhaps it was because she wasn't actually trapped in the way people underneath the rubble from bombs were trapped, she thought. She could still move her limbs, speak, look around. Or perhaps it was because when the worst happened, there was no longer anything to be afraid of any more. You could worry and worry and worry, but when the thing that you were worrying about happened, there was strangely no longer anything to worry about.

'It doesn't matter if we're trapped,' she said. 'The most important thing is that we help the dragons and beat back the splints.'

Pat looked at her sharply. 'That's the kind of thing a keeper would say.'

'What do the splints want, anyway?' Flora said.

'To get to the surface so they can kill us, of course,' Simon said.

'Simon!' Pat warned.

'What? It's true.'

'But why do they want that?' Flora said, struggling to understand. 'Why do they hate us?'

'I think it's because we get to live up there—' Simon jerked his finger up, 'and they have to live down *there*. In—'

'Leave off, Simon,' Pat said. He put the oars down and rummaged through his pockets then brought something out. It looked a bit like a clock, rimmed with shiny gold, but bigger.

'But it's what I think!' Simon protested.

Pat stared down at the gold object intently. 'They don't need to know what you think.'

'What do you mean, they have to live down there?' Isobel asked. 'Where's *there*?'

Simon glanced at his brother. But Pat didn't seem to be paying much attention. His eyebrows were pulled into a frown and he was looking down at the gold object, which Isobel realised was a compass. He shook his head, then moved it to the left.

Simon took a deep breath as Pat cursed quietly. 'So, you know people think heaven is . . .' He pointed upwards. 'In the sky. On clouds, or whatever.'

Isobel nodded.

'So, if heaven is up,' Simon said, 'what's . . .' He jerked his thumb downwards.

Isobel felt a strange tingling at the backs of her knees as she realised what Simon meant. Flora gasped. 'When you told us about them before, you called them another name. *Hellborn*.'

'Stop talking about it, Simon,' Pat said, his attention snapping back to them. 'You'll only scare them even more than they're already scared.'

'But it's true!' Simon protested. 'Think about it. They only come when humans have been bad. Well, that's when they get really strong, anyway. Like after the last war, when Dad and Lord Burlington defeated them, and like now. The vicar says when you do something bad, you're helping the Devil. It's like that but times a thousand. A million, even.'

Flora was horrified. 'So when you die, if you've been bad, you become one of those things?'

Simon shrugged.

'Of course you don't,' Pat said. 'It's a stupid theory.'

'It's not,' Simon said, looking a bit upset.

'It is and I'll tell you why,' Pat said, shoving his compass back in his pocket. 'It's stupid because there's no need to have a reason for things being evil. It doesn't matter why they're evil. Some things just *are*. If the last six years have taught us anything, it should be that. The splints are just evil, and we've got to stop them, and that's the end of it. Like Dad and your grandpa . . .'

He stopped talking and glanced at Isobel, then looked quickly away.

'Our grandpa?' Flora said, sitting bolt upright. 'What about our grandpa?'

'Nothing.'

'But you said, "our grandpa"!'

Pat went back to looking at the compass. 'I made a mistake, that's all.'

'No, you didn't,' Isobel said. 'You're lying. You said he never came down here but he did, didn't he? After the last war. When the dragon had the bone stuck in his foot.'

'Of course he didn't,' Simon scoffed. 'I told you, no one comes down here except for keepers. How many times do we have to say it? Pat, tell them.'

Pat put the compass down for a minute. He gripped the oars very tightly, shutting his eyes. Then he opened them. 'I suppose I may as well tell you,' he said, his voice flat. 'Lord Burlington did come down with Dad, after the last war.'

Simon was so shocked that he didn't say anything for a few moments. 'He can't have,' he said eventually, but his voice sounded unsure. 'Dad would never . . .'

'He didn't have any choice,' Pat said. 'There was no one else left. Uncle Ernie had died in that war, as well as Dad's cousin. Dad knew he couldn't get down to the dragon on his own, not with everything he had to carry to fix the wound. Your grandpa was the one who pulled the bone out,' Pat said, looking at Isobel. 'He killed a few splints too, with the poker. Dad said he was really brave.'

For a couple of minutes, the children were silent. Isobel was thinking about her grandpa and James, who would have been so much younger than he was now, maybe even Pat's age. How they'd gone down the tunnels just like they were. How they'd helped the dragons. How they'd kept everyone above ground safe, even though it was dark, and hot, and they were scared, and the splints were coming.

'But Simon's right,' Pat said. 'It shouldn't have happened. We're the ones who are keepers. We're the ones who are supposed to go down here, not your grandpa, and not you either.'

Flora groaned. 'Oh, you're not bringing that up again, are you?'

'Stop,' Isobel said, and her voice sounded clearer than she thought it would. 'We don't have time to argue. It doesn't matter who's meant to be down here and who's not. What's important is that we stop the splints. Like Grandpa and James did. That's the only thing that matters.'

Flora looked like she was going to say something, but didn't.

'You're right,' Simon said. Isobel looked at him with surprise.

Pat nodded slowly. He looked down at the compass and a shadow flitted across his face. 'I don't know how we're going to stop them, though, because we're lost.'

'Lost?' Flora said. 'What do you mean, lost?'

'What do you think I mean?'

'But how can we be?' Flora looked behind them, then in front. 'You said we just had to go in a straight line, then we'd reach the other side.'

'I know I said that,' Pat said, rubbing his forehead with frustration. 'But I don't think we've been going in a straight line. I mean, that's how I've been rowing, but the compass is now saying we're heading west. We're supposed to be going north, according to the map.' He uncrumpled the map and pointed to the lake. Someone had drawn an arrow across it, with the letter *N* clearly written by the side.

Pat got out the compass again. The needle swung left to right, north to south, then settled on east.

'East?' Pat said in disbelief.

'I don't think it's working,' Flora said. 'Maybe it doesn't work underground.'

Isobel looked around the boat, the hot, itchy panic returning. She still couldn't see the shore behind them, or in front. It felt like they were in the middle of the ocean. In fact, she could see even less than she could before. Previously she'd been able to see about twenty feet behind them or in front, but now it was only ten. She swung around, trying to understand why that might be, and her gaze settled on the lantern. The candle was dangerously low and the light it was giving out was now a dull orange, rather than bright white.

'Pat, look at the lantern,' she said. It came out as a whisper.

He glanced at it and she saw him freeze. His whole body tensed and she realised that even though Pat was older than them, and even though he was bigger and stronger, he was afraid.

Then it seemed that all the fear that Isobel hadn't been feeling was in her stomach, uncoiling and surging upwards like a snake about to pounce. It was one thing being trapped down here, it was quite another being trapped down here in total darkness.

'Everyone stay calm,' Flora said, though her voice didn't sound calm at all.

'But if the light goes out we won't be able to see anything!' Simon said.

Isobel felt something tap her arm. She looked down and saw it was Ratter. He nudged her again, then leaned over the side of the boat. It seemed like he was asking her to look at the water.

Isobel kneeled next to him and stared down into the lake. The brightly coloured creatures were back, she thought. But instead of swimming past them, this time they were hovering by the boat, darting back and forth. Then they all started swimming in a straight line to the left. After a few moments, they returned. They hovered for a little while again, then swum off in the same direction as they had before.

'What are they doing?' Isobel wondered.

Ratter whined, rapping the side of the boat with his claws. Behind them, Pat had grabbed the oars again.

'We might as well go somewhere instead of nowhere,' he said.

The boat jumped forwards, away from the creatures. The effect on them was instantaneous. They darted to and fro, so frenzied that a few of them even jumped out of the water and back in again. Strangely, their bright colours looked muted in the air, like they needed the water to show their true iridescence.

'Wait!' Isobel shouted at Pat, a thought forming in her head.

'What is it, Izzy?' Flora said.

'We've got to follow them! Follow those creatures.'

'What creatures?' Pat said.

Isobel pointed. Pat put one of his oars down and leaned over the side of the boat. Flora did too. 'What on earth are they?' she asked. 'They're so bright.'

'I don't know what they are, but they're going to show us the way to go,' Isobel said, tripping over her words in her haste to explain. 'They were right here, then they kept swimming in one direction, then they came back, then when you went the other way they started doing this.'

Pat looked doubtful. 'But—'

'I can't explain it but I know I'm right!' Isobel shouted. 'Please, you've got to follow them!'

'Go on, Pat,' Simon urged. His eyes slid sideways to the candle, which only had an inch or so left. 'She might be right, and even if she's not, you said we've got to go somewhere.'

Pat's hands hovered over the oars uncertainly for a second. Then he seized them determinedly. 'All right, but you'll have to give me directions. I can't watch them and row at the same time.'

Flora kneeled beside Isobel. 'They're going left!' she called.

Pat moved his right oar. It cut through the water easily and the boat surged forwards.

'That's it!' Isobel said. 'Now just keep going straight.'

'Now right a bit,' Flora said, a few moments later.

The creatures weren't easy to follow. They changed direction suddenly and without warning. 'Why do they keep doing that?' Isobel muttered, after shouting 'Right' for what felt like the fourteenth time. Then she felt Flora squeezing her wrist. Isobel looked at her questioningly. Flora's face was pale as she pointed at something Isobel hadn't noticed.

To their left, the direction in which they had just been rowing, a huge rock rose out of the water, dark and jagged. Then she saw another, about fifteen feet to their right, and then she realised there were lots of them. The creatures were forging a safe path through – that was why they were changing direction so often. The edges of the rocks were sharp and if the boat was to hit any of them, Isobel thought the wood would splinter like it had been hit with an axe.

Isobel looked back at Pat, completely unaware of the danger, then looked at her sister. Flora gave a tiny shake of her head. 'Left,' she called, keeping her voice steady.

Isobel's hands were shaking but she knew Flora was right.

If Pat knew about the rocks and was worried, he wouldn't be able to row as well as he was doing now. She looked down at the creatures again. 'Keep going forward,' she said.

After a few more nail-biting turns, Isobel grabbed Flora's arm. 'Look!' she said, pointing. 'It's the shore!'

About twenty-five feet ahead she could see the water lapping against a grey strip of beach.

'Thank goodness,' Flora said. 'We're nearly there,' she called behind her.

But at that moment, something thudded against the boat.

'What was that?' Simon said, sitting up.

'Did we hit a rock?' Flora said, whipping round.

'What rock?' Pat said, his oars freezing mid-row. 'You're telling me there are rocks here?!'

Isobel peered into the water and saw that the brightly coloured creatures had vanished. Her palms started to prickle with unease. Suddenly, the lake seemed even more still and silent than before. 'Hurry,' she said.

'You haven't told me which way,' Pat pointed out. 'And I want to know what hit the boat!'

As if to answer him, the boat thudded against something again, harder. This time the boat rocked violently and a small amount of lake water splashed inside.

'Ugh!' Simon said, shuffling away.

'Don't touch it!' Pat shouted.

'I'm trying not to! What was that?'

'I don't know but we've got to hurry!' Isobel said. 'Go left, quickly!'

Pat followed her instructions.

252

'Now right.'

Ratter nipped her on the hand.

'No, not right, look!' Flora shouted. 'There's a rock just there!'

Isobel's heart was in her mouth. 'Not right, left. No, there's a rock there too!'

'Which way should I go then?' Pat shouted.

Flora and Isobel looked at each other helplessly. There wasn't a clear path to the beach.

'Maybe we should swim for it,' Isobel said. 'It's not far.'

'I said, we can't touch the water!' Pat said. 'I don't know if it's dangerous or not. And me and Simon can't swim anyway.' He picked up the oars and rowed forward determinedly.

Flora opened her mouth to argue, but there was a loud creak, then the horrible, splintering sound of wood tearing. Isobel looked over the right side and saw a rock poking through the side of the hull. The boat shifted slightly from the impact. Black water started gushing in. Everyone scrambled to the other side, tucking their feet underneath them so they wouldn't touch it.

'We'll have to swim,' Flora said, rolling up her sleeves. 'There's nothing else for it. You'll have to hold on to our shoulders. Simon, you can hold Isobel's and Pat, you can hold on to mine—'

'Don't be stupid, I'll drown you!'

'Well, what else are we supposed to do?'

A few seconds later the back of the boat – where Pat and Flora were sitting – was pulled down by the weight of the water. The front, where Simon and Isobel were, wobbled as it rose.

'Woah!' Simon said, clutching the boat tightly.

Flora's eyes were huge and terrified. 'Pat, let go of the oars. You've got to hold on to my shoulders.'

'The meat!'

'I've got it, don't worry about that.'

Isobel looked back and saw Simon clutching his leg, his mouth opening and closing wordlessly. 'It's all right, it's all right—' She reached out to hold his hand, and then she heard splashing, and she knew that Pat and Flora were in the water already.

'It's not cold,' Flora called.

'Can you feel the bottom?' Isobel asked, but then she felt water flood around her ankles. Ratter was on her shoulders, whining louder than she'd ever heard before, and Simon's hand was gripping hers so hard it was hurting, and then there was water rushing up to her waist. Her feet wobbled on the boat until suddenly it wasn't underneath her any more – it was gone. The water rose up around her shoulders and she kicked her legs frantically to stay afloat.

'Isobel!' Simon shouted, his voice cracking with fear.

Isobel moved his hand to her right shoulder. 'Move your other hand to my other shoulder, that's it.' When he did so, his weight was heavier than she'd thought, and for a single, horrifying moment her head went underwater. But then her foot found something hard at the bottom – the edge of the boat. Isobel kicked upwards and took a breath, hearing Simon do the same behind her. Ratter was scrabbling in her hair. She licked her lips, realising the water was salty, like the sea.

Then, with a strength Isobel didn't know she had, she swam forwards.

'Izzy, you don't have to go too far and then you'll feel the bottom,' Flora yelled from somewhere ahead of her.

Isobel's arms and legs were burning. Her face kept dipping into the water and she had to keep wrenching it upwards so she could breathe. Ratter was no help, digging his claws into her ears and squawking louder than she had ever heard him.

'Keep going! You're nearly there!'

After another few seconds, Isobel kicked forwards and felt solid ground beneath her foot. She took a wobbly step, pulling with her arms. And then Flora and Pat were there, and Pat was taking Simon off her shoulders and Ratter was jumping off, and Flora was dragging her out of the water. They both collapsed on to a sort of beach, breathing hard.

The sand (if it even was sand) was hard and coarse underneath her hands. Isobel got gingerly to her knees. She felt her pocket instinctively for her dragon but realised it was gone. 'No,' she said under her breath as she scrabbled for it. 'No, no, no, no, no, no.' A couple of seconds later her fingers closed around its tail. She grabbed it so hard that the spikes dug into her hand painfully, but she didn't care. It was still slightly warmer than normal but not burning hot, like it had been when she'd seen the scout in Burley Caves. Isobel wondered if that meant the splints were still far away. She hoped so.

It was pitch black. Isobel realised the lantern was still on the boat, probably at the bottom of the lake by now. She couldn't see anything or, more importantly, anyone.

'Is everyone all right?' Flora asked.

'Just about,' Pat said. 'Thanks to you two. You're good swimmers.'

'I said we could do it,' Flora said. 'Though the water was salty,' she admitted. 'That made it easier to float.'

'Should make the water cleaner, too,' Pat said. 'That's good for Simon's leg. If the water was dirty, then . . .'

'I'll be fine,' Simon said. 'Anyway, the dragons will see to it, soon.'

'What do you mean, the dragons will see to it?' Flora asked.

'Wait a minute, where's Ratter?' Pat said, a note of alarm in his voice. 'Does anyone have him?'

'I don't,' Simon said.

'He was on my shoulders and then he jumped off,' Isobel said, looking around, then realising it was impossible to see anything in the darkness. 'He must be around here somewhere . . .' She moved to the side. The ground seemed to shift underneath her right foot, then something squawked angrily. Blue sparks shot into the air and a pair of red indignant eyes shone in the darkness.

'There he is,' Pat said, with relief.

'Sorry, Ratter,' Isobel said. 'I didn't mean to step on you.'

Ratter snorted, sending more sparks flying.

'If he could do that again, maybe we could see where we need to go next,' Flora said. 'Otherwise we're stuck.'

'You'd be lucky,' Pat said. 'He won't just do it on demand.'

'Maybe he will if Isobel asks him.' Flora still sounded slightly jealous. 'He likes her, doesn't he?'

Isobel didn't think Ratter was at all likely to do what she said but luckily, at that moment there was the telltale scuttle of a rat. Ratter leaped on it immediately but missed and was so cross that he roared. The bright blue flame illuminated the cave for a second, enough time for Pat to see the opening to the next tunnel.

'There! It's only a few feet away from you, Isobel. Just keep walking forwards till your hands touch the wall of the cave. Then go down and right. You can't miss it.'

Isobel did what he said. The wall of the cave felt smooth but grainy, and strangely warm. She followed the curve of it down until she felt it wrap underneath itself into a ledge. 'I've got it!'

'All right, now everyone just needs to get to where Isobel is. Simon, where are you? Can you walk?'

'I'm here. And yes . . . I think so.'

Pat stumbled in the direction of his brother's voice. In the meantime Flora found Isobel, grabbing her arm just above the elbow.

'You go first, Izzy,' she said. 'I'll wait for Simon and Pat.'

Something shot through Isobel's legs and scuttled into the tunnel.

'Was that Ratter?' Flora asked.

'I think so.'

'He knows he's nearly home,' Pat said, grunting with the effort of pulling Simon forwards. 'He'll be able to smell his parents. He'll be all right, the map says this tunnel's not very long, and there's only one way he can go so he won't get lost.'

It took Pat and Simon nearly a minute to get to the entrance of the tunnel, even though it was only a short distance. Isobel wasn't sure but she thought they kept having to stop because it was hurting Simon so much. When he finally bent down to enter the tunnel he couldn't stop himself crying out in pain.

'Not far to go now,' Pat said, trying to keep the worry out of his voice. 'Go on, then, girls, but remember, don't go into the cavern. You've got to stay in the tunnel while we return Ratter and check the grown-up dragons are all right.'

This tunnel was perhaps the tightest one yet. Isobel kept

feeling the roof of it scraping along her back. If it was like this for her, goodness knows what it was like for Pat. He must have had to practically lie down.

After a few minutes, Isobel saw a glimmer of light ahead of her. She kept crawling towards it and it got bigger and brighter until eventually she saw it was the end of the tunnel. Beyond it all Isobel could see was a dull, orangey glow. When she got there she hovered, uncertain. The cavern, or what she could see of it through the three-foot entrance, looked enormous – she wasn't even sure she could see the other side. There was a different kind of smell too. It was still that dank old-air smell that was in most of the tunnels, but here it smelled a bit like boiled eggs too. And it was hot. So hot that Isobel's forehead was damp with sweat.

Ratter was just outside the tunnel. He looked back at Isobel and thumped his tail on the ground excitedly.

The thudding marching sound had returned. In fact, it was getting louder and louder, Isobel was sure of it. Suddenly, she was afraid.

'Ratter, I don't think you should go in—'

But Ratter had already shot off into the cavern.

'No!' Isobel shouted. Without stopping to remember that Pat had told them not to go in, she scrambled out of the tunnel after him.

'Izzy, stop!' she heard Flora cry, but it felt like she was very far away.

The cavern was the biggest space Isobel had ever been in – bigger than any hall or shelter above ground. It seemed to go on for miles, not just across but upwards, too; she had to crane her neck if she wanted to even see the roof. The dull orangey glow was coming from branches that were lit and attached to the walls in iron frames. It was the first time since being underground that Isobel could see properly, and she blinked at the shock of it. To her left, about the size of a field away, Isobel could see a huge pile of rocks stretching up to the roof of the cave. Beyond, there was a shaft of light – real light, daylight-light, not the orange glow from fire – and her heart leaped. That was the way to get above ground again. Even if it was impossible to get to, it was comforting that it was there. Ahead of them was just empty space and, far away, the cavern's wall; to her right, the cave dropped into shadow.

'Izzy, I told you to stop!' Flora shouted, standing up beside her.

The word 'stop' bounced off the walls and echoed back to them. Suddenly, Isobel felt very small. Nothing moved in the huge cave, except for Ratter, who was scuttling around by the rocks on the left wall. He was so far away that he looked like a leaf blowing across the ground in the wind.

'Where are the dragons?' Isobel whispered.

'I don't know,' Flora said, also whispering.

Isobel looked around the cavern, slowly. Still, nothing moved. Then something caught her eye a little way in front of them. It looked like tree branches, scattered on the ground. Isobel moved closer to take a closer look.

'Izzy, where are you going?' Flora said, sounding desperate. 'Izzy, stop!'

Isobel didn't reply. She had seen what the thing was, and she couldn't stop. Flora caught up with her and they looked down at it silently for a few moments.

'I think it's the scout,' Isobel said eventually, her throat tight.

The skeleton was about as long as both of them, if they were lying down end to end. It had stretched, thin bones – which were blackened in parts – and its head was turned slightly away from them. Isobel knew the dragon had burned it to bits and it was no danger to them any more. But its claws were still intact, resting on the floor of the cavern and glinting in the light from the shaft.

'That's what I saw,' Isobel said. 'In the tunnels.'

Flora didn't reply. Isobel looked at her sister, who was staring at the skeleton, an expression of utter dread on her face.

'Flora, are you all right?'

Flora looked at her, like she'd forgotten who she was. Then suddenly she was grabbing Isobel's hands. She looked into Isobel's eyes, her expression wild.

'Izzy, you've got to go back to the tunnel. If you go now you'll be able to make it.'

'What are you talking about?'

Flora was gripping her arms painfully. 'Don't argue, just go! You'll be able to get back to the lake. That might keep you safe. Maybe those . . . those . . . things can't swim—'

'I'm not going,' Isobel shouted, brushing her off. 'You need me to help find Ratter's parents too.'

'Stop being silly and just listen to me,' Flora said, in her most irritating big-sister voice.

Isobel pulled back. 'No, I won't! You always think I'm such a baby, but I'm not. I'm not going back.'

Flora pushed her towards the tunnel and Isobel pushed back, so hard that Flora stumbled backwards, her foot landing on the splint with a horrible crack. For a moment, neither of them moved.

'I'm sorry—' Isobel began, horrified.

With a strangled sob, Flora lurched sideways, shaking her

foot, and banged her shoulder on the side of the cavern. She started to cry.

'I'm sorry,' Isobel said again.

Flora slid to the floor, her back against the cavern wall, and put her head in her arms. Isobel crouched down in front of her. 'Flora, please don't cry. I didn't mean to, I promise.'

'I'm not crying because of that.'

'Then why are you crying?'

'Because I'm supposed to look after you,' Flora blurted out.

'What?'

'I'm supposed to look after you. That's what big sisters do. And Mum said I should.' Flora put each of her index fingers in a horizontal line and swept them over her eyelashes to remove the tears. 'She said that if anything happened to her . . . at the factory, or, you know, in a raid. That I had to make sure you were all right. And when the War ended I thought I'd done it, but now . . .' Flora broke off. She looked at the blackened splint to her right, then covered her face with her hands. 'I just didn't think . . . I didn't know that it would look like that.'

Isobel realised that deep down, Flora hadn't really ever thought the splints were real. Isobel didn't think that her sister had thought the others were lying. It was just that some things were impossible to believe unless you saw them for yourself. 'I kept asking Pat and Simon to let us come, but I shouldn't have,' Flora said. 'We should have stayed in the air-raid shelter. It's all my fault.'

For a moment, Isobel wasn't sure what to do. Flora *never* said that anything was her fault. She expected to feel a flash of triumph, but she didn't.

She took her sister's hand. 'It's not anyone's fault,' she said.

'Pat's right. The splints are just evil. And I'm glad we came. I think Pat and Simon need our help, Flora. I don't know that they can beat the splints on their own. Not with the dragons being weak and especially not now Simon's hurt. If we'd stayed above ground, the splints would have found us anyway. But now, we've got a chance to stop them.'

Flora reached into her pocket for a handkerchief, then realised she didn't have one. She wiped her nose with the back of her hand instead. 'Maybe you're right.'

'I *am* right,' Isobel said. 'Come on. Get up.'

She helped Flora to her feet. They stood looking at each other for a few moments, then, without saying anything, they hugged. Isobel realised they had never hugged like this, without hugging Mum too. She was surprised at how skinny her sister was. She could feel each of her ribs through her thin jumper, and her heart beating against hers.

'Flora, are you scared?' Isobel whispered.

'Yes,' she replied a few seconds later. 'I've been scared ever since we left the air-raid shelter. You don't think you're the only one who's afraid of the dark, do you?'

The two girls hugged until there was a sound behind them and they whipped round, but it was only Pat and Simon.

'What are you doing?' Pat said once he'd helped Simon up. 'I told you not to go in here! Do you want to get burned to bits?'

'Simon, are you all right?' Flora said, looking at him with concern.

Simon was holding his leg tightly, his face pinched with pain. He nodded, giving Isobel the impression it was too much effort to speak, then sat down, his head resting against the cavern wall.

'You've both got to get back in the tunnel now!' Pat said, grabbing Isobel's arm. 'I'm not joking. NOW.'

'It's all right,' Flora said. 'The dragons aren't even here.'

'Of course they're here,' Pat said. 'They're always here.'

'So where are they then?'

'They'll be hiding.'

Flora let out a short, contemptuous laugh. 'How on earth can something that big hide?'

'Look, you don't understand,' Pat said. He ran his hands through his hair, so hard Isobel thought he might yank it out. 'You've got to get back into the tunnel right now.'

'Why's Ratter whining?' Simon said.

Isobel followed his gaze to see Ratter crouching by the huge pile of rocks. His tail was low on the ground and he was making that horrible screeching sound that set her teeth on edge. As if to reply, one of the rocks fell, bouncing down the others to land with a crash very near Ratter.

'We've got to get him away from there, it's dangerous!' Isobel said.

She moved towards him, but Pat yanked her back. She opened her mouth to argue but saw that he was staring at the rocks with something like fear in his eyes. Isobel turned her head back.

The mountain of grey rocks trembled, then shifted. No, Isobel thought, something *underneath* them shifted. No, it was something that was the mountain, and yet wasn't. There *were* rocks but some of the things Isobel had thought were rocks were actually huge grey bumps, which – now that the something was moving – were starting to look suspiciously like scales. The mountain moved further and something flapped out like a grey sheet, then lay flat again. *It's a wing*, Isobel thought, and then immediately thought, *It can't be . . .* Then a huge yellow eye opened, and she knew it for sure.

The dragon bent its long head down towards Ratter but couldn't get that far. Isobel realised its body was twisted underneath the hill of rocks. Ratter was whining louder than ever now, waddling fast round the edge of the rocks, then back again. He stopped and stuck his jaws high up into the air, then howled.

'It's his mother,' Simon breathed. 'Her bottom half's trapped by those rocks. It must have been the bomb. Part of the cavern's fallen in. That's why she sent Ratter to us, to get help.'

'You're right,' Pat said grimly.

'We've got to help her,' Isobel said. 'We've got to move those rocks before the splints get here!'

'I know we should be worried about the splints,' Flora said, 'but is no one else a little bit worried about the missing dragon?'

'What missing dragon?' Isobel said.

Flora looked nervously at the dragon underneath the rocks. 'Well, if that's his mother, then where's his father?'

There was a thundering crash, so loud that it rang in Isobel's ears for a few seconds.

Flora grabbed Isobel's arm. 'Izzy, I think Pat's right, we really should go back into the tunnel—'

But it was too late. There was another bone-shuddering crash, then another. The four children looked to their right. Out of the shadows came a huge, leathery foot with three bone-white claws which thudded down on the ground, making the cavern echo. Then another foot joined it.

Isobel had always imagined dragons as graceful creatures, with long necks like swans and patterned scales that shone like jewels – perhaps the size of a very large horse. When she saw Ratter's father, she realised how wrong she was. This dragon was huge. He was easily the height of a double-decker bus. His tail swayed menacingly from side to side, striking a rock in the process and easily tearing it out from its roots. Thick browney-black scales covered his body. Above his huge jaws two massive nostrils flared, and above those his blood-red eyes flickered.

Isobel gulped. The dragon was looking right at her.

CHAPTER SIX

'Don't move,' Pat said quietly. 'Dragons don't like any sudden movements.'

Isobel wasn't sure she could have moved even if she'd wanted to. She felt like a tree rooted to the ground.

'Don't take your eyes off him, either,' Pat said. 'Dragons think that's a sign of weakness.'

There was a noise from Flora, a little like a whimper.

Pat's voice was very calm. 'I'm going to distract him,' he said. 'I'm going to walk over to the rocks and pick up Ratter and give him to him. That'll take his eyes off you for a few seconds, at least. The second he looks away, you run for the tunnel. All right? It's not far.'

Isobel was too frightened to say anything but Flora nodded. Very, very slowly, she reached out and took Isobel's hand.

Pat started walking to his left. But the dragon didn't seem to like it. He stepped forwards and snorted. Like when Ratter snorted, sparks shot out of his nostrils, but each of his were the size of a fist. Pat tried again, but the same thing happened.

'All right,' Pat said, holding his arms up in surrender to the dragon. 'It's all right.'

'It's not all right,' Flora whispered, her palm sticky in Isobel's hand. 'What are we going to do?'

Suddenly, there was a high-pitched screech. Ratter ran across the cavern, flapping his wings so wildly he was almost flying. Isobel was sure she saw him leave the ground for a moment or two. He didn't stop until he was standing before his father.

When the dragon saw Ratter, his mood seemed to change completely. His whole body relaxed and he stretched down, almost like he was bowing, until his jaws were touching the floor of the cave. Ratter hopped up so that he was on his father's nose. Then he made a series of high-pitched screeches, squawks and those strange clicks again.

'What's he doing?' Isobel asked.

Pat was watching with fascination. 'He's talking to him.'

'You mean dragons talk?' Flora said.

'Of course they do. All animals talk.'

When Ratter had finished, he hopped off his father's nose. The dragon straightened up to his full – terrifying – height and fixed his eyes on Isobel and Flora again. Isobel swallowed painfully. The dragon flared his nostrils and Isobel shut her eyes tight, thinking that in any second flames would shoot out. But they didn't. Instead, the dragon made a long, sighing noise. It almost sounded like, 'Hmmm.'

'His tail's stopped moving!' Pat said. 'That means he's not angry any more. I think Ratter told him what's happened. About you bringing him food and Isobel saving his life.'

'Are you sure he's not angry?' Isobel asked, still feeling a little nervous.

The dragon stepped backwards, then sat on his hind legs with a crash, almost like a dog. Ratter hopped up onto the paw of his front left leg and screeched happily.

'I'm sure,' Pat said with relief. 'He wouldn't do that if he still felt threatened.'

'*He* felt threatened?' Flora said under her breath.

There was a noise from the rocks, where the other dragon was trapped. It was a low, mournful screech. The male dragon sighed in response.

'We've got to get her out,' Pat said, already rolling his sleeves up. 'That's the only way we'll be able to stop the splints.' He grabbed the bag of meat and emptied half of it in front of them. Isobel just caught sight of feathers and something brown and furry before it was gone, snapped up in the dragon's jaws.

'I don't think we've got long,' Flora said, her eyes round with fear. 'Listen!'

Isobel's fear of the dragon had shut out the sound of the splints marching. Now she realised it was impossibly loud. The splints must be close. Horribly close – underneath the axe-sharp sounds of bones hitting rock, she could hear the whisper of their hissing. A headache started to throb against her skull.

The male dragon could hear it too. He swung his head round sharply, then gulped down his meal. He nudged Ratter off his foot, pushing him in the direction of his mother. Once he was satisfied Ratter was going that way, he turned back into the shadows, the floor of the cavern trembling as he disappeared.

'Come on!' Pat said. 'That food will have helped, but he won't be able to hold them back on his own. We've got to get the rocks off *her*, but first we need to put Simon somewhere safe. Look at him!'

Simon's eyes were closed and his head was lolling on his shoulders. He grunted as Flora and Pat picked him up, with one arm over each of their shoulders, but his eyes didn't open. Flora and Pat carried him over to the rocks. There was a ledge set into the wall of the cavern a little way ahead and they put Simon there. He flopped on to it like a rag doll, his face grey.

'He must have lost more blood than I thought,' Pat said, his face worried.

'Will he be all right?' Flora asked.

'I hope so. But he won't be if we don't get this dragon free.' Pat turned to the rock mountain. 'I'll feed her first. You start taking the smaller rocks off, then I'll get the bigger ones off, once she's eaten.'

At first, Isobel thought it was impossible. There were so many rocks – hundreds, it seemed, and some of them were the size of tables. They were various shades of yellow and brown but left a white, chalky residue on your hands. Their edges were sharp. Isobel had carried only two rocks when she saw that her thumb was bleeding. But they couldn't give up.

Isobel was working close to the cavern floor, picking up small pieces of rubble covering one of the dragon's feet. It felt good when the foot was finally uncovered and the dragon flexed her claws. But Isobel realised it didn't make any difference as the dragon's leg was still trapped, meaning she still couldn't move.

Pat seemed to have had the same realisation. 'You need to climb up there,' he shouted from where he was standing by the dragon's head. Isobel saw her huge jaws working and she prayed that the few birds Pat was feeding her would give her enough strength to fight. Pat pointed halfway up the dragon's body, already climbing himself. 'We need to free the legs first. Then she might be able to stand up and shake the other rocks off.'

Isobel clambered up. One of the rocks she put her foot on broke free and she slipped, banging her knee painfully. But she picked herself up and scrambled to where Flora was helping Pat push a particularly heavy slab off the dragon's knee. She put her hands underneath it to join Flora's and Pat's and pushed. For a horrible second, it didn't move. Then it shifted a few inches, enough for Pat to bend down and put his shoulder underneath, and with a grunt and then a roar the rock heaved upwards then fell, flipping over and down on to the cave floor with a crash that reverberated around the cavern.

'Now these smaller ones,' Pat said. He gestured with his hand, and Isobel realised, with a jolt, that it was still shaking.

'Help me with this one, Izzy,' Flora said.

Isobel tucked a damp strand of hair behind her ear and leaned down to pick up the rock her sister was holding. This one wasn't nearly so heavy and they were able to pick it up and throw it down to the ground.

'Now this one,' Flora said.

Isobel couldn't say how long they worked. It felt like time had ceased to mean anything at all. It was as if the normal world, the one with sky and fresh air and grass, no longer existed, and all that was left was this terrible heat and the rocks, these endless rocks.

'We're doing it, Izzy,' Flora said, a flicker of excitement in her voice. 'Look, most of this leg's free now.'

Isobel looked down, past the rock she was holding, and saw she was no longer standing on rocks. She was standing on the dragon's leg itself. She looked uneasily up towards the dragon's head, hoping she wouldn't mind. Up close the scales looked dry and cracked, like silvery tree bark blackened by fire. She reached up and wiped the sweat away from her forehead. She could have sworn the heat was coming from the dragon itself.

'You were right, Izzy,' Flora said. 'It's good we're here. There's no way Pat could have done this all by himself.'

Isobel glanced up at Pat, who was working quickly, the sweat on his arms glistening in the firelight. 'I don't think Pat would say that,' she said. 'Maybe he thinks that Simon would have made it through the Cave of a Thousand Knives if we hadn't been there. I think that's why he's so angry with us.'

'Angry with us?' Flora said. 'Why do you think he's angry with us?'

'Because we shouldn't be here. He said so himself. We've just made things more difficult. That's why his hands are shaking, like Mr Godfrey's did when we stole the meat.'

Flora stayed looking at her for a few seconds, with an expression on her face that Isobel couldn't read. Then she sighed. 'Oh, Izzy,' she said, but for once she didn't say it in the way she normally did, like she thought Isobel had said something really silly. 'His hands aren't shaking because he's angry. They're shaking because he's scared.'

Now it was Isobel's turn to be confused. She looked back at Pat, working quicker than ever, rolling rocks off the hump of the dragon's back. He turned towards them to get a better angle and she saw his lips were pressed together with determination. 'But he doesn't look scared,' she said.

'Never mind about that now, we've got to finish this,' Flora said. 'Ooh, my feet! Can you feel that, Izzy?'

271

'Yes.' Isobel picked one foot up, then the other. It was like walking on hot coals. She peered at the scales beneath them, wondering if they were what was hot, then suddenly felt a piercing pain on her thigh. 'Ouch!'

'What is it?' Flora said, looking worried.

'My leg. There's something burning it.' Isobel reached into her pocket, then immediately pulled her hand out again. 'It's my dragon! It's boiling hot.'

'Just take it out if it's hurting. Come on, Izzy!'

Fear gripped Isobel as she remembered the last time her dragon had been this hot. 'No, Flora, this is what happened when I saw the splint in Burley Caves! I think it means the splints are coming.'

Before Flora could reply, the male dragon roared. It was so loud and deep that Isobel swore people would be able to hear it above ground, all those miles away. A river of blue fire shot from his jaws and the cavern was suddenly as bright as if the sun had been shining. It allowed Isobel to see that beyond the hulking shape of Ratter's father, the cave sloped down into a narrow tunnel. At the end of this tunnel Isobel caught a glimpse of something moving. No, Isobel thought, the right word was *swarming*. It reminded her of the way ants moved when you poked their nest with a stick – climbing on top of each other in their haste to escape. Even though she was hot – hotter than she'd ever been before – ice ran through her veins.

We'll come for all that you hold dear.
There's no escape. We'll come. We're here.

'Hurry!' Pat shouted.

Forgetting all about their feet, Isobel and Flora went back to moving the rocks, working faster and more frantically than they'd done before. The dragon roared and roared and the heat was nearly unbearable. Pat moved a particularly huge rock off the top of the female dragon's left leg and her whole body moved, making Isobel stumble and nearly lose her balance.

'We're nearly there!' he yelled. 'Keep going!'

But the splints were nearly there too. Isobel resolutely refused to look, but from the flickering movements she kept seeing when the cave lit up, she knew they were closer. She looked up and saw Flora had stopped moving the rocks. She was staring at the splints, her mouth half open, a look of absolute horror on her face. One of them reached up and slashed the male dragon's leg viciously with its ten-inch claws and Flora flinched.

When the dragon roared, Isobel caught a glimpse of the grasping, clawing creatures filling the tunnel. The ones at the front were soon turned to ash by the dragon's fire, but they kept coming, and the dragon had to take a few seconds between roars to catch his breath. During the time in between, a couple of the splints made it to the entrance of the cavern. The dragon roared again, incinerating one of them and grasping the other in his claws.

'Pat's right. The dragon can't hold them on his own,' Flora said. She got to her feet and pulled Isobel up. 'Come on!'

The two girls climbed up to Pat, who was still straining to move the same rock. As they pushed, Isobel looked down and saw something terrible. There were now five splints that had made it past the dragons, and they were heading for Ratter. He blew a tiny blue stream of flame at them, keeping them at bay, but Isobel knew there would be more.

Pat screamed with frustration and at that moment the rock

finally moved. It wobbled, but that was enough for the dragon to push up on to its leg. The rock tumbled off with a crash.

'Woah!' Pat said as the children stumbled, trying to keep their footing as the dragon shifted underneath them. As she struggled to get to her feet, the remaining rocks on her back started to slide downwards.

'We're going to fall!' Flora screamed.

'Jump!' Pat said, grabbing their hands.

They half jumped, half fell down the dragon's body, landing uncomfortably on the floor of the cavern. The dragon roared triumphantly as she finally shook herself free of the rocks and stretched up to her full height. She was huge – even bigger than the male dragon, with bigger spikes on her back. Scanning the cave with her lemon-yellow eyes, she flared her nostrils with anger.

'Ratter!' Flora gasped. 'Look at him.'

Ratter was surrounded by a group of five or six splints – it was impossible to tell, because they were moving so fast. He was spinning around, making a blue circle of fire, but Isobel could see that he was getting tired. One of the splints reached out its long claws and Isobel moved forwards, knowing it would be too late—

But Ratter's mother was already there. With one swoop of her neck she took all of the splints in her jaws and shook them angrily until they went limp, then tossed them aside. Then she bent down and Ratter hopped on to her nose. She turned and set him down on the other side of the rocks, out of reach of the splints.

'I think we should go there too,' Flora said, tugging at Isobel's sleeve. 'We'll be safe there. Come on, Izzy!'

But Isobel broke free and ran the other way, ignoring her sister, towards the ledge where Simon was. She caught a flicker of something out of the corner of her eye and saw a splint racing towards the ledge too. It was going to reach Simon before her!

Isobel looked around desperately for something, anything, to stop the splint. She saw Pat charging towards her, his mouth open with panic, and knew he was too far away, he wouldn't be able to do anything. Then she felt the burn on her thigh again and reached into her pocket.

'Leave him alone!' Isobel screamed, hurling the toy dragon at the splint.

The splint hissed with pain as the toy struck its body. It stopped about ten feet away from Simon and looked at Isobel. She quailed under its gaze. Not because it was angry but because there was nothing in its expression at all. She didn't doubt that it had once been angry – the kind of anger that is all-consuming, that makes it impossible to think of anything else. That was the only kind of anger that could make your body as wire-thin and bone-sharp as the splint's was. But its eyes were set back in its skull, black and empty, unseeing. It was like it had forgotten what it had been angry about in the first place. At that moment Isobel knew that Pat was right. There was no kindness, forgiveness or compassion. There was only the desire to hurt, to destroy. There was only evil.

The splint snarled. It leaped towards Isobel and she screamed, but then – out of nowhere – a burning torch crashed into it. The splint shrieked as it burned, withering into a heap on the floor. Isobel looked to her left and saw Pat and Flora running towards her, flaming torches in their hands.

'There are too many in the cavern now!' Pat shouted. 'The dragons can't kill them all; they've got to stop the rest of them coming in. We're going to have to fight these ones. Here, throw this.'

Isobel took one of the torches. There were splints coming towards them – maybe ten, maybe more, it was impossible to count. Isobel knew she was awful at throwing, but she couldn't think about that now. She threw the torch with all her might and heard a shriek as it hit. Flora and Pat were doing the same. The splints they hit howled terribly as they burned into ash. She'd thrown three torches when she reached for the next and found there were no more.

There was still one splint left in the cavern and now it was hurling itself towards them, angrier than ever, and they had no way of stopping it.

'What do we do?' Flora cried in panic.

Isobel picked up a rock, but then a huge black spiked tail knocked the splint off its feet and threw it against the side of the cave.

'That was close,' Pat breathed. 'I've never seen them get that far before.'

Isobel was already running to the ledge. 'Simon, you have to wake up!' she said, shaking him. 'It's not safe here.'

Suddenly Pat and Flora were by her side. Together, they eased Simon out of the ledge. He groaned and mumbled something as Pat put him over his shoulder. Then they stumbled up over the rocks. Ratter was waiting at the bottom on the other side.

Isobel looked back for a final time to see the female dragon next to Ratter's father. Both the dragons opened their jaws and roared, so deafeningly that Isobel had to put her hands over her ears. The cavern was instantly bathed in blue fire.

'Isobel, come on!' Flora shouted, pulling at her dress.

Feeling a wave of blistering heat on her face, Isobel stumbled down the rocky hill. Ratter jumped into her lap and the five of them huddled together against the rocks. Most of them had their heads down but Isobel was looking up. Towers of blue sparks were rising and falling and Isobel saw that the roof of the cavern had tiny tunnels criss-crossing all over it, tunnels that probably led up to the surface, becoming rabbit burrows and sink holes and joining with tree roots. There was another huge roar, and the blue flames surged so high that some of them escaped through the tunnels. Isobel realised, as she finally put her head in her arms to avoid the scorching heat, she now knew the cause of the blue sparks they had seen on their way to Splint Hall, what seemed like a lifetime ago.

CHAPTER SEVEN

*I*sobel couldn't have said for how long the dragons fought the splints. She thought it was only minutes but she had closed her eyes, and when she opened them again the light from the shaft next to them had changed. It was now light blue instead of golden, the sort of light you get in early dusk.

The cave was strangely silent. The hissing and thudding of the splints had gone. Isobel thought she could hear water running somewhere, far away. It was still hot, desperately hot, but not quite as blistering as it had been. Looking at each other nervously, Pat, Flora and Isobel got to their feet and slowly climbed back up the mountain of rocks.

When they got to the top, the splints were nowhere to be seen. The dragons were resting, lying on the floor of the cavern with their tails touching. As soon as he saw them, Ratter struggled out of Isobel's arms and zoomed down the rocks and across the cavern floor, making strange yelping sounds that Isobel had never heard him make before. When he reached his parents he hopped into the crook of his mother's arm. She nudged him with her head and licked him gently. Isobel felt tears welling up in her eyes.

'We did it,' she said. 'We brought Ratter back to his parents.'

'We did more than that,' Pat said. 'We saved their lives. Our lives too. *Everyone's* lives. If we hadn't brought the food and got his mother free . . .' He trailed off, shaking his head at the thought.

'Are the splints really gone?' Flora said, not quite daring to believe it.

Pat had a huge grin on his face. 'Yep, they're gone.' The grin wavered slightly. 'They'll be back of course, they always will, but they're gone for now. The dragons kept them back, like they always do. Though this was a close one.'

'Too close,' Flora said, with feeling.

Pat cleared his throat awkwardly. 'If you hadn't been there, I don't think I'd have got her out in time. Or fought those splints off, the ones that made it into the cavern. So, you know. Thanks.'

Isobel looked down at the dragons, her cheeks warm.

'That's all right,' Flora said. 'We always said we wanted to help.'

Simon groaned behind them and Pat's grin faded. 'Flora, will you help me carry him?'

Flora looked a little confused, then a little nervous when she realised where they were going, but she helped carry Simon over the pile of rocks and towards the dragons. They stopped a few feet away. Pat looked the dragons over carefully.

'What are you looking for?' Isobel asked.

'I want to see if they've got hurt,' Pat said. 'Dragon blood's got healing properties. Ah, there. You see, on her leg?'

The dragon blood was silvery like moonlight. A little way off from the dragons, there were some discarded scales, as big as dinner plates. Isobel picked one up, looking over at the dragons a little nervously, but they didn't seem to mind. The scale was hard but with a bit of give in it, like a cross between metal and wood. 'Their scales got burning hot, during the fight,' Isobel said. 'Except Ratter's.'

'Yeah, they do that when the splints are here,' Pat said. 'It's something to do with them breathing fire. Ratter's too young, though.'

Pat opened Simon's bandage, showing the red, angry wound. 'It'll heal in a couple of hours,' he said.

'A couple of hours?' Isobel said.

Pat dipped a clean bandage in the silvery blood and dabbed it on Simon's leg. Simon's face crumpled and he murmured something, but he didn't wake up. Before her eyes, Isobel saw the redness disappear. The wound was still there but it looked both cleaner and older, like it was a week old rather than fresh, and healing nicely.

'That's incredible!' Flora said.

Simon opened his eyes and sat up. He looked around him wildly, then his eyes fell on Pat's. He gripped Pat's shirt. 'Where are they?' he cried. 'Where are the splints? They're coming! We've got to be ready—'

'It's all right, Si, it's all over,' Pat said.

Simon shook his head. 'No, but they were coming—'

'The dragons drove them back,' Pat explained. 'And killed a fair few of them in the process.'

Looking around the cavern to satisfy himself that Pat was right, Simon slumped back on the floor. 'Good,' he said, with relief.

Pat reached into his pocket for another clean bandage, then tried to fasten it around his brother's leg but his hands were still shaking too much. Wordlessly, Flora took the bandage from his hands and did it for him. Pat sat back on his heels. He caught

Isobel looking and twisted his lips into a smile, embarrassed. 'Like they'd have let me be a pilot,' he said. 'It's a good job the War ended before I got called up. I'm useless when I get scared.'

'Don't say that,' Flora said, tightening the bandage.

Isobel thought of how Pat had pulled her and Simon out of the Cave of a Thousand Knives when stalactites could have fallen on his head. How he'd gone back for Simon in the Cave of Beating Wings, even though the bats had then scratched him to pieces. How he'd rowed them through the Lake of Forgotten Things and tried to distract the dragon when he'd thought Isobel and Flora were going to get scorched to death.

'You're not useless,' she said. 'You wouldn't have been useless in the War, either. They'd have been lucky to have you.'

Pat smiled, but it didn't reach his eyes. 'Well, we'll never know, will we?' He shook his head, sounding half relieved, half wistful. 'I still can't believe the War's over.'

Simon struggled to a sitting position again. 'You know what I can't believe?' he said, sounding dejected. 'That I still haven't seen a splint.'

Pat laughed as Flora said, 'You don't want to see one, believe me.'

'Course I do! I'm a keeper and I've never seen one before. You have. Even your grandpa did, and he wasn't a keeper either.'

'I wish I hadn't seen one,' Flora said.

Pat laughed again. 'You probably wish you'd never set foot underground. All the stuff we've put you through.'

Flora shook her head. 'We don't.' She glanced sideways at her sister. 'Well, I don't anyway. Though I do wish there was a way out.'

Isobel had almost forgotten that they were trapped. The old, familiar panic bubbled in her chest, but then it died down again.

'We might not be,' Pat said, a determined look on his face. 'Maybe we can get back into the main tunnel. It might be easier from this side to clear a way through the rubble. You stay here while Simon rests. I'm going to go and see.'

Pat strode off down the mountain of rocks, the dragons barely stirring as he passed. He ducked down into a tunnel that Isobel hadn't noticed, and was gone. Flora looked at Isobel and Simon, then sat down again, hugging her knees. 'We shouldn't get our hopes up,' she said.

Flora was right. Maybe they really would be trapped down here forever. But Isobel looked at the dragons, together again, and thought that maybe, it was worth it. She could understand why Grandpa had been so keen on them. Now that they weren't fighting or submerged under rocks Isobel saw they were extraordinary, better than she'd ever imagined. The female dragon wasn't the same browney-black colour as the male – she was a dull silver, which glistened in the light from the shaft. *They're the same colour as the toy dragons*, Isobel thought, imagining Grandpa in his study, drawing his pictures. Then Isobel remembered. She'd thrown her dragon at the splint during the fight!

It didn't take long for her to find it, nestled among some ash but still shining brightly. Isobel picked it up. It was still faintly warm. Isobel looked at the toy carefully. It was *exactly* the same colour as the scale she'd picked up.

'Flora, I think Grandpa made the toy dragons out of real scales,' Isobel said slowly. 'That's why they get hot when splints are near!'

Flora sighed a long-suffering sigh. 'It wouldn't surprise me.'

It was hardly any time at all before Pat was back. Isobel would have known the answer even if he hadn't shaken his head. It was in the disappointed slope of his shoulders and the way he looked at the ground. Flora sighed next to her and Isobel squeezed her hand. It was still worth it, she told herself. It was worth it because everyone above ground was safe. Including Miss Stewart, Aunty Bea and Mum (though when Isobel thought about Mum she felt tears welling up again, which she had to blink away).

'I still don't wish we'd never come,' Isobel said. 'Even if we are stuck here.'

'You might not say that when you've been stuck here a few weeks,' Pat said, sitting down next to them.

'And when you've eaten a few rats,' Simon added.

'Ugh!' Flora said, folding her arms. 'I'm not eating a rat. I'd rather starve first.'

Pat raised his eyebrows knowingly. 'We'll see.'

Now that it was all over Isobel felt weary. *Weary to her bones,* Mum would have said. It was just the same down here as it was above ground, she thought. Bad things happened and good people tried to stop them, and even when they did, even when they thought they'd won, even when they thought it was all safe again, sometimes even more bad things happened. It wasn't fair. Perhaps it was because evil was too powerful to be got rid of completely. Perhaps some of it lingered, like the thick black smoke after a raid. Like the splints, who had been defeated but would be back.

Isobel sighed as she got to her feet.

'Wait, where are you going, Izzy?'

'I'm looking at the shaft,' Isobel called, climbing over the rocks. 'I want to see if we can get out that way.'

'We can't,' Pat called back.

He was right. When Isobel got down the other side, she looked up. It was like being at the bottom of a well. Far, far above her she could see a circle of light, so far away that it was about the size of the round window in her bedroom at Splint Hall. The shaft was the exact opposite of the tunnels they'd used to get down to the cavern. Where the tunnels were narrow it was extremely wide, more like a quarry or a mine, where they were dark, it was light, but it was far too steep for them to climb. Plus, the walls were fairly smooth, meaning there wasn't even anything to hold on to.

'Ow!' Isobel exclaimed. She looked down to see Ratter. 'Why did you do that?' She sucked her finger where he had nipped it.

Ratter didn't answer, but shot back over the pile of rocks, his little legs scrabbling to propel him upwards. When he got to the top, he looked back at Isobel and squawked impatiently.

'All right, all right,' Isobel said under her breath as she followed him.

When she got back to the others, Ratter was on his father's back. He flashed his beady eyes at each of them in turn, squawking constantly.

'What do you want, Ratter?' Pat said, sounding exasperated as Ratter scrambled off the dragon and flitted around the children.

'Ow!' Simon said with surprise. 'He nipped me!'

'He did that to me, too,' Isobel said. 'It's like he wants us to do something.'

Ratter scrambled up on to his father's back again. He fixed his red eyes on Isobel.

An idea started forming in her mind, as faint as the glimmer of light from the shaft. 'Hang on . . .' she said, looking over at the shaft, then back to Ratter again. 'Do you think . . . do you think he wants us to go on the dragon's back too?'

There was a shocked silence.

'Go on his back?' Flora said. 'Are you mad? He'll shake us off like flies!'

'But dragons can fly, can't they?' Isobel said. 'And the shaft is big enough for the male dragon to fly up. So maybe that's how we can get out—'

Pat was shaking his head. 'I've never, in all my years being a keeper—' He stopped, then lowered his voice, like what he was saying was blasphemy, '*ridden* one.'

'It's just not done,' Simon said.

Isobel stood up. She slowly walked towards Ratter, keeping her eyes half on him and half on the dragon's head to her left. When she'd reached Ratter she tentatively stretched out one hand and put it on the dragon's back.

'What are you doing?' Flora said. 'Stop it!'

Isobel had half expected the dragon to rear up on to its front legs with outrage, sending her flying, but nothing happened. Ratter squawked impatiently. The spike she was holding on to felt strangely smooth, like polished wood. Praying she was right, Isobel swung her leg over and sat down in between two of the spikes.

The dragon raised its head very slightly, making Isobel's heart jump in her chest, then settled down again. Ratter hissed triumphantly.

'Izzy, get off there *right now*,' Flora said, her hands clenching into fists.

'No,' Isobel said, feeling strangely calm. 'This is what he wants us to do. You should get on.'

'I'm really not sure about this,' Pat said.

'His tail's not moving,' Simon pointed out, looking at the tail with fascination. 'That normally means he's not angry.'

'Well, I'm not getting on,' Flora said. 'I'm just not.'

'But Izzy's right,' Simon said. 'This might be our only chance of getting home.'

Flora shook her head.

'It's too dangerous!' Pat agreed.

Ratter had been moving his head from side to side, following the argument. He hissed long and deep in his throat. Then, his eyes glittering so much they were almost purple, he bounced off his father's back again, towards the others.

'Ouch!' Flora cried. 'He bit my leg.'

'Ratter, stop it!' Pat shouted. 'Stop biting us. I'm your keeper and I'm telling you to stop. Now!'

But Ratter didn't stop. Simon was the first one to get up and hastily fling himself over the dragon's back.

'He doesn't do it if you're on his back,' he shouted. 'Izzy's right, that's what he wants us to do!'

Pat and Flora were stubborn, but Ratter wouldn't give up. After a few more seconds, and more than a few more nips, Pat and Flora were both sitting on the dragon's back too, grumbling under their breath.

Isobel hid a smile as Ratter perched in front of her, his throat clicking with satisfaction. It was strangely comfortable. Her back was resting on one smooth spike and she was holding on to another. Then everything wobbled. Isobel gripped the spike as they surged upwards. In a couple of seconds, the dragon was on its legs and the ground was suddenly twenty feet below them.

'Hold on, Izzy,' Flora said, sounding terrified.

Everyone held on to whatever spikes they could as the dragon crashed its way through the hill of rocks, sending boulders flying in all directions. At one point, he lost his footing and everyone was thrown to the right. Flora nearly slid off but Pat pulled her back just in time. Then they were propelled forwards as the dragon went down the other side, the spike pressing painfully into Isobel's belly.

At the bottom, the dragon thundered into the shaft then looked up. He seemed to hesitate and an awful thought appeared in Isobel's mind. The dragons had wings, but she'd not actually seen them fly. And the cavern was huge, but Isobel wasn't sure if it was big enough for them to fly around in. Maybe they could fly, once upon a time, but they never did any more and they'd forgotten how . . .

'Pat, Simon,' she said, twisting round. 'These dragons can fly, can't they? It's just, I've not seen—'

But then Isobel was thrown back as the dragon reared upwards. His huge wings extended out and flapped once, hitting the air with a loud slap. They did it again and then Isobel looked down and realised they'd left the ground.

Riding on a dragon's back wasn't the nicest way of travelling, Isobel thought at first as the dragon's back jerked beneath her, her legs rubbing against its rough scales. As the dragon flapped his wings they shot forwards, then they came to a nail-biting almost-halt in the air before the dragon flapped his wings again. But as the dragon gained speed it got better. It still went faster then slower but it was smoother. Every time the dragon surged upwards, Isobel felt a tingle in her chest, like she used to get when she went too high on the swings.

'This is amazing!' Simon shouted from behind her.

The round window of blue light got bigger and bigger. Isobel sneaked a glance back down and saw they were already so far from the ground, the rocks were just a blur beneath them. She gulped, imagining what would happen if one of them fell off. But when she looked back up, the light was so close that she could see it was coming from the left. It looked like there was some kind of cave at the top too. It wouldn't be long now, Isobel thought, her palms wet. Just another four flaps, or maybe five . . .

After another few seconds, the dragon surged upwards into the light, landing with a bump in a cave at the top. Isobel took a long, shaky breath. As she eased herself off the dragon, her legs felt wobbly, like she'd forgotten how to use them.

'I'm glad that's over,' Flora said, looking a little green.

'We should do that again,' Simon said, looking miles better than he had underground. He got to his feet and Isobel could see that his leg wasn't hurting him any more.

Pat didn't say anything, but when everyone was off he reached out and touched the dragon's back. 'Thank you,' he said quietly.

The dragon turned its head round to look at them. His red eyes flashed as if he understood and he thumped his tail once, so loudly that the sound echoed round the cave.

Isobel looked around. The cave they were in was different to the cavern they'd come from. It was a sandy yellow colour rather than dark brown and it wasn't nearly as big, though it was hard to see in the disappearing light. The sky was deepening into a darker blue and Isobel realised the sun had long set. They'd been underground all afternoon and now it was evening.

'This is one of the parts of Burley Caves that they've closed off,' Flora said. 'Look, I can see the rope! We're not far from the entrance at all.'

Ratter had started to whine again. He was still on his father's back and she walked towards him until she was close enough to reach out her hand and touch his head.

'We'll come back soon,' Isobel said, not knowing if it were true. 'Well, I hope we will.'

'Of course, we will,' Simon said, coming over to say goodbye too. 'We're keepers, aren't we? We'll have to find a way.'

'Bye, Ratter,' Flora said, reaching her hand out shyly. Ratter snorted suspiciously, but then he let her touch his head as well.

'But we're not keepers,' Isobel said, wishing in her heart that they were.

'I don't know,' Pat said, looking at Ratter, who was nuzzling his head against Isobel's arm. 'You've risked your life to save the dragons. You've stolen meat to feed them. You've gone on a terrifying journey deep underground, facing the two caves of peril, and you've even fought the splints – well, some of them, anyway – with your bare hands. Plus, dragons let you touch them.' He grinned. 'I reckon you're honorary keepers, at least. Like your grandpa was. And I reckon we'll need your help again, sooner or later.'

Isobel's heart soared. Then she caught sight of her sister, who was looking at Pat with horror on her face. She saw Isobel looking and her expression softened.

'I suppose we could help,' she relented. 'Maybe. But I'm not going in that cave full of bats ever again.'

289

'I think I'll give the one with stalactites a miss myself,' Simon muttered.

The dragon shifted away from them. The four children stepped back as he trod towards the shaft, Ratter twisting on his back so he could look at them for a final time.

'We'll see you soon!' Isobel said, knowing, this time, that it was true.

Ratter snorted blue sparks into the air as a final farewell. Then the dragon tipped forwards – its dark wings folded close to its body – and disappeared down the shaft.

Everyone was quiet for a few moments as they watched the dragons go. Isobel thought of them in their strange, dark home far below the ground, watching and waiting for the splints to come back.

'We'd better get back, I suppose,' Pat said eventually. 'Dad'll be going spare, wondering what's happened. It's already dark.'

'So will Mum,' Flora said.

When Flora said 'Mum', something twisted in Isobel's belly, and suddenly she couldn't wait to be back at Splint Hall. But soon afterwards she thought of something else, like a stone clunking into a well.

Mr Godfrey.

Isobel wondered if he was looking for them. If he was still cross. Perhaps Flora was wondering the same thing too because her face was troubled as she took her sister's hand and followed Pat and Simon, who was barely even limping any more, out of the cave and towards the village. As they got closer to the houses Isobel thought of the people inside. They'd have gone about their day as normal: buying bread, weeding flowerbeds, mopping their floors, with no idea what was happening beneath them.

'They're lucky,' Isobel said. 'The people, I mean. All safe inside their houses, not knowing about the splints. Not knowing how close they were to . . .' She broke off, not wanting to say the words.

'Yeah, I was thinking about that too,' Simon said.

'It's how it should be,' Pat said, giving his brother's arm a squeeze. 'It's how it's always been. With any luck, the splints won't be back for a good while.'

Flora looked at Pat with narrowed eyes. 'How long exactly will it be? Till they come back?'

Pat shrugged. 'It's impossible to say. Years. Decades, even. There might be a few stragglers but there won't be another attack like this until the next time there's a war, maybe, or something else awful happens.'

'I hope that's a long time,' Isobel whispered.

By the time Isobel and Flora approached Splint Hall, it was pitch black, and cold. If they hadn't been used to the darkness, they might even have been afraid. But Isobel didn't think she'd be afraid of anything above ground now, ever again.

They left the shaded path and stepped on to the gravel of the driveway. It crunched under their feet, impossibly loud. Without speaking, they walked up to the house and then up the steps to the main door. They both waited for a second, suddenly not sure what to do.

'Do you think we should knock?' Flora asked.

But then the door was wrenched back and Miss Stewart stood

before them. One of her hands was balling her apron into her fist. The other one flew to her open mouth and she took a couple of steps backwards.

'Ma-am!' she said, but it came out as a croak. She cleared her throat. 'Ma'am!' she shouted. 'Mrs Johnson! Julia! They're here.'

A door opened and then someone was tearing across the hallway. Isobel only had half a second to realise that it was Mum before her arms were around them.

'You silly girls,' she sobbed, when she could speak. 'Where have you been? Where on earth have you been?'

She pushed them away so she could look at them, her red eyes taking them in fiercely, then drew them to her once again.

Behind Mum there was a clattering sound. When Mum let them go again Isobel saw Aunty Bea running down the stairs. In the next moment, she was hugging them too, squeezing their arms too tight. Her face was pressed against Isobel's and it was wet with tears.

'Sorry,' Isobel said, feeling uncomfortable. 'We didn't mean to make you worry—'

'I thought you'd run away,' Aunty Bea said, releasing them so she could look into their eyes. She put her hands on Isobel's cheeks and squeezed, like she was trying to convince herself that they were really here. It hurt a bit, but Isobel didn't say anything.

'They're safe now, Bea,' Mum said, gently removing Aunty Bea's hands.

'I thought you'd run away and it was all my fault,' Aunty Bea said again, clenching her fists so tightly, Isobel knew her fingernails would leave marks.

Isobel didn't understand why it would have been Aunty Bea's fault. She glanced at Flora, who was looking equally puzzled.

'We didn't run away, Aunty Bea—' she said, but Aunty Bea didn't seem to be listening.

'I'll never let you down again,' she said suddenly, looking from Isobel to Flora, then back again. 'Do you understand?' She clutched their arms. 'Never. As long as I live.'

'What do you mean?' Flora said.

But before Aunty Bea could answer, they heard another sound from the house. This time, it wasn't the sound of someone rushing. This was slow and regular, like the person making it had all the time in the world. It was the clunk of a stick hitting the tiled hallway, again and again and again.

No one spoke as Mr Godfrey appeared from the corridor that led to his study. He stopped in the middle of the hallway and looked at the scene before him. There was no relief on his face, only satisfaction.

'Didn't I tell you they'd come back?' he said, jerking his stick in their direction. 'Didn't I tell you not to worry?'

No one replied.

Mr Godfrey tutted as he shook his head. 'What a wild goose chase you've led us all on,' he said. 'Your mother beside herself with worry, Rigby driving the car all across the county. You even had the police out looking for you. Do you have any idea of the trouble you've caused?'

Before they had gone underground, Isobel had been afraid to look at Mr Godfrey. Now, she raised her head and looked him firmly in the eye. Perhaps it was because of the splints, but he didn't seem so terrifying any more. It was as if she could see him clearly for the first time and what she saw was pain, anger and disappointment, spun together over many years like strands in a spool of wool. She almost felt a little sorry for him.

'We didn't mean to,' she said.

'It doesn't matter what you meant,' Mr Godfrey said. 'What matters is what you did. Which was cause a great deal of trouble. Honestly, Beatrice, I can't understand how these girls are even your relations. They have no idea of the proper way to behave.'

'I'm sorry,' Aunty Bea whispered. Isobel's heart sank, but then she realised her aunty wasn't speaking to Mr Godfrey. In fact, she hadn't even turned to look at him. She was looking at Flora and Isobel, though again, Isobel didn't have a clue what she was apologising for.

'I'm so sorry,' Aunty Bea whispered again. She turned to her sister. 'Can you ever forgive me?'

Mum's face softened. 'There's nothing to forgive, you silly goose.'

Isobel wondered if Flora was also wondering why Mum and Aunty Bea were speaking in riddles. But then Mum gathered all of them together in another hug and they stayed like that for a few moments, Isobel breathing in Mum's soap-and-lilies smell.

Mr Godfrey's grip on his stick faltered, just a little. 'So you're all giving me the silent treatment, are you?' he said. 'Well, you'll have to talk to the police when they arrive. They'll want to know exactly what you've been up to. Wasting police time is a criminal offence. Did you know that? And that's not to mention the stealing. They'll be wanting to talk to that boy and his father, make no mistake.'

Later, Isobel wondered if what happened next was because

294

the splints had been beaten back. Perhaps it wasn't just that splints fed off the evil that was happening in the world. Perhaps it worked the other way too: when splints were strong, evil drifted upwards like smoke, making the people who did bad things stronger and the people who tried to stop them weaker.

'You're the one the police will want to speak to,' Aunty Bea said as she got to her feet, her voice calm and clear. 'I'm sure they'll be very interested to know about your black-market operations, not to mention the money you've fraudulently claimed from the War Damages Commission.'

Mr Godfrey was speechless for a few moments. 'What?' he blustered eventually. 'Beatrice, what on earth are you talking about?'

Or maybe it was nothing to do with the splints at all. Perhaps it was the dragons getting stronger. Yes, Isobel thought, it must have been the dragons. That was the only thing that could explain the strange fire in Aunty Bea's eyes as she put her hands on her hips and told her husband to leave Splint Hall at once.

EPILOGUE

THREE MONTHS LATER

'I'm freezing,' Flora complained.

Isobel looked at her sister. She had a hat pulled so far down her forehead that Isobel was surprised she could even see. Noticing her looking, Flora stuck her tongue out, then shoved her hands even further into the pockets of the dark blue woollen coat she was wearing. 'What?' she said. 'I *am* freezing. You know I hate winter.'

'I think we all know that,' Aunty Bea said under her breath, flashing a smile at Isobel.

Isobel hid a smile of her own as they crunched their way up the main street of the village. As it happened, she was freezing too. The snow was nearly a foot deep in places – where it hadn't been trodden into ice, that is. The black boots she was wearing were thick-soled and sturdy but it had turned out that they weren't quite waterproof, and even the two pairs of itchy socks she had on were no match for the icy water seeping through.

'Merry Christmas, girls.'

Isobel and Flora looked to their left and saw Miss Joyce, bundled up against the cold. She was smoking a cigar.

'Merry Christmas, Mrs Godfrey. Merry Christmas, Mrs Johnson,' Miss Joyce added cheerfully.

Isobel wasn't exactly sure what Simon and Pat had told the people who lived in the village about them. But she knew they'd said something. The next time they had gone into the village, people were much friendlier: nodding and smiling, rather than pretending they didn't exist.

Isobel didn't know if anyone in the village knew about the dragons though. Sometimes she thought they might. Like when Tony the butcher had slipped them an extra ration of bacon with a meaningful wink. Or when Miss Joyce kept the path to Burley Caves clear all through the autumn, sweeping away the dead leaves every day so it was easier for them to get up there. Somehow, the rubble in the tunnel had been cleared as well. Isobel didn't think James and the boys could have done it by themselves. She wanted to ask Simon and Pat about it but something stopped her. She knew that some secrets were best left alone.

And anyway, the people being friendlier might have nothing to do with the dragons and everything to do with Mr Godfrey. When Aunty Bea had asked him to leave, there was a long moment where he just stared at her. Isobel had thought that he would shout so loudly that he would explode, but he didn't. He was white and trembling, and he didn't look anyone in the eye as he stormed out of the house, Rigby scuttling at his heels.

Since he'd gone to live in London, it was like a cloud had lifted from Burlington Village. Everyone had felt it. Miss Stewart now sang as she dusted Flora and Isobel's new bedroom (which was the pink one, where they'd found the toy dragons all those weeks ago). Mum hummed under her breath, an auburn curl escaping from her scarf as she sewed new winter clothes for them all in the Breakfast Room. But the biggest change of all was in

Aunty Bea. Isobel realised that she had hardly known her before. The old Aunty Bea was shy and quiet, only speaking if she really had to. The real Aunty Bea loved nothing more than to talk for hours on end, until the tea had gone cold and it was getting dark outside. The old Aunty Bea used to jump if there was a loud noise. This Aunty Bea delighted in driving the car around the Sussex countryside, honking the horn until birds flew out of the trees. And while the old Aunty Bea wore plain dresses, this Aunty Bea had sequins on underneath her brown worsted coat. After all, it was Christmas.

Isobel didn't think she'd ever forget the look on Aunty Bea's face when they showed her the dresses. It was the day after Mr Godfrey had left and Aunty Bea had been looking out of the window for ages. Isobel had thought perhaps she was waiting to see if he would come back. But he didn't, and in the end it was Miss Stewart who suggested taking her to the coal cellar, to 'take her mind off things'. Aunty Bea had looked down at the cases, covered in coal dust, like she couldn't believe it. Then they'd told her the story of how they'd rescued them and she had laughed so hard she'd had to sit down, right there on the gravel, with tears running down her cheeks.

'Merry Christmas, Miss Joyce,' Aunty Bea called back. 'Though you can stop calling me Mrs Godfrey. We got the news from London a couple of days ago. I'm soon to be Lady Burlington.'

Miss Joyce sucked on her cigar. She nodded. 'It suits you better, I'm sure. And a little birdie told me that the house is going to be opened to the public. Is that right?'

Aunty Bea nodded. 'Just Tuesdays and Thursdays for now.'

Mum had told them that letting people come and look round

the house would mean they didn't have to sell it. She'd asked them if they minded. Flora had shrugged and asked why on earth people would pay to look round 'this crusty old place' but it seemed that people did. They'd already had over twenty letters booking appointments.

After waving goodbye to Miss Joyce, the four of them continued on their way, up the winding path to the caves. It was nearly lunchtime and the sun was high and bright in the pale sky.

'I'm really not sure why you've dragged us all the way up here,' Mum grumbled. 'We should be helping Miss Stewart with the Christmas dinner.'

'It's nice to get some fresh air,' Aunty Bea said, breathing in deeply.

'Yes, but we could have just gone for a walk in the grounds. I don't see why we needed to come here.'

'You'll see in a minute,' Flora said. 'When we get there.'

Flora and Isobel stole a look at each other. Isobel's heart thudded as she felt the weight of the chops she was carrying in her coat pocket. They had talked about what was going to happen next for so long that she couldn't believe the moment had really arrived.

It was warmer inside the cave than it was outside, but Isobel could still see her breath. James, Simon and Pat were already there, waiting by the rope.

'Ready?' James said, a smile dancing in his eyes.

'What are you doing here, James?' Mum said. 'I hope the girls haven't persuaded you into doing something. You've got the day off, you know!'

'Not at all, Mrs Johnson,' he said. 'I'm delighted to be here.'

James had been reinstated as the groundsman of Splint Hall after Mr Godfrey and Rigby had left. Isobel had got used to seeing him, Simon and Pat, chopping wood and stacking it in the air-raid shelter to dry out.

'Now, if you please.' He gestured towards the rope barrier.

'You want us to go past the rope?' Aunty Bea said. 'Isn't it dangerous?'

'Not if you watch where you're going.'

Isobel ducked underneath the rope, ignoring her mother's shout of, 'Hold on a minute, Izzy,' and slipped past the rock that led to the cave. Her gaze settled on the other side of the space, where she knew the huge shaft dropped downwards. Her palms prickled.

'You shouldn't get too close to the edge,' Pat said.

'Too close to the edge of what?' Mum asked.

Flora took Mum's hand as Isobel took Aunty Bea's and they walked further into the cave. They stopped a short distance from the opening. For a few moments, no one spoke.

'Girls, what is going on?' Mum said, laughing uneasily.

Flora took a deep breath. She looked at Pat and Simon for support. James nodded.

'That day when we got lost, we didn't really get lost,' Flora began, then immediately backtracked. 'Well, we did actually, a bit, but it wasn't in the countryside like we said. It was down there.' She jerked her thumb towards the floor of the cave.

'What do you mean, down there?' Aunty Bea asked. 'In the caves, like Isobel got lost before?'

'Sort of,' Isobel said. 'Well, no, not really. Further down than that. In a secret network of tunnels and caves, including some quite scary ones with flesh-eating bats and even a lake with a boat.

301

We rowed on it to the other side to find the cavern, which was where the splints came—'

'Stop!' Mum said, holding her hands up. 'Girls, stop this. You're not making any sense. What on earth do you mean, talking about hidden tunnels and strange creatures? And what are splints?' She said the last word like she was trying it out in her mouth.

Isobel looked at Flora, who shrugged helplessly. 'We'll explain everything, I promise. But we knew you wouldn't believe us. We knew we had to show you first.'

'Show us what?'

Flora nodded at Pat, who walked closer to the shaft and whistled a long, high note into the air. For a few seconds, there was silence. Then, from deep below, there was a sound. A clatter of rocks, then a screech, then a slap like leather hitting the air.

'What on earth's that?' Mum said, a note of alarm sounding in her voice.

'Don't worry,' Flora said. 'It's perfectly safe.'

Then Mum and Aunty Bea gasped as the dragon rocketed out of the shaft. It hovered in the air for a few seconds, gazing at all of them. A stream of blue sparks shot up into the cave. Then Ratter glided down to land – more heavily than he intended – a few feet away from Isobel. Now the size of a small pony, he had only been flying for a few weeks. His tail curled round his body and thumped on the ground impatiently as he nudged Isobel's pocket. Isobel grinned as she got the meat out.

'You can't eat it all,' she warned him as she threw him a chop. 'You've got to take some back for your parents, understand?'

Ratter snorted as he wolfed down the meat.

Isobel turned to look at Mum and Aunty Bea. They had both

taken a step backwards involuntarily when they'd first seen Ratter. But now that he was eating, they stepped forwards again. They looked scared, Isobel thought, but there was something else in their expression too. Something like fascination, and also understanding. Like they had finally found the answer to a question that had always been at the back of their minds.

'I might sound a little silly for saying this,' Aunty Bea said, her voice faltering, 'but is that . . . is that a *dragon*?'

Ratter snorted as he gulped the chop down. He flapped his wings again then peered with his red eyes at Aunty Bea and Mum, curious but not concerned.

'Oh my goodness, it is,' Mum breathed. 'It can't be, but it is.' She looked at Isobel, questions written all over her face.

Isobel nodded. 'This is what Grandpa wanted you to know,' she replied, her heart soaring. 'This is the secret of Splint Hall.'

ACKNOWLEDGEMENTS

It is a dream come true and the fulfilment of a lifelong ambition to have a book (a real book!) published. While it's my name on the cover, there are many people who are also responsible. Firstly, my agent, Penny: thanks for believing in my writing and for your stern words not to lose my nerve when receiving early rejections. Secondly, to Charlie, for publishing this book just because you liked it, and for your insightful edits. It's a far better book because of you. Thank you to Eloise for meticulous copyediting, Chloe for equally meticulous proofreading, Paul for expert championship, Kate and Becky for the absolutely magical cover, which surpassed all my expectations, and everyone else at Andersen Press for publishing this book so wonderfully. I'm so proud to be a part of the team.

Huge thanks must go to my loving friends and family, particularly my mum Emma and my brother Freddy: thank you for your comments on earlier drafts.

And finally, to my long-suffering husband Val: I'm sorry for the many weekends that I spent writing this book instead of doing fun things with you. Thank you for being my first reader and supporting me wholeheartedly in the pursuit of this foolish dream. I love you.

EVERNIGHT

ROSS MACKENZIE

THE EVERNIGHT
HAS BEEN UNLEASHED...

As far back as she can remember, orphan Larabelle Fox has scraped together a living treasure-hunting in the sewers. In a city where emotionless White Witches march through the streets and fear of Hag magic is rife, Lara keeps her head down. But when she stumbles upon a mysterious little box in the sewers, Lara finds herself catapulted into a world of wild magic – facing adventure, mortal danger and a man who casts no shadow.

'Epic good-versus-evil fantasy'
Guardian

'Beautifully cinematic, *Evernight* is a spellbinding tale'
The Scotsman

9781783448319

SEASON OF SECRETS

SALLY NICHOLLS

On a wild and stormy night Molly runs away from her grandparents' house. Her dad has sent her to live there until he Sorts Things Out at home now her mother has passed away. In the howling darkness, Molly sees a desperate figure running for his life from a terrifying midnight hunt. But who is he? Why has he come? And can he heal her heartbreak?

'A stand-out story . . . exciting [and] profound'
Guardian

'A wonderful, evocative, lively book'
Literary Review

9781839130465

PHIL EARLE

1941. War is raging. And one angry boy has been sent to the city, where bombers rule the skies. There, Joseph will live with Mrs F, a gruff woman with no fondness for children. Her only loves are the rundown zoo she owns and its mighty silverback gorilla, Adonis. As the weeks pass, bonds deepen and secrets are revealed, but if the bombers set Adonis rampaging free, will either of them be able to end the life of the one thing they truly love?

'A magnificent story . . .
It deserves every prize going'
Philip Pullman

'An extraordinary story with historical and family truth at its heart, that tells us as much about the present as the past. Deeply felt, movingly written, a remarkable achievement'
Michael Morpurgo

9781783449651

LIGHTNING MARY

ANTHEA SIMMONS

WINNER OF THE MIDDLE GRADE STEAM BOOK PRIZE

One stormy night, a group of villagers are struck by lightning.
The only survivor is a baby – Mary Anning. From that moment
on, a spark is lit within her.

Growing up poor but proud on the windswept Dorset coast,
Mary faces danger to bring back valuable fossils to help feed
her family. But tragedy and despair is never far away.

Mary must depend upon her unique
courage and knowledge to fulfil
her dream of becoming a scientist
in a time when girls have no
opportunities. What will happen
when she makes her greatest
discovery of all . . . ?

9781783448296